To my wife Millicent;
my daughters Karen and Karlene
my son-in-law Russell Pierre,
my brother, Orville
the Jamaican Media;
Mike Henry of LMH Publishing
and to all who have directly or or indirectly assisted
Bateman Carter Jr.
on his Road to Damascus

Contents

Chapter 1

JAMAICA -NO PROBLEM

One thing I know, that whereas I was blind, now I see. (John ix:25)
Empowered to see the light... having been blinded
on the road to Damascus (Acts ix:3)

*H*e wasn't bored. It wasn't that he had got inured to long hours in the air, having recently logged thousands of miles throughout Europe and to and from the Americas on special assignments. It was only that he had not been home for a long time and the expectation of seeing Pappy, his grandfather and Raymond, his last brother, was giving him a queasy feeling.

Pappy had fathered and mothered them after the death of their mother and after their father was stabbed to death by his best friend in a dispute arising out of a game of dominoes. He reflected with slight amusement at how strict and harsh Pappy was. Every day, rainy days regardless, he and George, the eldest of the brothers, went to Denham Town All-age School under the tyranny of Miss Rhule. After dinner, around seven o'clock, Pappy, equipped with his thick leather belt, would listen to each boy's account of himself. Books would be examined, questions asked and accolades, censures or stripes meted out. After a while, they overcame the fear of the strap and were secretly entertained by the threats and colourful verbal reprimands which gradually supplanted the floggings.

He was aroused from his drowsiness by the crackling of the

intercom, followed by the metallic voice of the captain: "Arriving Montego Bay 0500 hours. Touch-down in ten minutes. Hope you enjoyed the flight. Please fly with us again. Thank you."

He didn't bother to listen to the routine instructions of the pretty stewardess looking rather smart in her cream blouse, blue skirt and matching jacket. He had sub-consciously fastened his seat-belt at the sound of the captain's voice.

He looked at Montego Bay while the plane was slowly banking towards the airport and butterflies of excitement fluttered in his stomach. It was ten years since he had visited the island. The momentary sight of Montego Bay, from the air, was unnerving. Montego Bay from the air! It did not look as orderly as Miami from the air. Montego Bay despite its lush greenery looked like a huge, muddy splash thrown beside a great basin of blue and white soapy water.

"Jamaica, here we come!" he said to the smiling Englishman who said that he was from Liverpool. The Englishman was reticent, but his wife kept up lively conversation. She wanted to know everything about the island. He told her that it was impossible in a single flight from London to Jamaica. "Tell me about the sun and the beaches and the calypso music," she asked. "What language do the natives speak? It sounds like English, but it isn't. I tried to procure a book of the native language, but it doesn't seem there are any."

"The natives, as you call them, speak English," he replied. "As for books in the native language, unfortunately, I don't think there are many."

She was surprised to hear that the natives speak English. "English! It sounds rather outlandish to me," she cried. "When I visited, I could not understand a quarter of what they say."

"So are Cockney and Welsh and the provincial dialects to me," he replied. "Not much difference, is there? If you understand as much as a quarter of the language in Jamaica, you are doing well. I, sometimes, understand less than that," he teased.

"But it is your language, isn't it?" she continued. "You said that you are Jamaican, ain't yah?" she reminded him. He explained that he grew up in England. He had not been home in ten years. He had a British passport. He could hardly be called a Jamaican. He was out of touch with many things Jamaican.

"Calypso is Jamaican music, isn't it?" she asked.

"Oh, no," he replied. "Reggae is our music. Calypso is Trinidadian."

"Sorry for being so confused and mixed-up," she blushed and apologized.

He told her that she would have to go to Trinidad for Calypso. In Jamaica, she would certainly have her fill of reggae music. However, since it was Carnival time, she would hear a lot of calypso, as well as soca. She wanted to know the difference between soca and calypso. He had to admit, to her dismay that he didn't know. "I don't think I am of much help here," he said, "I am a Beatles fan. Ask me anything about John Lennon."

"Oh, those!" She exclaimed, wrinkling her lips in disgust. She was under the impression that all 'islanders of the Caribbean' knew the difference. He laughingly reminded her that, unfortunately, he could not be truly called an 'islander of the Caribbean', having grown up in the island of Great Britain.

"*Sparrow* is a rhapsodist, ain't he?" she asked. He replied that he hadn't thought of it, not being an authority on calypso. She said that she was in the movie business and, therefore, ought to know.

"Actress?" he asked.

"Oh, no," she replied. "Nothing as glamorous as that! Scriptwriter."

"I see," said he. "I have always wanted to write stuff like plays and so on."

"So why don't you?" she said.

"Well, I have to set myself to it," he replied.

"All you need is a little talent and some paper," she teased.

"I think it takes a little elbow grease, as well. I think I lack that," he bantered.

"My husband seems to have a lot of that," she said. "He is a producer." She gripped the arm of her husband. "I was telling this gentleman that you have a lot of elbow grease. Don't you, Darling?" The Englishman adoringly smiled at her, but said nothing.

She added that she would like to meet "The King" – *The Mighty Sparrow*. He told her that now was her chance to meet him as he would be performing with his troubadours, in a day or two, at the Carnival. It could easily be arranged. Her husband, all this while, kept glancing at his wife, admiring the buoyancy of her conversation, as well as her vibrant knowledge. He silently smiled, a soft glow emanating from his pale blue eyes. At least, unlike her husband, she had some idea of what Carnival was about. She said that she had never missed attending the London Carnival – not once.

"Darling," she said to her husband, "the natives are having a Carnival. How exciting! We shall take it in, shan't we?"

"A Carnavol! You don't say!" her husband replied.

"I am thrilled at the prospect of meeting the Mighty Sparrow and Bob Marley, of course!" she exclaimed.

"I suggest that you delay the thrill until you meet *The Sparrow*. As for Bob, he is dead. Some twenty years now. You could probably meet with his wife, Rita, and his sons and daughters, scintillating artists in their own right," he explained.

"Oops! I am sorry. I had forgotten that he is dead!" she said, blushing and putting her hand over her mouth in feigned apology. "There is a museum and a shrine to Bob Marley's memory, ain'it?" she asked.

"Yes," he said. "Tuff Gong, I think is the name." He was hoping that he was right.

"I should like to visit those places honouring the memory of Bob," she continued with the excitement of a child.

"Do you intend to do likewise?"

He felt slightly guilty and embarrassed not having a similar desire. He did not have any immediate plans to visit on this trip, he told her, but he was thinking that he would. "Where are you staying?" he asked.

"We booked at the Sandals," she replied.

"Jamaica, here we come," he repeated, as the plane touched down with a feathery bump, a screech of wheels and an awesome rumble towards the end of the runway.

"Joy-maker is it?" the silent Englishman asked.

"Uh-huh! Jamaica," he replied. "Land of wood and water."

The pulsating strains of a song filtered from the intercom. "That's Belanfonte. I recognize him!" she said.

"Yeah," he replied, "Island in the sun, willed to me by my father's hand." He softly crooned a couple of bars and realized that he had forgotten most of the song. He once knew all of it. He surmised from her air of assurance and knowledge that she had visited Jamaica before, probably on a previous honeymoon. Her husband looked awkward and over-attentive as if he was new. He didn't bother to ask if they were honeymooning – though he was tempted to do so.

"It's beautiful!" she cooed, stretching across her husband to look through the porthole.

Her husband was as pleased as a bruckin's king. He was smiling more than ever. He was probably thinking that his wife was not only beautiful, but she was also very smart "Man-tiger Bye, is it?" the Briton said.

"No, Darling," she corrected him.

"Mon-tigger Bye. It's Mon-tigger Bye."

He was privately amused at how far one was from, and how near was the other to pronouncing Montego Bay correctly. He silently concluded that it was a matter of different strokes for different folks, even when some are yoked together. He was also privately amused with the manner in which the Briton asked, as if doubting the discovery that he had actually reached his destination, after spending eight hours in the sky. He seemed to be seeking reassurance that he was back on Mother Earth.

"Yeah, Montego Bay," he replied.

By then, the plane had come to a stop. He put his hands together and applauded. He had not forgotten the Jamaican custom of passengers clapping hands whenever a plane landed, as if the pilot had performed a breath-taking theatrical act or an acrobatic stunt or it might be a subconscious and explosive form of release of energy from suspense pent up in the narrow and pressurized confines of the passenger cabin for such long hours. He swiftly realized that no one else was clapping. He felt slightly foolish and embarrassed when she asked why he clapped. Ten years ago, every Jamaican passenger would have clapped. He explained, to her amusement, that it was a peculiar habit of his, whenever he got back to earth.

He unfastened his seat-belt, sprang up, pulled his blue and silver executive valise from the over-head compartment, and stood in the slowly moving queue, the reticent Englishman and his vivacious wife standing behind him. He turned sideways to continue conversing with her. "Be sure to see the Carnival," he said, among other things.

"Surely!" she replied.

"You're coming home, ain't yah?" her husband asked.

"Yeah, coming home," he replied.

He stood before the English couple in the queue of passengers at the clearance desk for passengers who had nothing to declare. "What do you think about the upcoming nude wedding?" she asked.

He thought that if a flock of late hens and some crafty old cocks wanted to pluck themselves in front of one another, what the hell? He couldn't see what the hullabaloo was about. It was no business of his. Yet, that was the reason why he stopped off at Montego Bay. He wanted to be there, at Hedonism II, absorbing the vibes of place, people and event. "So long as it doesn't interfere with other people's rights I see no harm in some crazy people parading in the buff," he replied. "What do you think?"

"I think it's jolly good fun," she replied.

"Would you?" he asked, then realized that he shouldn't have asked her such an impolite and *gauche* question, at least, not in the hearing of her husband.

She blushed and laughed sweetly, then turned to her husband, "Would you get married in the nude, Darling?" she asked.

"I think not, but in a grass skirt maybe," he replied, flashing his perpetual smile.

"It would be un-English to get married in the nude," she observed.

"It is also un-Jamaican," he said, "whether in the nude or in grass skirts."

"Hev a good toime, mite," said the Englishman, when he bade the couple goodbye.

"Thanks, have a good time," he replied. He hadn't had a vacation for a long time, and, although that was not his primary purpose for arriving, he hoped to have the opportunity to holiday a bit. It did not take long for him to leave the airport. He always traveled light. Whatever he needed, he purchased wherever he went. He rarely carried a firearm with him on an assignment. A gun was supplied to him by a contact on the site of the operation. But on this occasion, he had his Beretta in R2AMD/XRD, a secret radio-active anti-metal detector/ X-ray depressant compartment in his valise (controlled by a state of the art electrode designed to cause momentary dysfunctions of detecting X-ray device scanning an object in the resistant compartment). Lord X insisted that his secret service operators be conversant with the physio-electro-mechanical elements and the capabilities of such sophisticated devices. He donned his dark glasses, and with his valise in one hand and a portmanteau in the other, he casually stepped into the tropical sun. It took five minutes to hire a JUTA limousine. "The Grand Lido," he nonchalantly said to the driver.

On the road to Negril, comfortably settled in the luxurious car, he could not help but take stock of himself, and reflected on why he was in Jamaica on this occasion. He was one of the few coloured men, and the only Jamaican – as far as he knew-who was a part of a special FBI intelligence unit who kept eye on, and, when necessary, intervened in the dirty work of agencies and persons, here and there. The operators attached to this Unit received orders from no one and reported to no one, except Lord X, the doyen of the British Secret Service. Lord X could be contacted only by secret code, no two operators having the same code, and also by the click of SAM (Solar Automated Mode) a pea-sized one-way communication module which had a single long range radio wave, and is compatible with any computer installed with STERL (Selenium Tele-Radio Linkage), using the secret code – of course. Wily fox that he was, Lord X contacted his operatives by devious means, hardly ever repeating the same route twice in a row.

He began to wonder if he wasn't facetious to have acted on a sudden whim to deplane at Montego Bay just to gain on spot feelings about the nude wedding event. He had surfed the internet, and good heavens! If those folks had anything of virtuous value to protect, they would put it into yards of wrap! What were the moralists griping about? There were more critical issues in the island to be addressed, including the death of George, his brother.

What he knew about George swiftly flowed from his mind like a torrent. George, his senior, always wild and adventurous, had fled from justice from Britain to America via questionable means. He had lived obscurely in New York City on the narrow crooked and not so easy street called *drugs*. He was eventually caught. While in prison, he met another Jamaican, Ralph Pearson, alias 'The Knife', a small-time drug-pusher. When George left prison, he linked up with 'The Knife' in Brooklyn, and resumed his nefarious trade. To establish himself as a citizen, he married Greta Mier a.k.a. 'The Horse' a.k.a. 'Kersene Ile,' a notorious Harlem whore and drug-pusher. Greta ran away, while George was in jail, and linked up with another Jamaican in Miami.

George and 'The Knife' fell out. 'The Knife' took two Puerto Rican friends to George's apartment, apparently to soften him up. But George proved too tough for them. A few days after, the residents of the shoddy apartment building, disturbed by a bad smell emanating from apartment H27, called the Police.

"Hell fire!" shouted the Police Officer who first entered H27. "What the hell...?"

There were three bloated bodies sprawled about. Stale blood everywhere, money, clothes and drugs, but no documents – not even a shred of paper to identify the occupants of the apartment. According to the Police, not a clue. He learnt from a contact in New York that George was not among the dead in H27. George had mysteriously disappeared. He knew nothing about George's whereabouts until George was found by the Police in Jamaica under the assumed name of Vinton Case. He did not think that either Pappy or Raymond, their younger brother, knew. Pappy, in the rare phone calls between them, had been complaining that he wasn't hearing from George.

He suddenly jerked from his reverie, and told himself he ought to be looking through the windows to see if he was able to recall landmarks, and to see what developments had taken place in ten years. The road suddenly narrowed after a bend and the driver barely slowing down, angrily tooted his horn at a red bullkin indifferently crossing the road. "Dese cow, dey won't move out a' di road when dey see car comin'. Dem mus' t'ink dey can buy car! Dey t'ink dem own di road!" the driver complained.

"That's a lot of bull, man!" he said.

Turning around his head to gaze at him, the driver asked, "What yuh say?"

"Never mind," he replied. "You have to keep your eyes on the road. There seems to be a lot of development about here."

"Yes Sah," the driver answered. "Lots a' development. Big hotel, big house, plenty touris'. Dem callin' fo' casino now. But church people bawl out an' di government say 'no casino'."

"Ah, I see," he said. "How is crime in Montego Bay?"

"Crime?" replied the driver. "Well, it not so bad in MoBay, but a 'hole heap o' bad t'ings a' gwaan. Di Police a' kill off di yout' dem an' di yout' a kill Police. 'Yuh 'ear 'bout di killin' of seven yout' in a place dem call Braeton?"

"Yes, I learned about it on the *net*," he replied.

"It's di biggis' talk dey 'ere right now," the driver explained, waxing warm to the subject. "But dem dey yout' deserve fi dead! Dem bad! Dem ac' like dem nuh did 'ave no parents. Nobody response fi dem. Dem nuh innocent! Yuh t'ink dem nuh fi dead? What 'appen to dem parents? Dem nuh did ha' nobody fi talk to dem, no uncle? No aunt? What 'appen to dem school an' di church an' di community weh dem did live? Yuh t'ink is di Police alone kill dem?"

"My friend, I can't answer your questions until I have a chance to look into the whole issue," he replied. "But I am willing to join you in asking them. What do you think about the nude wedding tomorrow? Is there much excitement about it?"

"Di nude wedding? Nutten much 'bout it. Only some church

people ha' screw," said the driver.

"Ha-ha! Screw!" he exclaimed, amused.

"Is none o' my business, but I don't agree. Those t'ings mus' 'appen in yuh bedroom," the driver asserted.

"A nude wedding in your bedroom!" he said to himself. "How about that? It has a romantic streak, doesn't it?" He said to the driver.

"A wedding is a public affair. You can't have it in a bedroom unless one or both parties are bed ridden.

"Yuh see di photographs of di nude bride dem?" the driver asked.

"Nope," he replied. "Why?"

"Well, I look at di photograph in di paper an' dem look well bedridden to me," the driver commented.

The driver had missed the point, but had inadvertently invented the pun of the day. He was not a man to whom laughter came easily, but he could not resist laughing his head off. *The driver wondered what his passenger was laughing about, was he a mad man?*

"Right now, Hedonism II, full up a' Jamaican turn touris' fi go see di wedding, but yuh cyaan go wit' yuh clothes. Yuh ha' fi go naked," the driver continued.

"How is the Carnival going?" he asked.

"Di Carnival?" replied the driver. "I believe it alright. Nuff t'ings a' gwaan. Dey say it biggah dan las' year. Nuff jumpin' an' wine-in', soca, calypso, reggae an' jammin'. Boss, if yuh want to see Carnival, yuh should go straight to Kingston. Is dere Carnival deh!"

He said that he was thinking that he ought to have done that.

"Yuh can go to Kingston by air-taxi," the driver advised.

"Yeah, thanks. I must do that," he replied.

By then, they had arrived at the Grand Lido. A uniformed porter opened the door of the limousine, and another insisted on taking his valise and portmanteau. He was surprised that shortly after, while he was waiting at the reception desk to be registered, the English couple came into the foyer.

"How exciting to see you again!" she exclaimed.

"Noice plice!" said her husband, smiling and shaking hands.

The Briton was sweating profusely and his hand-shake was limp and clammy.

"Yeah, this is a beautiful country," he pleasantly, remarked. "Enjoy your vacation. As they say here in Jamaica: 'JAMAICA? NO PROBLEM'!"

"No problem, indeed!" he said to himself. "So much irony in living a lie?"

He turned to her. He didn't desire to know their names. They were only a passing jot in his journey. After this, he may never see them again. It was enough to be polite, helpful, if necessary, and friendly. In fact, he was attracted to her porcelain beauty, her petiteness and her vivaciousness. "I thought that you were staying at Sandals?" he said.

"Pardon me," she sweetly apologized. "I made a silly mistake, I guess. I stayed at the Sandals last year with my former husband. I was probably thinking of the great time we had."

"Well, I wish you a grand time at *The Lido*," he said. He signed the hotel register using his newly adopted name, Edmund Price, and collected the key to his hotel room.

"See you around," he said to the English couple. A bell-boy took his slim luggage and led the way towards the lifts. He was pleased that he had chosen the Grand Lido. Pleasant surroundings always exhilarated him. He went to the window of his room and looked out on to the spacious grounds of the hotel. He was pleased with what he saw. Life at first, for him, did not come easy. He had been through the ropes. Now he was determined to enjoy some living.

"Yah," he said to himself, "I love what I am doing!" He loved danger. He was born for the convolutions and subtleness of the hunt. He was clever and he worked hard. "I am good at what I do. There have been no complaints, at any rate not from Lord X."

He turned from the window and sank into a commodious chair He rummaged through a pile of papers, brochures, tabloids and magazines neatly piled on a table. He rifled through the day's copies of the local papers and a couple of back numbers, feeding his eyes on columns about Carnival and crime. 'A BETTER AND

BIGGER CARNIVAL' screamed from several pages.

As he read, he was impressed with the quality of the local writers and journalists. "Some good writing in this country. A bit wordy," he murmured, "and a bit difficult to follow. But British writers could learn a thing or two from these local writers. I find most British writers too stiff, lacking in sensation, colour and humour, and their command of language too conservative. Jamaican writers do not know how to be miserly with words."

He dialed Room Service, and when a bell-boy appeared, he ordered fish fillet, rice and peas, a soufflé and a Red Stripe beer. He turned a number of pages, reading through the profiles of the up-coming Carnival. He was not only a Beatles fan, but he was also a disciple of Byron Lee, and had several of his albums in his collection. He read from one of the pages entitled, 'JUMP AND WAVE', he read.

Further on, he read about the Beach J'ouvert held in Ocho Rios and that Michel Montano and Xtatik had performed at a place called Chukka Cove. Information about the Road March and the Last Hurrah held his interest.

"I would like to visit the Calypso Tent," he muttered, "and probably meet Byron Lee. But the Road March and the Last Hurrah is certain. I won't miss the big event."

When the bell-boy appeared with his dinner, he asked which was the quickest way to travel to Kingston the following day. The bell-boy explained that the hotel could arrange for him to travel by air-taxi. He instructed the bell-boy to make the arrangement at the reception desk. While he ate, he glanced at a caption in one of the tabloids. The words sensationally screamed at him like the title of a Dracula movie: *The Spectre of Braeton*. He placed the page together with another captioned: *Grim Reaper and the Braeton Seven*. He intended to read them after his dinner. He also reminded himself that he had to phone Raymond to inform him that he would arrive in Kingston the following day.

After several tries, he got his brother who sounded as if he was in the room with him. "Hello, Ray, it's me," he called. "I am in Montego Bay. I am coming to Kingston, tomorrow. No, no, I will be staying at a hotel in Kingston. Ask for Edmund Price. Why the false name? I will explain when I see you. Don't tell anybody that I am here…Not even Pappy. Understand?...No, no, I will inform Pappy myself...Let us not discuss it on the phone...I will call you from the hotel…Oh, yes, bring the clippings. It is important for me to look through them. Ok, Ray, tomorrow."

"Irie, Big Breddah," Raymond replied, leaving him to wonder what the outlandish word 'irie' meant.

What more he knew about George, he learnt from the long telephone discussions he had with Raymond, since he had called to inform him that their eldest brother was detained in jail awaiting his extradition. It was alleged that George had killed 'The Knife' and his two aides who had gone to his apartment apparently with the intention of working him over.

Then, he cleaned out all vestiges of his occupancy of H27 and disappeared. Unknown to Pappy, to Raymond and to him, George turned up in Jones Town and set up himself firstly, as a big taxi-operator and secondly, as a philanthropist, under the name of Vinton Case. The DEA eventually put the pieces of the crossword puzzle together and found the missing piece, George, in his homeland, Jamaica. The local Police picked him up, before he realized they had got wind of him. He was acting as a reputable and responsible businessman and good citizen sitting in his air-conditioned office when the Police came. He offered no resistance, was actually urbane and did not affirm or deny that he was Burnel George Carter wanted in the United States for multiple crimes. George, however, filed petition in the courts against the extradition order.

He set aside his thoughts about George and took up the pages he had put together about the Braeton affair. What he gathered was that seven young men ranging from fourteen to nineteen were surrounded in a two-bedroom house in the wee hours of the morning by a contingent of sixty members of the Police - Incredible! It couldn't have been so many - and executed at close range. The Police lost their heads! The Police alleged that two or three men were wanted for the murder of a policeman and a school principal. According to the accounts on the pages, the fatal event of Braeton was causing a division in the nation as some people agreed with the ruthless action of the Police, while others condemned them as brutal murderers.

"Couldn't the Police have used tactical methods to apprehend some if not all of those suspects?" he asked aloud. "We make a lot of mistakes in policing in Britain, but such incompetence and disregard for life in capturing suspected persons, and even hardened criminals, could not have happened. Why was teargas or a watercannon not used? Why weren't the occupants of that house starved into surrendering? Jungle justice, indeed! They kill us, and we kill them. It's all in the game! No prisoners are taken! Much is lost. Little is gained!"

He crushed the page in his fist, and his forehead became corrugated with intense concern. "If this report is correct," he murmured, "then the Police need to be trained to differentiate between killing suspects and killing those that they necessarily have to kill in self-defense. This is where the scientific and tactical aspects of policing show up." He agreed with the journalist who wrote: " In Jamaica, we have serious problems preserving the right to life." Here, he thought, we have to separate the *sheep* from the *wolves that are usually wrapped in sheep-skins.* If the Police are shepherds, to what extent are they expected to use their discretion and common sense to decide when to shoot and when not to shoot? In shooting wolves, sheep will be shot, at times.

"That is the rub!" he exclaimed. "How, when and where to discern sheep and wolves and wolves in sheep's clothing, without error, every time! A million dollar question! Citizens in condemning ought to make allowance for human error. It is merely human for people not to tolerate error in others, but only in themselves. What is crucial is that the right of people (including, 'the weeping and gnashing of teeth' agencies, such as AI) to protest be respected and preserved equally with all other rights.

"For members of the Police not to be impelled by their own human feelings of frustration, fear, disgust, hate and desire for revenge, and not to resort to irresponsible and callous conduct in trying situations or to act extra-judicially, require up-to-date specialized training in areas such as shooting to disable rather than to kill, overpowering or subduing prisoners without the use of excessive force, alertness in self-protection and expertise in the use of strategy. Amnesty International cannot be doing a good job if they see that their primary role as publicizing their efforts to vindicate the so-called rights of the convicted. This human rights organization would serve a nobler cause if it set out to muster resources and expertise to assist countries that need to upgrade their policing and justice systems. Probably there is, but not sensationalized by the organization as the so-called infringements and the denigration of the rights of the criminal. The role of the organization, it would appear, is to intimidate and belittle small *'renegade countries'* like Jamaica, to toe the line according to their code, or else…"

Chapter 2

RAYMOND:
GUN CULTURE INTRODUCED

*T*he flight from Montego Bay in a single-engine air-taxi was a bit cramped, but the breath-taking view of the landscape more than compensated. He was surprised that Kingston looked almost the same as he remembered it ten years ago. Before he settled in his room on the tenth floor of the Hilton, he phoned Raymond. From the wide window of his room, he looked on the Boulevard below and noticed, to his amazement, that the unending procession of snorting cars, trucks and buses looked like ants bustling in disorganized lines, human bodies from on high appeared minute – flattened close to the earth, moving awkwardly by means of flapping their arms and legs in clumsy forward and backward movements like insects that had lost two or more of their legs. Quite irrationally, his thoughts drifted to the ineptitude of the human form.

He intended to call Pappy in due course. Pappy would surely appear to be offended and would insist on knowing why he had not informed him that he was coming. He would explain that he had planned his visit as a surprise, not that the ol' man would buy it and allow himself to be mollified, but it was worth the try. He turned away from the window and threw himself on the bed from which he could enjoy the panoramic view of the Kingston Harbour.

He was shaken out of his reverie by a knocking on the door and by the sound of the buzzer.

"Who is it?" he called.

'Is me big breddah," the voice replied.

He rose to open the door. "Ray, I wasn't expecting you so early. I am glad to see you."

"Me too, Big Breddah," Raymond replied, as they embraced. The brothers viewed each other for a while, and then Raymond threw himself into a chair and draped his left leg over its arm and caressed its back with his right arm. Raymond was his last brother. After a checkered career at Wolmer's Boys School, Raymond was sent to England to him to continue his schooling. But Raymond would not settle. He became unmanageable and ran with a London gang who called themselves "Jute Boys", rivals of the "Teddy Boys". Raymond, after a number of run-ins with the Police, confessed, "I hate di English people dem. I want freedom from di slave-master dem", and finally, "Me waaan go back a Jamaica. Mi waan go 'ome!" Pappy wrote to say that he was happy to have Raymond back: "But I hardly see him. The boy sly and lie like any mongoose."

Raymond had grown into a tall, bearded and rangy young man, and his language and deportment were more outlandish than when he was in England. His dress was bizarre, a green shirt and tight yellow jeans, a woolen cap of red, yellow and black drawn closely over his ears, huge dark glasses which accentuated the thinness of his hairy face, and a large expensive looking pair of Nike sneakers. He was the caricature of an English rake with whose sister he once had more than a platonic relationship. With his head on his chest, his left arm hanging listlessly, fingers nervously tapping the carpet, Raymond appeared a boneless, exhausted and dejected creature.

"I hope that you haven't told anyone that I am here," he said to Raymond. "It is important that I remain incognito. Remember; do not address me as your brother. The name is Edmund Price, as I told you on the phone."

"Irie, Big Breddah. I mean Missa Price. I get di message. Do not address Missa Price as big breddah," Raymond said, mockingly. "Irie!"

"It is important," he warned, ignoring Raymond's theatrical effort to treat his instruction lightly. "Did you bring the clippings I asked you to collect? Have you heard anything further?" he asked.

"Yeah, I bring di paper," Raymond replied. "But I sure dem kill 'im. What di Police seh yuh t'ink anyt'ing coulda go so? Him nuh did a' mek nuh bomb! A lie dem a' tell! Dem kill 'im! Mi good, good breddah!"

"Who killed him?" he asked.

"I don't know who," Raymond replied. "But I sure somebody kill 'im! Him nuh mek nuh bomb! Is not true!"

"You can't say for sure that he was murdered, without the facts or evidence," he gently admonished his brother, "We have to get the facts and that's where you come in. You have to help me."

Raymond raised his head, his thin and lanky frame trembling, and his voice hoarse with anxiety and excitement. "How you goin' find out if is kill dem kill 'im?" he asked. "How I goin' help yuh? Me is no Babylon police!"

"Go easy, Ray," he calmly said to Raymond. "I can't tell you when I don't know myself. We have to play it by ear, until something comes our way, know what I mean?"

"Irie," Raymond answered. "We play it by ear till somet'ing penetrate. Irie!"

With so frequent repetition of the word, *irie,* by Raymond, he took it to mean that his brother understood and agreed with what he said. "The first thing which you are to do is to remember never to disclose my true name or identity to anyone, not even to Pappy," he warned. "Don't tell him that I am here."

"But 'ow long yuh goin' not tell Pappy seh you is 'ere? Dat not right! You can't come so far an' don't go look fi 'im!" Raymond complained.

"I intend to see him soon," he replied. "But as I said, let's play it by ear."

Raymond loudly scratched his beard, cocked his right eye and twisted his mouth, revealing strong nicotine-stained teeth, while he reflected on the implications of the conversation. Then he murmured dejectedly, "As yuh say, big breddah, play it by ear. Irie!" Sifting the four paper clippings and swiftly glancing through them, he said, "I will go through these later. What have you been doing to yourself?"

"Ahm!" Raymond cleared his throat. "Nothin' much. I do a little work for a Chiniman name Missa Chew. Rememba him?"

"Vincent Chew?"

Raymond nodded.

"Of course, I remember him!" he exclaimed. "We went to Wolmer's together. I should like to see him. How is he?"

"Irie!" Raymond replied. "Big man now. Big supermarket, villa, fishing business an' two boats."

"Sounds like a big man, indeed!" Of course, he remembered Chew. He must see him soon, or at least, before he returned to England. "Chew! What kind of work do you do for him?"

"I go to di fishermen on di Cay. I collec' di fish an' pay dem an' take supplies fi dem," Raymond replied.

"Sounds interesting," he remarked.

"Not really," said Raymond, a vacant look fluttering across his brow. "It dull. But I have to live."

He noticed that Raymond laughed uncomfortably at his own remarks, but he refrained from commenting.

"I could do with a Red Stripe," Raymond said, looking at the decor and at the ceiling as if he expected to find a bottle of beer hidden someplace in the room.

"Sorry about that," he said. "I was about to ask you." He rang 'Room Service' and ordered half dozen bottles of Red Stripe. "How is Pappy?" he asked.

"Still chawin' fire," Raymond replied. "Irie!"

"Irie, eh?" He was getting used to the term. "Ray, tell me! What's happening in the country, these days?" he asked,

"A long time it ha' gwaan," Raymond grossly replied. "Whole 'eap o' killin'. Man a' kill Police an' Police a' kill man. 'Whole 'eap a bad tings a gwaan."

Raymond's unexpected incursions, in and out of English and patois, were disturbing him. He thought that he was well versed in patois, though Pappy had strongly discouraged the speaking of it, but long separation from its everyday use was making it difficult for him to understand Raymond, especially when it seemed that new inflections and unfamiliar nuances had crept in.

"Yuh hear 'bout 'ow di Police kill di yout'man dem at Braeton?" Raymond asked.

"No, I haven't heard how they were killed, though I have read about it on the Net. How did the Police kill them?"

"Babylon surroun' di house an' shoot dem up!" Raymond angrily shouted.

He remained calm at Raymond's outburst. "I thought you had reliable details on how the police operation was actually carried out. We can't depend on hear-say."

"Di Police bwoy dem a do bad!" Raymond hotly complained. "Da's why gunman a kill dem."

"Ray, let's... just say 'Police', for the time being. I don't think I have ever seen a Police 'bwoy'. You're saying Police are bad. That opinion depends on which side of the fence you're on. If you're looking from the Police's side, you may agree that they are only doing their duty. However, I would rather learn more about this Braeton business or even of police operation throughout the island, so as not to be too prejudicial. It is easy to become blind to the truth."

"What about Breddah George?" Raymond asked, his voice hoarse with anger and desperation. "Di Police arres' him fi nutten! Nex' t'ing we hear say him dead! Nuh bad t'ing dat? Dem kill him!"

"We have no proof of that!" he sharply replied. "I will discuss it with you, as soon as I go through these bits of paper you brought me. I have a hunch I may pick up something. Remember, Ray, my name is Edmund Price. I have registered at this hotel by that name, as well as at the Grand Lido. Don't mention to Chew that I am here, nor to anyone of your friends or associates."

"The Lido! You steppin' high, big breddah!" Raymond exclaimed. "Yuh nuh easy!" Raymond pushed a nicotine-stained finger into the neck of his third beer bottle, knitted his brow and pursed his lips, as if in deep thought. "Irie!" he muttered. "Yuh don't have to keep on soakin' yuh new name into mi ears so much time. Irie?" He silently watched his brother for a half minute or so, translating into English what he said, evaluating the possible connotations of his several *iries,* and then he said, "I see you later. I will call you tomorrow."

Raymond sensing, that his brother meant that his visit had ended, unwound himself from the chair and rose to his feet. "Yuh have to get a gun, Big Breddah," he said.

"For what?" he sharply asked, greatly surprised that Raymond suggested such a thing. "I don't need a gun. You have to have a permit or a license to acquire a fire-arm, if I recall rightly!" He exclaimed. "Has the law changed?"

"No," Raymond replied, "di law don't change, but t'ings change. Plenty man ha' gun without no license. Plenty gun out deh!"

"I don't need a gun, and by no means, an illegal one!" he repeated.

Raymond shrugged his shoulders. "Di way how t'ings a guh now, if yuh ha' anyt'ing, yuh ha' fi ha' iron fi protec' it."

"But I don't have anything to protect," he replied, laughing sardonically.

"Yuh have yuh life!" Raymond replied. "Life don't wort' much in dis country so man ha' fi bar an' grill up dem 'ouse an' put burglar alarm an' dem t'ings deh, an' ha' guardsman an' guard-dog an' gun fi protec' dem. Is di runnin's in dis country now."

"I still don't think I will need a gun," he insisted. "Listen to me. Guns don't provide protection. Guns are instruments of death, for intimidation, extortion and extermination. They are useless for protection or self-defense whenever you need them most. We deceive ourselves into thinking that they can protect us. Many families suffer grief because someone was left with a loaded gun. Guns are disloyal and are often turned on their own masters. Whatever a gun is pointed at, that is what it shoots at."

"I overstan' yuh, but if yuh goin 'seek out 'ow Breddah George dead, yuh have to get a gun," Raymond insisted. "Penetrate?"

He looked at Raymond, raising a disapproving eyebrow.

"I mean overstan' – understan', Big Breddah," Raymond explained, grinning and chuckling, amused at his brother's perturbed look.

"Well, I'll be damned!" he swore beneath his breath. He did not wish to prolong the argument. "OK, Ray, see you tomorrow," he said. He opened the door to show Raymond out.

"Irie! See you tomorrow, Mr. Edmund Price. At what time do you want to see me, Mr. Price?" Raymond bantered.

He remained impervious to Raymond's attempt to humour him. "I will call you," he promised.

When the door was closed behind him, Raymond leaned against the door frame. "Look 'ow far me come fi see dis man! Waste mi time come look fi him an' him don't drop even a 'undrid quid 'pon me!" he grumbled. He was tempted to knock on the door and ask for a hand-out, but he could not muster the courage. "Fuck!" he swore as he bopped along the corridor of the hallway towards the lifts. "What mi gwine tell Needham? Him a screw seh 'im want 'im money."

No sooner had he closed the door, he took up the bits of paper he had thrown on the bed. Sitting on a chair, he read softly, *"PRISONER BLOWS UP SELF. On January19, at about 3:00p.m. there was an explosion in a cell of the General Penitentiary occupied by one George Carter, age 46. According to the Police, it is alleged that Carter was manufacturing a bomb and accidentally blew up himself. Prison authorities reported that the Police are investigating, and forensic experts have been called in. Mr. Carter was remanded in jail, awaiting the hearing of an extradition order against him, in the Corporate Area Resident Magistrate's Court. Mr. Carter was wanted by the FBI as the mastermind behind an elaborate drug ring in which women were used to transport cocaine and marijuana from Jamaica to the United States. He was also wanted for questioning in connection with the death of three men found in an abandoned apartment in Brooklyn. Carter, a Jamaican, was living in Jamaica up to the time of his capture, under the assumed name of Vinton Case. Case was identified as one of the men found dead in the Brooklyn apartment. Mr. Carter had been living in Jones Town as a law abiding citizen, taxi-operator and philanthropist.*

He browsed through the other bits of paper, and then put them aside. "They're all saying the same thing, as if written by the same news-man. No indication of *sleuthhound* efforts by some sharp-nosed newsman to ferret out the truth," he yawned and muttered. "Nothing, not the slightest clue to go on! Good old George, you finally ran out of luck. You came to the end of your narrow and crooked road, with nowhere to run and hide. Nowhere! The sum total is you were blown into thin air, and I need to know how and why. That is the most I can do for you, George. Probably, I should have turned you in myself. But then, I didn't know where you had disappeared to. Who would believe that you would turn up in Jamaica? There are so many other places you could have hidden. You were bound to be traced and picked up sooner or later."

He was non-committal and unemotional, almost too cold in his reaction to what he had read. He stretched on the bed and retrieved from the pile an oldish newspaper that had caught his interest earlier. A caption, *"The New Face of Terrorism,"* screamed menacingly at him. He quickly turned the page to be confronted with, *"Brits find cocaine in J'can callaloo. Cocaine contamination,"* he read. *"of Jamaican exports has reached its highest levels, local trade experts estimate, with two major seizures within a week. The latest haul of cocaine valued at $1.6million (J$350million) disguised in callaloo exports to Britain, comes after 72kilograms of cocaine and other drugs were found among Jamaican exports to Miami. The drugs, in both cases, were smuggled in pallets... Exporters are warned to be vigilant in shipping exports...Five men, including a Jamaican, had been arrested."*

"Ah-ah! What's for breakfast? Cocaine and callaloo?" he sardonically exclaimed. "Oh-no! You can't stop a Jamaican, eh? Doctah Bird! He is a cunning bird, hard bird fi dead! Jamaicans will find ways to install air-conditioners in hell and force the Devil to pay the bill. When ingenuity was being given away, they collected bags of it. Why won't they put their dexterity to good use and invent things great enough and powerful enough to change the world? Instead, they pack their insides with drugs and fill the insides of Britain's jails. Jamaica's past has been of a people exploited by masters. Now they exploit themselves and are exploited by their own. Do Jamaican drug dealers and couriers think of the thousands of lives and families they help to destroy by trading in cocaine, marijuana and other illegal drugs? Have they no feelings? Have they no conscience? If I didn't have a cast-iron stomach, I would and vomit every time I think of it!"

He dialed Room Service and ordered two dry martinis, then returned to re-read the cocaine in callaloo account. The removal of the cocaine and replacing it with flour drew a chuckle from him. This belied general opinion that British Police were dour and lacking in humour like bull-dogs, he thought. *The Rampage of The Gun* shouted at him from another page. *"If the account of the Braeton shooting that claimed the lives of seven young men, as reported in the GLEANER of March 18, 2001, is factual,"* he read from one of the columnists, *"then some reprehensible, awful and ignominious seven men were stupid not to have come out with their hands in the air. Yet it cannot be overlooked that the handling of the whole affair by the Police was inept and brutal. Didn't the Police think that as many of those men as possible ought to have been captured for interrogation?"*

"Yes, of course!" He said looking through the open picture window of his room. "I agree that the Police should have handled the situation with professional skill, from the fact that the wanted men were holed up and pinned down by a possibly exaggerated number of armed policemen, but enough to capture all or most of them alive."

"Guns bark in Tivoli," he nonchalantly muttered, scanning a page. He downed the rest of his martini, and mused on what he had read about guns. "It would appear that gunmen are always human target-practice in Tivoli. I am sorry for the children and the bulk of law-abiding citizens living there. If I were the government of this country," he said dryly, "I would build a firing range and invite all

gunmen to freely do their shooting there. It would be probably more effective than offering them an Amnesty to bring their guns in."

"Good God! Even when a person carries an illegal firearm, and it must be assumed that the intent of that person is to kill or rob or maim, real effort must be exercised to ensure that the culprit be subjected to the due course of law. Compromises and any other recourse, endanger the life of every citizen, law abiding or otherwise." *BEATTITUDES FOR GUNMEN* preached at him in a splash of red blood colour from a tabloid. He read the benign article written by a pastor advocating the restoration of morals instead of using guns to fight crime.

Tongue in cheek and benevolently, as if he were a cleric himself, he muttered, "My Pastor Friend, your article is what I call pulpit drivel. When since has morality ever solved the world's problems? Your ramblings and religious ranting are a Utopian pipe-dream." He murmured to himself, "Many people may read your article or listen to it, and agree or disagree with it; the people who you hope should read or listen never do. To some people it does some good; it does no harm to any, so what the heck? Continue doing what you're doing. Pastor, world without end!" He knew he was getting tipsy. If it wasn't due to the martinis, it must be the tropical ambience. "Jamaica land we love! Tourist paradise! Jamaica, no problem!" He muttered.

He dialed Room Service and ordered another brace of double martinis. He was not much of a smoker, since as a rule secret service operatives do not smoke because of the possible danger of one's presence being detected by the faintest tobacco aroma when one least desired to be discovered. However, he kept a choice selection of cheroot, Royal Crown Brand, in a slim wooden case in his portmanteau. When the martini arrived, he tipped the bell-boy again, bit off an end of the cigar, lit it and drew its essence into his lungs. "Tackle crime with morals, not bullets! Go tell that to the birds in bird-shooting season! The advice to use morals instead of bullets to tackle crime is little consolation to those who are liable to find themselves at the wrong end of the game." But he agreed, in part, with the well intentioned and reverend gentleman. He agreed that in no way could the problem of crime and violence be solved by simply fighting force with force. *An eye for an eye will leave the world blind.* He reflected for a moment on this epigrammatic thought of the writer. He held his martini high, downed it and shouted, "Well said, Parson. I give you full marks! Let's solve the world's problems with morals! Where shall we begin? Where shall we start? With UNO? With NATO? With the World Bank? With the EU, the Middle-East, the President, the Queen or the Pope? With the whippings of Islam? With India or China or Cambodia? With Palestine, Tivoli or Sharpesville? Where shall we start? The world has too many places lacking in morals from which to start. We can't focus. Defeat is inevitable, even before we begin."

He tried to recall how long ago the last time he was drunk. It must have been a long time. Failing to recall how long, he gave up and, succumbing to the Caribbean breeze that gently entered the room, fell into a doze.

Chapter 3

THE MEDIA,
CRIME AND POLICE

*I*t was morning when his hunger awakened and reminded him that he had not dined. Despite a dull headache, a bad taste in his mouth and a miserable feeling in his stomach, he pulled himself out of bed. He shaved and showered, donned light-blue linen shorts and a pale blue, silver embroidered jacket, *a guayavera*, he had bought in Mexico. White leather-soled tennis shoes on sockless feet completed his dress. He descended to the grand dining-room and had black coffee, ackee and saltfish with boiled bananas for breakfast. After breakfast, he strolled about the hotel grounds listening uninterestedly to the clatter of cutlery and the chatter and laughter of the guests. His walk took him to a huge billboard still flashing, though it was day: JAMAICA NO PROBLEM.

He crossed the Boulevard, took a newspaper from the news stand in the foyer of the hotel, and returned to his room without realizing that he had lost his hangover. An attendant had already tidied his room and had neatly re-arranged the newspapers, magazines and clippings he had strewn about the table. *Guns Seized: Two Arrested,* he silently read. Then he fixed his eyes on a well-written letter entitled "*The Police are People too,*" which he found eloquent and thoroughly reasoned: "*The death of seven young-sters in Braeton has stirred much alarm and horror in the society...It must be recognized that 'due process of law' is a preferred course for administering justice. The society must accept that there are rules governing the process and must ad-here to those rules. The due process of law is hampered, frus-trated and mutilated when accused persons and their comrades in crime, cannot be convicted, because no one dares to testify against them...It is, therefore, imperative that those to whom it is entrusted to protect the citizens against crime, act so as to safeguard against the complete over-running of the society by criminal elements. Witnesses must be effectively protected. Courts must be efficient in trying cases ... The media has a responsibility to sift the information they get so as not to sensa-tionally distort thus putting the Police and the citizens in a bad light. Those who are trained and are entrusted to protect the society, on the other hand, should professionally execute their dangerous and difficult tasks at most, if not, at all times.*"

"Excellent bit of writing!" he said to himself. "And a timely and sound warning to the nation. The Police, to be competent and ef-fective, must have the trust and support of the people they are working with and are risking their lives to protect. But the citizens whom the Police serve cannot condone their taking the law into their hands. I stand for the fundamental right of citizens, in a democratic society, to examine, criticize, praise or condemn the level of policing in their country. The Police, despite the many frustrations that confront them, and their personal sense of danger, must observe due pro-cess. The highly sensitive and volatile practice of extra-judicial mea-sures should be discouraged by the police officers and policemen themselves." Looking through the window, far out at sea on a clump of downy clouds floating lazily against the pale southern sky, he said aloud, "But the Police are only human. They will make mistakes. They can be carried away by frustration and fury, by desire for revenge and by the resentment against those who kill. Good God! People, don't be too hard on them! They are only human!"

"What is the point of apprehending a criminal, if they can't be held securely?" glared at him from an editorial. "Yes," he addressed, with a sardonic smirk, the question to the wide picture-window revealing a great expanse of placid water, "What's the point? Defects as these in the system inevitably breed callousness in the Force." *"Harsh Measures Needed To Fight Crime"* cackled at him like a toothless old lady. *"The country's murder rate has reached alarming proportions,"* the article groaned in horror and fright. *"A harsh reality is that in the process of undertaking to reduce the incidence of criminal activities, some innocent people are liable to come to harm. But it is also a troubling fact that innocent people are being killed almost every day with signs of getting worse, if the Police do not endeavour to contain it, even at the expense of losing a few innocent lives."* Not a confronting prospect, but what has to be done, must be done, he was thinking. *"But there doesn't seem to be an alternative which is free of the risk of innocent people coming to harm, caught in a cross-fire or found in the wrong place at the wrong time."* he read. *"The stark reality must be faced that no amount of concern for human life can stand in the way of safeguarding the lives of the many. There is always a painful price to pay."*

"Yes," he remarked. "Even at the expense of sacrificing a few innocents for the safety of the majority!" he muttered aloud. CARIBBEAN COURT screeched like a wounded hawk beside a column captioned: *How Much More Violent Can We Get?* "Tell it to the judge," he almost shouted sardonically. *"Violence of any kind is criminal,"* the article intoned. "You may be right," he murmured, with a chuckle, "but I beg to disagree." The article however, did succeed in capturing his attention for a while. *"Senseless violence undermines the structure of good communities and depletes social and economic energies."* "That is the reason I kill sometimes," he casually muttered to the wide window facing the direction of the vast inscrutable wisdom of an ever restless sea, delicate seabirds exquisitely floating, reconnoitering on their curved wings or swooping down in almost perfectly symmetric arcs to violently pluck flapping fish from the waves in the distance. "Violence! There is beauty with agony in some forms of violence," he remarked with a sardonic chuckle. "For instance, I am paid to kill –to rid the world of the violence of criminals on society." In the Secret Service, authorized to kill, they have never asked him how and why he killed. They asked if the assignment was complete. Violence is a relative term, to each his own in that what is repugnant to one person may be attractive to another. CRIME NEEDS NEW APPROACH sprang at him. *"The country is now faced with an escalation in violent crimes in inner city communities...The Police tried in the past to maintain law and order by the use of intimidation and force. They used this method in the 1960's, and again in the 1980's, when the killing fields and all manner of abuse of civil rights reared their ugly heads."*

There was a knock on the door. On recognizing Raymond's voice, he rose and opened the door.

"Mawnin'," Raymond greeted him with a sly grin. Raymond had with him a companion whose nondescript appearance, haphazard dress and dark glasses made him look like a ferret. "Dis is mi bredrin, Speng," Raymond explained, "Can I an' I come in?"

He stepped a few paces backwards into the room and beckoned them to enter. Raymond immediately wrapped himself about the chair he had occupied the day before. Speng refused to sit and assumed a slouched stance in the middle of the room.

"Dat awright," said Speng, when he offered him the other chair in the room. "I man want to grow tall."

"Big Breddah, di bredrin 'ave a gun fi sell you," Raymond informed him.

"What?" he shouted, "Sell me a gun? I explicitly told you I don't need a gun!"

"Sh! Not so loud, Boss," Speng said as coolly as if they were trading a bunch of bananas.

"Hey! Big Breddah!" Raymond cried in alarm, shifting his supine form to look around as if he expected the police to leap at him from the window, the carpet or the walls.

"Yuh nuh ha' fi gwaan so!" Speng said in a matter-of-fact tone, flashing his teeth in a diabolical grin, as if he was impersonating the devil in a school play. "Yuh don't want nobody know yuh business? As I man say, we ha' fi go t'rough evillous times in dis yah country."

"Seen! Dese evilous times!" Raymond agreed. "Show him di iron!"

Speng pulled a gun from beneath his shirt and handed it buttwise to him. "Boss, is good iron dat!" he drawled.

He checked the chamber of the pudgy-looking German Luger, and then balanced it on his palm. An old serviceable weapon with its serial number erased, it looked cumbersome and benign like an obese, old priest. "How did you come by this gun?" he asked. "Obviously, it isn't licenced!"

"Yuh can get anyting yuh want in dis country, Bass, if yuh know weh fi find it," Speng replied.

"And I suppose yuh wouldn't tell me where," he growled.

"Dat depen' on what yuh want, Bass, an' it kinda dangerous!" Speng replied. "We would ha' fi negotiate. Money ha' fi pass."

"Money, eh?" he asked slightly amused. "You slimy son-of-a-gun," he murmured, to himself. "I bet, you'd sell your grandmother. Every mother-son wants money and wouldn't care how they come by it. Contemptible bastards!"

He pointed the empty gun towards the window and pulled on the trigger. "Rather hard on the trigger," he said aloud. "A pretty old gun."

"So you know 'bout gun Boss!" Speng exclaimed.

"Yeah," he boasted. "I collect old guns as a hobby!" he chuckled softly at the lie. He was amused that Speng was impressed. "How much do you want for this old fellow?" he asked.

"Two hundred quid," Raymond quickly said.

"Yeah, 'ow much dolla' dat?" Speng said, looking intently at Raymond.

" 'Bout twelve gran'," Raymond replied.

"Twelve? Irie," Speng said, contemplating the numbers in the air by gesticulating with the fingers of his right hand, coiling and uncoiling them around a bundle of imaginary notes, as if he already had the money in his hands.

He decided to purchase the gun, justifying his unlawful action by telling himself that by possessing the weapon, he was securing one less illegal gun from the hands of the criminals. He put the gun down and took up his wallet from the night table. "I am paying a hundred pounds, not a pence more," he said, looking at both of them.

"No, Boss," they exclaimed in unison, "Di gun cyaan't sell fi dat!"

He looked hard at Speng, "You yourself said I know about guns. This gun is hot stuff, and you and Ray know it." He snarled savagely, but not too loudly at them.

"Don't' talk so loud, Boss. Dat kinda low fi di gun. Make it up to one-fifty!" Speng whined.

"A hundred," he said adamantly. "Take it or take back the gun!" He was buying an illegal gun for the first time in his life and he felt as if a bucket of icy water was being poured slowly down his spine. There was one other occasion when he had a similar feeling. He was sent to Brussels to shadow a British diplomat suspected of certain irregular practices. He had to climb up to a window five stories high and into the room of the diplomat, at night, only to be attacked by a Tabby cat and a yapping poodle. He swiftly drew the spread from the bed and enveloped the cat, quietening its nine lives in a few seconds, and he made friends with the poodle. Even now, he still chuckled at what he imagined to be the consternation of the diplomat as to how his cat became fatally entangled in the bed-spread.

The roar of motor vehicles on the Boulevard far below seeped through the window into the silence as Raymond and Speng, behind their dark glasses, peered at each other in some sort of telepathic communication.

"It nuh irie," whined Speng, stretching out his hand to accept the money. "It kinda thin, fi true!" Speng held the note up towards the light coming from the window, then blew on it as if he saw specks of dust on it, flicked its stiffness between his gingers to listen to it, and then put it to his thick lips. "Blood money, to blood!" Speng swore. It required a bit of effort to shove the money into a pocket of his over-tight jeans. With similar effort, he extracted half dozen cartridges from another overly tight pocket, which he placed beside the gun.

"Yuh need more slug," Speng said. "I can get more fi yuh, Bass, but it cos' money."

"Yeah," he mocked. "You said that, you can get anything, if you know where to ask for it."

" No lie, Boss! I 'ave contac'," Speng boastfully replied. "I guarantee dat!"

Raymond took up one of the cartridges and the gun. He swiftly snatched the weapon from Raymond. "Don't play with guns, Ray," he coolly said. "People are often accidentally shot, by careless and irresponsible handling of guns." Raymond inspected the cartridge, blew on it and kept tossing it and catching it on his palm. "Beautiful baby!" he said repeatedly, and when it fell on to the carpet, he went on all fours to retrieve it from under the bed. When Raymond rose, their eyes met and Raymond said to Speng, "See yuh later, Star!"

He opened the door to let Speng out. Raymond said to Speng, "Irie!"

"Boss, see yuh!" Speng said to him. He did not reply. He was angry with Raymond, as well as disturbed with the criminality of the transaction with Speng. Not that consorting with questionable characters and indulging in illegalities was new to him, but he preferred to arrange such matters by himself, and at least on his own initiative. But this occasion with Raymond and Speng triggered in him a premonition that he was destined to enter into a region where some things were not going to turn out right – one which made him believe that he should probably take the next plane out.

Chapter 4

NOSTALGIA

*I*t hot!" Raymond remarked. "I could suck a Red Stripe." He ignored Raymond's wish. "How could you do such a thing, Ray?" he exploded. "You bring this bloke here, without asking me! Suppose he planned to hold me up?"

"Speng?" Raymond asked, laughing uneasily. "Da's di las' man on eart' to do dat! Di bredrin is as 'armless as a dove an' hones' as a lamb! No, big breddah, I don't deal wit' criminals!"

"I have seen a lot of doves and lambs in my time. They rip off the gullible. Don't tell me about it! Does Pappy know about the friends you keep?"

"My friends is my business!" Raymond angrily replied. "Pappy can't tell me what kinda' friends to keep!"

"You're quite right!" he coldly replied. "I suppose it's none of my business either! But remember what we agreed on. Nobody must know that I am here. You have to remember that. I told you that the investigation of George's death is a dangerous operation. Do not act without my specific instruction and never before consulting with me. You are intelligent enough to understand. Don't go about putting me danger, for Christ's sake! And you learnt to speak English. I have no objection whatever to you speaking Jamaican to your friends, but I need to understand quickly and clearly what you say, therefore speak in clear English as much as you're able. That outlandish gibberish you and your friend speak is difficult. What is his real name? I'm sure it is not Speng."

"Needham, but 'im don't use Needham. Everybody who know 'im, call 'im Speng."

"Well Speng or Neeedham, whoever he is, I hope I don't see him again!" he growled.

"Jus' res', Big Breddah," Raymond replied. "I penetrate."

"Penetrate? Penetrate what?" he asked. "I am afraid I don't understand!"

"Yeah, da's what I did mean say if yuh can't penetrate is di same as to say yuh don't understan'," Raymond explained.

"Ray, I am out of touch with patois subtle nuances, and fresh inflections that have crept into the language which is making it difficult for me to 'penetrate' so to speak. I have no objections as to how *you* speak ordinarily, nor do I have a right to object, but I repeat that I would be greatly obliged if when you speak to me, you use the Queen's English, as you learnt to speak it in school," he explained. "And remember my name is Edmund Price."

"Irie, Mr. Price," Raymond replied smiling roguishly. "That I will try, but the real and true language is what me an' mi bredrin talk. We understan' one anoddah, much better. So one language for me and you, an' one language fo' dem an' I. Irie! I get the message. Big Brother. Jus' res'!"

"I am glad that you understand my position," he said. "I told you that I don't need a gun, and you went and got me one. What am I to do with it?

"Everybody in this country need a gun," Raymond replied.

"But not an illegal firearm!" he growled. "It must be taken that a man with an illegal gun can have only one intent, and that is to rob and kill. Based on spate of almost daily killings, I conclude there are too many illegal guns in the island."

"I was t'inkin' di same t'ing, – too many illegal guns!" Raymond said.

"And yet you went and got me one, instead of informing the

Police where to recover it."

"The Police! Informah nuh las' long in dis country!" Raymond loudly remonstrated. "Informah not popular in this country! They en' up wid' no tongue an' full a' shot in bone yard!"

He laughed at his brother's vehemence. "Bone yard, indeed!" he muttered. "No wonder the policeman's job is so difficult and dangerous. The Police cannot be effective, if civilians are reluctant to pass on information."

"The Police have to learn to work close with people an' don't dis, I mean disrespec' them," said Raymond. "The Police know that some a' them jus' don' know 'ow to talk to people. Some don't care. Dey make people afraid of them an' don't trust dem."

"I totally agree with you. It seems to me that some policemen undo the good that other policemen are trying to do. I see a dilemma. You're afraid to give information to the Police and so you condone with criminals, even bringing a man here to sell me an illegal gun. I am wondering what more you know of the crime circle. What you know might be valuable to me to crack open the mystery of George's death."

"What yuh talkin' 'bout, Big Breddah? Gun illegal only when Babylan ketch yuh wit' it!" Raymond said.

Seething with anger, he did not bother to counter Raymond's obnoxious remark.

"Good!" he growled, and Raymond seemed to wilt under his glare. "I think we are going to make a great team with that opinion and attitude of yours. I have looked through the bits of paper you brought me, and I have not discovered even a tiny clue on which to work. Have you any information, no matter how unimportant it may seem, that might give me a lead? If I could talk to anyone who was closely associated with George in the prison, we could begin from that angle, and pick up the pieces as we go along."

Raymond remained silent as if he were not listening, his lips pursed and the fingers of his right hand tattooing softly on the carpet.

Brooding, he turned to look through the window at the pedestrians lazing about, and he watched the unceasing and feverish cavalcade of snorting vehicles along the Boulevard, in a hurry to go some place.

"I t'ink I could find a man," Raymond said, "but it goin' cos' money."

He turned from the window to look at his brother. "You can get anything in this country, eh?" he sneered. "You only have to know where to search. How much money it will take?"

Raymond became animated, apparently, by the thought of money. "About a hundred quid," Raymond suggested, after reflecting for about a minute.

He plucked a hundred pounds from his wallet, and then as if responding to an afterthought, he gave Raymond fifty more. "That fifty is for your personal expense," he explained.

No sooner than Raymond received the money, he headed for the door, lingering a moment to say, "Well, Mr. Price, dat is irie. I will call you tomorrow. Seen?"

He opened the door in angry silence, let his brother out and watched his back disappearing down the hallway, his Nike making soft brushing sounds on the plush red carpet. Surveying the room after Raymond left, he swiftly devised a hiding place for the gun. He pulled the bedding on to the floor, and over-turning the divan frame, he pierced the housing of the posturepedic mattress and cutting into foamy mass, he removed a small section of it. Then, he wiped the gun free of finger-prints, wrapped it in sheets of paper and shoved it into the aperture he had made. "Great hiding place for you, Ol' Fellah! I hope that I can reach you, if I need you," he murmured. "I must call Pappy, now."

"I don't want to hear anything from you!" Pappy shouted in feigned anger, over the phone, "I don't even want to see you! You tell me that you leave Mother Country (Pappy always referred to Britain as Mother Country,) an' come 'ere wid'out infoming me? Suppose I get heart failure?"

"I didn't know that a tough fellow like you have a heart, Pappy?" he teased. "I thought of giving you a surprise by just dropping in to say, hello, without notifying you, Alright?"

"It not alright at all! Surprises ain't good for my nerves. It is bad manners to drop in on people without notice. Don't do it again! Where you is now?"

"Don't do it again!" he muttered. Just like being reprimanded in his childhood and in the same harsh tone. The Ol' Man hasn't changed. He still has a lot of spunk. Only contradictory metaphors could describe him. "I am staying at a Hotel," he replied.

"Hotel?" Pappy shouted with derision, "And we have big house right here? 'You 'ave a woman wit' you why you gone to hotel?"

"No, no! No woman!" he shouted back.

" How long it will take for you to come look for me?" Pappy asked.

"In a day or two," he replied.

"Make it today, and not in one day nor in two, three days. Lift up your ass, leave di woman an' get 'ere fast. I dyin' to see you, you bastard!" Pappy bantered.

"So you hear 'bout George?" Pappy asked.

"Yes, Ray told me," he replied.

"As for Raymond!" Pappy exclaimed in pained tones.

"What about him?" he anxiously asked.

"Is not every t'ing good fi eat, good fi talk over phone," Pappy replied. "An' ol' people say dat walls 'ave ears. When I see you, we will talk. What Raymond tell you 'bout George?"

"Not much to go by. Well, in addition to what little Raymond told me, I have clippings that he brought me. I learnt a little from them. I suspect that there is a cover-up. I don't think the media got hold of the truth," he replied.

"Well, I don't 'ave anyt'ing to tell you," Pappy truculently replied, "except that George spread his bed tough an' he lie down on it. He has sown di wind an' reap di whirlwind."

"Did you go to see him in prison?" he asked.

"No, I didn't, but I sent Raymond," Pappy replied. "All dese years he hidin' in Jones Town, he never say, 'hi dawg, how yuh do?' to me. He didn't tell Raymond anyt'ing to tell me neither. Never even ask' fo' me'! He must be did shame! Or Raymond hiding what George said from me. I don't trust dat boy!"

"OK, Pappy, I will be seeing you." He swiftly replaced the

phone so that Pappy couldn't get in another word. "Crabbed Ol' Man!" he fondly remarked. "He still has a lot of spark. He is as acidic and sweet as iced lemonade on a hot summer day." He threw himself on the bed, closed his eyes and tried not to think. But what Pappy said about Raymond kept signaling his brain with increasing intensity. He didn't like the ease with which Raymond was able to contact a man to sell him an illegal gun. He didn't like his dress and mannerisms, the furtive look in his eyes, and the nicotine stains on his teeth and fingers. At 3.00 p.m., when he awoke, he shaved, showered and dressed, then ascended to the grand dining saloon. He had a bouillabaisse and broiled lobster which he finished with a sundae and a Red Stripe beer. He returned to his room and recommenced browsing the papers, including the day's issue. The caption, *'Revolving Partner Plan Promised Too Much,'* attracted his attention. "Another scam," he muttered sardonically. "The road to hell, people say, is paved with good intentions. As long as there are gullible people, there will be others less gullible to pull off scams on them. Gullible people enjoy being taken for a ride, it seems. Some, obviously, have been burnt already," he said to himself.

He was amused at the irony of the juxtaposition of an article entitled, *'Time To Focus On Agriculture'*, beside *JUNGLE JUSTICE*. "This world is never short of humour, even in grave situations," he chuckled sardonically. He was drawn to the caption *'Amnesty International To Report On Braeton Killing'*. He read, *'The Secretary General of Amnesty International says he intends to release, in a couple of days, the report of the forensic pathologist sent to Jamaica to observe the autopsies of seven young men killed by Police at Braeton. What has been called The Braeton Massacre which took place on March 14, was widely condemned by civil rights movements led by the local group called 'Jamaicans for Justice.'*

'Seven young men between the ages of 15 and 21,' he read, *'reportedly led during a shoot-out with members of the Police.' There are conflicting accounts of what actually happened.'* He had to ask himself a number of questions: " Whose truth will the

human rights people believe? It is obvious that they will believe what they wish to hear. If it is true that the Police called out the seven to come forward with their hands on their heads, and were answered with bullets, what did they expect the Police to do? Throw their hands up in the air and run for their lives? The Police, however, could have exercised good police procedure by flushing them out with teargas or with water cannon or starve them out. Patience, strategy and ingenuity, criminal psychology and respect for life and the process of law are prerequisites of good policing." He had never killed wantonly. Killing for him was a cold, calculated, premeditated process. His emotions were never involved. He killed surreptitiously, No fanfare, No public weeping and gnashing of teeth for the dead! He had never had to apologize.

'*Police are our sons too,*' an article insisted. '*…we also need to feel their pain when they are hurting, and be careful that* we *do not frustrate them unduly. The media should carefully sift through charges of police brutality, so as to assist the public, and should avoid as much as possible hysterical or over-sensationalized presentations of public reaction against the police…*'

"A well written piece, well reasoned and a well balanced statement. I hope that everybody may read it." '*A Mockery of Justice,*' shouted from the page. '*Misguided,*' screamed another. He read: '*Jamaica has become one of the most dangerous countries on earth.*'

"Ah! Ah!" he laughed. "Earth became the most dangerous of all places ever since it was occupied by that bloody beast called Man."

'*In today's society, a thousand or more people are murdered annually. The carnage on the roads each year is senseless and irresponsible. Children are unable to attend school because of violent disruption of communities. The tragic incidents of unprotected and neglected infants left in houses where they are burnt to death are heart-rending. People are attacked daily by criminals. Yet, there is not a whimper from those one-sided human rights groups.*'

"Superb writing! Tell it to AI. You may probably extort a whimper from them!" he said. "This country is like 'Danté's Inferno'."

From another page, he read: *'The Police have a right, like all other citizens, to defend themselves. We ought not to ask them to preach beatitudes to gunmen. We, however, have no other recourse than to demand a higher quality of police procedures requiring that police training be updated. It is imperative that policeman be trained and be equipped to use armed force only when other means of capture have been ineffective or impracticable.'*

"Yeah, damn right!" he exclaimed, addressing the writer. "I agree with you one hundred percent! But what is this beatitude thing you are advising people not to ask the Police to preach? I have never heard of it in policing and I was a policeman. Is it a thing with the local Police?"

'Falling Fortune For The Windies,' The Sports Page warned. *'The West Indies, if they are to win or even draw the Fourth Test against South Africa will need a spot of good luck mixed into their pluck. Up to now their fortune has been falling as fast as their wickets. At close of play yesterday, the third day, South Africa had gained 247 and 122 runs for their two wickets. Fortune seems not to be smiling with the Windies with only 140 runs and two days to go.'*

He took up the phone and called Raymond. "Ray, it's me. Any progress?" he asked.

"Some progress, Mr. Price," Raymond replied. "I still working on it."

"Ray, I need to rent a car," he said.

"Irie! Big Breddah!" Ray replied excitedly. "I will come get yuh later."

He called Room Service and ordered two Red Stripe beers. While he was reading a column captioned, *'Challenge For Young Men'*, Raymond arrived, all breezy and exuberant. "You ready, Mr. Price?"

"Yeah, I am ready!" he replied.

As they walked towards the car-park, Raymond proudly reported to him on what progress he had made. "Yeah, Big Breddah, I speak wit' two warders an' give dem half a di money. We will pay di balance when dey fix us up wit' di prisoner name Delroy Parson who was gofer for Broddah George."

"Are you telling me that George had a servant while he was in prison?" he asked slightly amused.

"Not really a servant, but a prisoner man who carry-go-bring-come fi im. But Broddah George could get anyt'ing him want. Him have electric fan, television an' posturepedic bed in him cell. Jus' pass a money to di warders an' everyt'ing cool. Everybody turn weh dem eye."

"His own servant in prison!" he exclaimed. "What shall we hear next?"

"You will hear more when you get fi talk to de man dey call Parson," Raymond remarked.

"How do you know that?" he asked.

"Di warder dat set it up tell me," Raymond replied.

By then, they had reached Raymond's battered old Toyota.

"Dis is mi Numknack," Raymond proudly claimed, giving a mighty thump to its bonnet.

"Dis car will take yuh anywhere an' everywhere you want to go. She nevvah bruk down yet! Not even a belch when she climbin' hill!" Raymond continued to praise the virtues of his car, while he bridged the ignition wires under the dashboard to start the engine.

"How did you manage to get a road license for this old bone-shaker?" he asked, as Raymond bumped into a pothole, and the old thing shook and rattled as if it would fall apart.

"Road license?" Raymond asked wrinkling his face as if he had been asked an obnoxious question. "Dat is the easiest t'ing fi get. It is as easy as goin' to the supermarkit!"

He didn't bother to ask how easy, anticipating a devious and disturbing answer. "Where are we going?" he asked instead.

"Hertz RentaCar," Raymond replied. "Yuh have yuh driver's licence?"

"Yeah!" he replied. "I got it." He had an international driver's licence with his assumed name, Edmund Price, on it. It was just as easy to get it, if not easier than going to the supermarket. Thanks to Lord X, he didn't have to go any place for it.

"We goin' to di airport," Raymond said. "Da's where Hertz have dem office and is out dere di cars deh."

"Norman Manley Airport?" he asked.

"Irie!" Raymond replied.

"Hey! You promised to speak English. Remember?" he gently admonished.

"Yes. Mr. Price!" Raymond replied, smiling broadly, "But patois is sweet an' di people I deal will penetrate mi bettah. I keep on forgettin'." With that, Raymond changed gear and savagely pushed the gas pedal down, and the old Toyota belched, back-fired and merrily sped in the direction of the airport, leaving a trail of acrid smoke behind.

He wasn't as merry as the old car, and asked Raymond to slow down. "Slow down, Ray," he begged. "Take it easy! I want to remain in one piece."

"This Numknack?" Raymond replied, glancing at him. "Nuttin' can 'appen when I behind di wheel!"

"Numknack?" he asked. "I think I am knowledgeable on most make of cars. I have never heard of it. What brand is that? Japanese?"

Raymond grinned broadly. "A Numknack is just a car dat is still running. Vintage!"

"Aah! I see!" he exclaimed.

Passing Harbour View on the left, as they went around the roundabout, they joined the maddening file of vehicles roaring, snorting and rushing towards the airport. Raymond parked the old Toyota in the car-park, paid the cost and collected a parking ticket. Then they strolled towards the office of Hertz Rentacar. Business with Hertz was quickly transacted, and he selected a silvery blue and sleek looking Datsun.

"All you got to do is fallah me close," Raymond instructed him, as they were about to leave the airport. When they reached the Boulevard, Raymond said that he had to leave immediately. "I goin' to do Missa Chew business now. When I come back, I will tell yuh more 'bout di prisoner business. Drap a tenner 'pon me. I runnin' short a' capital."

He took twenty pounds from his wallet and handed it to his brother.

"Dat cool, I see you tomorrow. Irie!" Raymond said.

Chapter 5

A WICKED OLD WORLD:
AN EVENING WITH PAPPY

*N*ext morning, he breakfasted on black coffee, fried eggs and beans, boiled bananas, shrimp de Jonghe, steamed callaloo and a mango. After he had eaten, he decided to stroll across to the Bank to change travellers' cheques into local currency. He planned to tour the Conference Centre and do some window shopping before returning. He intended to phone Pappy when he returned to his hotel room. He was planning to stay with Pappy for a few days.

On his way back to the hotel, two hours later or more, he stopped at a petrol station and procured a road-map. He still retained a mental image of Pappy's old green and white house with a green roof also with the twisted mango tree leaning over his neighbour's rusty zinc fence. He needed the road-map to fix a geographical diagram in his mind on how to get to Pappy's house, under his own steam. Back in his room, greatly invigorated by the morning heat and his walk, he ordered a cold Red Stripe, while he studied the map and plotted his route to Trench Town. As he read and fixed the positions including the stoplights in his mind, he realised that his memory of locations came back easily to him.

"We losin' de match!" greeted him as he came into the house. Pappy was holding the Gleaner dejectedly crushed and clutched in his right hand while he shook his nephew's hand with an iron grip. "How are you, Pappy?" he asked.

"Fine!" Pappy replied. "Only that this country is getting me down. If I had known that t'ings was goin' to go so bad, I wouldn't have left the Mother Country. I made a wrong move."

"Ah! Come off it, Pappy," he replied. "You're looking pretty good to me."

"Maybe the hard times agreeing with me," Pappy remarked. "So you come in the country like a thief in the night. You didn't tell me that you was comin'."

"I wanted my visit to be a surprise for you," he said.

"Well, it nearly became a surprise for yourself. I nearly drop down when you said that you was here!"

"You look extremely good Pappy," he repeated. "But what you're saying is contrary to what you said when you decided to come back to Jamaica. You said that that there is no place like home. Remember that song you used to sing, 'the green grass of home'?"

"Yeah, I remember" he said and he hummed the melody. "You're damn right! I take back what I said, but I still feel like runnin' away."

"Ah! Take it easy Pappy," he said, "Everything, as Bob Marley sang, will be alright. Things are always turning out right for you, Ol' Fellah!"

He threw his arms around Pappy and held him in a brief and close embrace. "How are things with you, eh? Still ticking away on all eight cylinders?"

"Not much to complain about," Pappy replied. "What's the use of crying?"

"I didn't think so when I just came in. You were like a whistling kettle on a hot stove."

"Well, I have to let off steam," Pappy explained, "When things don't look right to me. What 'appenin' here, can't 'appen in the Mother Country."

"That's where you are mistaken, Pappy. A lot of what is happening here and even more is going on in Britain and in other parts of the world. Human behaviour is a universal problem, especially with failing economies, moral degeneration, corruption and fraud, robberies, murders and social injustices, AIDS and disillusionment, you name it."

"It's a wicked old world," Pappy remarked. "I read in yesterday's paper that in Khartuum, a city in Sudan, the government cruelly beat 53 Christians, men, women and children for demonstration." Pappy angrily shook the newspaper and turned to a page, "what is 'appenin' in Jamaica today is a baby to what is 'appenin in some parts of the world. But what is 'appening' in our country is too close for comfort. Anyone of us can be dead any minute. I made the mistake of comin' home!"

"No, Pappy," he consoled, "I think you made the correct decision at the time you did."

"No, sah!" Pappy vehemently disagreed. "It was a wrong move. If I did get the slightest hint, I would not have put foot out of the Mother Country," Pappy shook the paper savagely and dug his fingers into another page. "Listen to this, 'EMERGENCY.' These people have the gumption to come here and try to treat us like delinquent schoolboys. Those weepers and wailers have no right to come here so arrogant and high-handed in their estimation of us. Who give dem dat right? Imperialism finish! I think the Braeton massacre ought to be a lesson to the gunmen to throwaway their guns and seek gainful employment. It should be a lesson to young people to mind bad company. If there were any innocent among them, then it is unfortunate that they were in the wrong place at the wrong time and with the wrong crowd. You can't lie down wit' dog an' don't get fleas. It is a lesson to parents not to leave their children to their own ends. I hope that the Police learn a lesson – there are better ways to deal wit' criminals wit' out murdering them. The killing of those youngsters was a matter of lack of proper planning to capture them alive. I still maintain, however, that we have competent people to censure our Police. We don't need foreigners to jump down our throats."

"I see your point, Pappy," he replied. "But your stand needs some modification. You must bear in mind that we are a part of the so-called global village. We can't act *ex parte.* International censorship and critique and assessment are vital to our survival. I suggest that controls be put in place that no so-called Jesus might enter this country and pass judgment that might be deleterious to our well-being. It is like bearding the lion in his den."

"There we are again!" Pappy chortled. "You will be suggesting suppression of freedom of speech next!"

"Amnesty International is a reputable organization. They even won the Nobel Peace Award for aiding the release of over ten thousand political prisoners. It's an independent movement working for the international protection of human rights. Established in 1961, it campaigns against the detention of prisoners of conscience, detained because of their beliefs, colour, sex, ethnic origin, language or religion.

"The organization advocates fair and prompt trial of political prisoners and the torture of prisoners and the end of extra-judicial executions and disappearances. It seeks to promote awareness of, and adherence to, the values promulgated by the Universal Declaration of Human Rights. It has a membership of over a million people worldwide. It has been doing some solid work."

"I am not condemning them," Pappy averred. "I only saying that dem too aggressive against small nations like ours. Why don't they condemn China or America and threaten them? Why pitch on little us? They shouldn't come into our country with hostility and level threats at us. They are feisty and rude!"

"Globalization, Pappy!" he replied. "Globalization is the new word, the 'in thing' that has caught up with us and no nation, these days, can act without other nations looking over its shoulder. Amnesty International is supported by the UN organization."

"Eh! You know a lot 'bout this Amnesty thing!" Pappy exclaimed.

"You're also well informed Pappy," he returned the compliment.

"It is important to be well informed and enlightened, these days, because a lot of things are happenin'. I read the newspapers every day and I watch television, the BBC news goes all night on television. We have a Police Corruption Authority. Let the Authority carry on the investigation of complaints against the Police. To top it all, West Indies lose the match which means they lose the series. Dat is addin' injury to insult. Just listen to this! It 'appenin' too often !" Pappy shouted, the crumpled newspaper angrily crackling in his hand: "Dat Amnesty man tellin' lie that we have the highest police killings in the world. I do not believe that! Tell me! Where is the proof? Don't they suppose to present statistics and evidence to substantiate what dey sayin'? The government should tell dem where to get off and mind dem own business!"

"Wow, the Ol' Man is hopping mad!" he said with a chuckle.

"Listen to this," Pappy fumed. "Make mi read it to you! *The West Indies dream of winning the Cable and Wireless Test against South Africa at the Antiguan Recreation Ground ended in disappointment when they were beaten in the Fourth Test.* What I want to know is where was Lara an' Chanderpaul? The Cricket Board should a' keep Adams as captain. They dish' dat man dirt!"

"After his performance against Australia and England, you would keep Adams as captain?" he asked, greatly surprised. "That's cricket, Pappy, as in other games you win some and lose some."

Pappy glared at him for some time, then flopped into a chair, brushing his forehead with the palm of his left hand.

"Pappy, is something wrong?"

"Naw," Pappy replied, "Nutt'n is wrong. Everyt'ing seems so awry in this country. Everyt'ing goin' from bad to worse."

"Well," he said, "You and I alone can't fix it, so why fret about it?" he asked. "We can only try to hold up our little part by doing what we have to do in our own corner."

"How can you do when the whole damn thing is coming down on top of you and everybody is breathing down your neck?" Pappy savagely asked.

"Pappy, you're as spunky as ever. You haven't changed one bit!" he exclaimed greatly amused.

"Yeah, I have changed," Pappy retorted. "You ain't seeing right. I used to run after the world. Now I feel like running away from the world. I can't cope. You better drive in and park the car and bring in your things."

Pappy piloted him between the house and the twisted Bombay mango tree half of which still hung over the neighbour's fence. He recalled that Pappy used to quarrel with old Mrs. Crowly about her numerous grandchildren stoning the mango tree, and in anger she would throw her soapy water from her washing over the fence at the mango tree. This used to drive Pappy completely crazy. "What happened to Mrs. Crowly?" he asked as he came from the car.

"Bless her soul," Pappy said with a broad grin. "She is gone to the happy land. And her grandchildren scattered."

"Who lives in the house now?" he asked.

"One of her grandchildren, I believe," Pappy replied. "I miss Mrs. Crowly though. The mango tree seem to miss her soapy water too. The mangoes were sweeter when she was alive." They both laughed heartily. "Take your things out of the car," Pappy said. "Here let me help you." He insisted on taking one of the cases. "You hungry or something?"

"I ate before I left the hotel, but I could use a beer. May I smoke?"

"Do any damn t'ing you want to do," Pappy replied, "though I don't approve of smoking. It is dangerous to your health. It is also a bad habit. A man musn't become a slave to habits. Put your luggage in your old room. I go get the beer."

"Don't go to so much trouble, Pappy," he said.

"No trouble at all," Pappy replied. "The shop is just by the corner." Pappy was out of the house before he could say another word of protest.

Ten years ago when he visited, the room with its old paint and old iron bed, looked the same, but he had not slept in it. He had stayed on the north-coast. He was about to sleep in that old room again. *Had he turned back the clock?*

He returned to the living room and throwing himself on the old wooden-frame settee. He clasped his hands behind his neck and staring blankly at the blotched ceiling and the old photographs on the wall, he hummed a few bars of 'The green grass of home'. Pappy hadn't done much to the old house in ten years!

Pappy, on his return, opened a beer and handed it to him, then opened another for himself. "Welcome!" he said.

"Cheers!" he replied.

For a short while, only the ticking of the wall clock disturbed the silence, as they surveyed each other. "Bats, how is Mother Country and the Queen?" Pappy eventually broke the silence. Bats was a short for his real name, Bateman.

"The Thames and Big Ben are still intact," he answered. "So is the Queen" (Pappy was an ardent admirer of the Queen and a self-styled advocate of the royal family).

"Prince Charles don't stand a chance of sitting on the throne, eh?" Pappy said. "Why she won't abdicate?"

"Ask the Queen," he mischievously suggested.

"I may just do that," Pappy replied, laughing. "I long to see Mother Country."

"Why don't you come on a vacation? I would pay your return flight," he offered.

"To tell you the truth, I am afraid of traveling, airplanes and such things," Pappy said.

"You, Pappy? You afraid?" he asked, amused and feigning shock and surprise.

"You'd be surprised at what I am afraid of these days. We live in dangerous times."

"I must call Raymond and let him know I am here," he said.

"Dat boy!" Pappy almost shouted. "I hardly see him these days, since he took up with that Chew. I believe that boy is in bad company. I don't like how he dress an' I don't like how he talks."

"Vincent Chew!" he exclaimed. "I haven't seen him in years! How is he?"

"He is a big shot now," Pappy said. "Supermarket and fishing boats. He has the biggest supermarket in Allman Town. He is a big boy!"

He remembered Chew very well. "I should like to see him. I must give him a call."

"Yeah," said Pappy. "We were in Mother Country when his parents were murdered. Remember?"

"Yeah, I remember," he replied.

"You can look up his number in the Directory. It's Family Plus Supermarket."

He called Raymond, but he was apparently out. He looked up Chew's number and dialed. "Chew, this is Bats," he said. "How are you, Man?"

"Bats?" Chew asked incredulously.

"Yeah. It's me!" He replied.

"How're you Bats? I haven't seen or heard of you for centuries.

"Hey, come off that! It is only eighteen years! "

"Eighteen years? Eighteen years is a long time in which to forget a lot of things including long-lost friends," Chew remarked.

"Well, I haven't forgotten you," he said. "In fact, I want to come around to rap with you about the old days. How about that?"

"Sure!" Chew said, "It would be good to see you. Where are you now?"

"I am staying with Pappy. Remember him?"

"Oh yes! Pappy! Of course I remember him!" Chew replied. "Haven't seen him since he came back from England. But I ask Raymond once in a while for him."

"So how're you doing, Man?" he asked.

"Things are rough with the economy not moving, crime and all that, but I am holding on – only that we losing the series."

"Series?" he asked.

"Test Cricket against South Africa." Chew replied.

"Oh yeah! Pappy is here hopping mad about it."

Chew laughed. "Come around to see me for old times sake," he invited.

"Ok! When shall I come?" he asked.

"How about tomorrow afternoon? I close the supermarket half-day on Thursdays."

"No problem Pappy and I will come tomorrow. Expect me."

"Tomorrow will be fine," Chew said.

Pappy cooked a delicious supper of seasoned rice, fried plantains and steamed fish which they washed down with a generous supply of beer, Pappy trekking down once again to the shop on the corner to replenish the supply. During the meal, he asked Pappy, "What do you think about the bare-bottom wedding?"

"No big thing!" Pappy declared. "I see no reason for the hue and cry and the hullabaloo. Rather boring I think! The only amusing thing I noticed about it was the photograph of the brides with casket-pieces of flowers around their you-know-what."

"Ah! Ah! Why?" he asked, bursting into laughter.

"Well, when I was a boy in Jones Town there was a Jew by the name of Bloom who had a small shop where he made and sell coffins. In those days, undertaking wasn't as sophisticated and lucrative as it is today. Because the shop was so small, Mr. Bloom used to lean the coffins outside, upright against a wall of his shop during the day. He used to tie a wreath of artificial flowers around the waist of each to pretty them up. That photograph in the papers of dem girls remind me of Mr. Bloom's coffin shop."

Pappy's laughter was infectious. "I think that the owner of Hedonism II is a bit thin skinned and mean to lash out at the church as he did. You don't give people gifts and then turn round and use your giving to insult them because they offend you. Besides, he ought to expect that if people have something that is *gauche* and not *kosher,* they will talk. If you give people things to talk about, they will talk. If I were like him, I would ignore what the people say, and get on with my business. I defend the right of every man to talk his head off. I also defend the right of every man to choose whether he listens or not. I don't have to look or listen. And if you don't pay them any mind, they are likely to forget what they were protesting about. They will soon stop talking."

"I intended to be a guest at that wedding, but I understood that I would not be accommodated with my clothes on, so I came over to Kingston without delay."

"I read in the papers that the brides bare their asses, but there was no information as to what the men did with their jacks and dangles, whether they let them loose or harnessed them. But what was the fuss about? The country has more crucial issues to address. Have you ever seen a goat butting at flies?"

"No," he replied. "Why?"

"The flies evade the butts, yet they persist in harassing the goat. Well, we shouldn't waste our time and energy hitting out at frivolities, such as uncovered tails, like a stupid goat butting at flies!"

"Never mind," he said. "Let's forget the nude wedding. We are sure to get our eye-fill of nudity at the Carnival!"

"Me? Not me!" Pappy exclaimed. "I have seen enough of naked women to last me the rest of my life!"

"Come on, Pappy, don't be a wet blanket," he bantered.

They chatted through the night, he adjusting to the many and changing moods of his grandfather until Pappy eventually said, "I am turning in. No sinner ought to sit up so late, he will burn in hell – if there is somewhere worse dan here."

Chapter 6

ENTER MR. CHEW: PEACE, AND ILLUSION

*P*appy had already prepared breakfast of fried dump-
lings, liver, bread and coffee and a grapefruit when
he entered the dining room. Pappy turned from the
television in the living room to look at him. "Breakfast is ready, but
I refuse to starve waiting for you until you choose to come out of the
bathroom, so I ate already. So we going to Chew today?"

"Yes, Pappy," he replied. "A lot of water has flowed under the
bridge from schooldays. I didn't get to see him when I was here ten
years ago."

"I tell you what," said Pappy, "I want to go down by the shop
before we go to Chew."

"OK by me!" he replied. "I'll first wrap myself around the
breakfast. It smells pretty good. It ought to be good."

"You're welcome to all of what is left of it," said Pappy, crackling the newspaper in his hands as if to emphasize the invitation.

"So you get your paper early," he remarked.

"It isn't early. It is after nine," Pappy replied.

After he had breakfasted, Pappy piloted the Datsun around the
crooked mango tree and out onto the street. Pappy instructed him
to pull over three blocks down the street by a little shop painted
black, yellow and green. "Stop by that shop there," said Pappy,

pointing his finger. "It's hot already. Let's have a beer." As they approached the Shop, he noticed that two stoutish women were dancing in the shop to Marley's 'Wait in Vain'." "A lone young man, his legs coiled around a bar-stool was sipping a Red Stripe while he nonchalantly watched the gyrations of the women, repeatedly shouting at them, "Yeah, Man! Yeah, Man! Wo'k yuh body!" He barely glanced at the new arrivals and returned his gaze to the women.

"Two Red Stripe," Pappy called to the bartender. "Make them cold, Bertie," Pappy jovially added.

"Dem always col'," Bertie replied, swiftly opening the bottles and banging them on the counter top. The fatter of the two women stopped dancing, wiped the sweat from her face with a green rag, and, picking up a bottle from the counter, sucked noisily at its contents. "Paula, Gal, yuh good fi true. I cyaan keep up wit' yuh. Yuh run mi!" she pleasantly remarked, at the same time eyeing the men.

"Yuh t'ink mi easy!" exclaimed the other who continued dancing until the song ceased and was followed by the unintelligible gibberish of a DJ. "Yuh t'ink mi easy?" she repeated, wiping the sweat from her brow with a ringed and curved forefinger. "Mi wi' run yuh off anyday. Boy, di mawnin hot sah! Maltie, buy mi anaddah beer, nuh?" she said to the man on the stool. Maltie said that he didn't have any money. "Yuh ha' money. Is mean yuh mean," she pleasantly remarked, lightly thumping him on the shoulder and playfully attempting to enter his pockets.

"Jamaica no problem!" Pappy uttered beneath his breath. "Bats, let's go."

They left the shop and went towards a Poinciana tree in full orange coloured bloom. There was a gathering of some eight men under the tree from among whom an old toothless man called out to Pappy. "You bring di paper?"

Pappy irritably replied. "Say mornin' first nuh, Man! You tink a little good manners and a little patience goin' to kill you?"

"Good mawnin', Missa Carter. Good mawnin', sar!" The old man mocked. "Please for the paper, sir!"

Pappy pretended to ignore the banter and greeted a foursome of strong young men who were playing dominoes so early in the day when most men ought to have already completed three to four hours of work. "Peace, Pappy!" They returned his greeting almost in unison and without a pause in their intense concentration on the game. A young man who had a radio on his left shoulder close to his ear said nothing. Two men squatted on the ground throwing a pair of dice on a square of cardboard. The silence of all seven men was broken only by the rattling of the dominoes, the drone of an occasional car passing, the dun click of the dice and their dull thud as they were cast onto the cardboard and the exclamations of the men as one of them hoarsely read the dice.

"Me seh weh di newspaper deh?" the old man called out.

Pappy threw the folded paper at the old man and it fell from his hand as he attempted to catch it. "Why you won't buy you' own paper!" he shouted light-heartedly at the old man.

"Mi wouldn' waste my money by paper fi you fi read," replied the old man. "An' what yuh would a do wit' you' money? Give it to 'oman, you ol' Nanny goat?"

Pappy humorously appealed to the other men. "Gentleman, you see my trial? Dis man insult me over my own things an' call me a Nanny goat. Ah not bringin' him any more paper. Dis is di las' las' time I ever bring him even a page! Ol' James, you hog yuh! Yuh hear me?"

"After mi nuh deaf", the old man cackled. "But mi nah hear yuh. Mi deaf right now, yuh ol' Toad."

This last repartee was greeted with whoops of laughter from the domino players who had become somewhat transfixed by the friendly exchange between Pappy and the old man who by then had spread out the sheets of paper on the ground, sheet after sheet and sitting on a piece of board had commenced reading aloud. Pointing at the words, word by word, with an arthritic and knobbly forefinger he spelt loudly as he read.

Pappy stood, keenly watching the men who were playing dominoes.

"Six love to rhatid!" triumphantly shouted the smallest of the men, aggressively slamming down some pieces of the dominoes in rapid succession, rising with hand erect above his shoulder to render his dramatic *coup de grace.* One of the men — he probably weighed three hundred pounds — lifting his bulk from the table, shouted in a voice as raspy as an empty barrel being rolled on a stony road, "Winners buy di beer!"

"No," protested the smallest of the four domino players. "Ha' losers fi buy!"

The big man, his stomach bulging over his pants, pulled out his wallet. He took out a note, gingerly holding it between two fingers and flicking it with the thumb of his other hand, before giving it to the man with the radio-cassette player. "Buy beer fo' everybody," he said. "Bring back change."

"Care for a game, Pappy?" the little man challenged.

"Why not? Come on Bats, let's play a game."

"Alright! Let's have a game," he said. He sat at the table. He hadn't played dominoes for years. The dice-players ceased their gambling to watch the contest. He and Pappy lost three sixes. Pappy got up in disgust and sent the radio-cassette man to buy more beer.

"Pappy, yuh haffi go back a school go learn fi play domino," the small man taunted.

"Go away, Half-pint," Pappy scoffed. "Where was you when I use' to teach yuh grandfather to play domino?"

"Dem days gone!" The little man retorted. "Is modern days now."

"Modern days hell? I can beat you wit' my eyes shut an' one han' tie behind mi back on the darkes' night," Pappy quipped.

The men who had paused in their gambling led the laughter. "It's better to joke than to quarrel," rasped the three-hundred pound giant.

"Dat is true word, Pappy!" said one of the gamblers. In the midst of all this the old man unconcernedly kept spelling and reading aloud.

When they finished drinking and after some more banter, Pappy said, "Come, let's go. Give me the key. The way you play domino, I can't trust you with my life."

Chew's supermarket was an imposing two story edifice constructed on the site of his father's ancient grocery shop. Although it was daylight a very high and very wide neon sign dimly winked, 'CHEW'S FAMILY MARKET *If we haven't got it, it's nowhere available.'*

"Eh, this is a grand affair!" he remarked to Pappy.

"You ain't see nutten yet," Pappy replied, as if he owned the place.

He followed Pappy to a narrow orange painted door. Pappy pressed a red button on a small grey marble panel marked 'PRESS' on the right column of the metal door frame. A stainless steel panel on the door flashed the word, 'ENTER' as the door slid aside with a gentle hiss and a soft rumble. Chew stood at the top of the stairs looking at them. "Come on up," he cheerily called. "Welcome!"

He noticed that Chew, in his voice and features, had not changed much over the years. His wiry *shock* of hair was still long and raven black except for a streak of grey here and there; his moonlike face, high cheek bones, flat nose and squinty eyes were still there, excepting that his slight body seemed thinner, bonier and slightly stooped. He sensed at once that Chew with his slight figure and mannerisms exuded wealth and confidence. Behind him a huge hound or mastiff growled at them. "Down, Pluto," Chew ordered. "These are friends."

"How are you Chew?" he asked, as they shook hands.

"Half and half," Chew said. "Bateman Carter! It's a long time we haven't seen each other. Not since school days."

"Yeah," he replied. "We have been too busy chasing after life, I suppose."

"Nothing happens before the time," Chew said, then turning his gaze on Pappy. "I haven't seen you this long long while, Mr. Carter. Still living in Trench Town?"

"Oh, yes," said Pappy. "I have live' their all my life, except when I was in Mother Country. Born an' grow in Trench Town."

"I knew when you came back from England and repaired your house," Chew said. "Come with me."

They followed Chew toward tall double doors beautifully ornamented with an intricate oriental design and Chinese hieroglyphics. The doors slid open with a soft rumble and hiss like the door downstairs to reveal a red carpeted saloon. Beautifully patterned tapestry of eastern designs hung from the walls. At one end of the room psychedelic lights intermittently flashed, 'Welcome to the bar'. As they approached the bar, bar-stools automatically sprang out of the floor. He observed that Chew was using a remote gadget to perform these miracles. Pappy sat near an ice-dispenser which traveled on a rail the length of the counter top, flashing and repeating the word, "Ice", while an unseen, seductive and metallic female voice kept asking, "What's your desire?"

"What do you wish to drink, Gentlemen?" Chew asked.

"Gin and water," said Pappy. Bateman requested a Red Stripe beer. He noticed that Chew chose a Pepsi for himself.

"Ice, ice, ice," said the ice-dispenser, its single green eye blinking. Chew silently demonstrated, how it worked by placing his glass beneath the spout of the machine. It paused and dropped ice cubes into the glass. Pappy did the same. "Be damned if I am not seeing the last of everyt'ing!" Pappy said. "Di worl' comin' to an end."

"You ain't see nutten, yet," he mimicked Pappy.

Chew pointed his gadget at a panel on the wall of the room, and soft symphonic music poured from the ornate ceiling and filled the saloon. "Do you gentlemen like classical music?"

"Yes," answered Pappy, "though I don't understand it, classical music touch me."

"That's the mystical essence of classical music," Chew remarked. "To pretend to understand lessens your enjoyment of it."

"I have a pile of The Beatles," Pappy continued, "Bob Marley, Toots and the Maytals, Millie Small's 'My Boy Lollipop', Ernie Smith, Kenny G, Luther Vandross, Beres Hammond and so on, you name it," and he hummed a few bars of 'Oh Carolina'.

"There's not much classical stuff in your collection." Chew remarked with a complaisant smile. "How about you, Bats?"

"I stay clear of music I don't understand," he replied, "though I sometimes try to, keep awake on an occasional evening of Chamber music at Albert Hall with friends, for appearances sake, not wanting to be rated a philistine. I, however, have a fair collection of Bach, Mozart, Beethoven, Mendelssohn, Tchaikovsky, Brahms, Liszt, Schumann, Chopin, Verdi, Smetana and Dvorak. I also go to listen to the London Philharmonic Orchestra where I join the London cream of society in the audience, pretending to conduct the orchestra or tap my feet to the beat of the cello or bassoon, sitting in cushy red plush chairs. But as you say the less you understand, the more you enjoy. Ignorance is bliss."

His sardonic remarks drew laughter from Chew, in which Pappy lustily joined. Pluto awakened from his slumber by the commotion, lifted his huge head from the carpet and growled a warning angrily at them, as if he objected to being disturbed. "Down, Pluto," Chew growled back at him. "Pluto doesn't like classical music. He likes Bob Marley, but abhors the likes of Ninja Man, Buju Banton and Beenie."

"How about Luciano? I like him." Pappy mischievously remarked.

"I am not sure if Pluto likes him or not. I believe he tolerates him," Chew replied.

Pluto bared his teeth and growled ferociously at the next peal of laughter. The three men greatly amused all turned their eyes on the dog.

"Down, Pluto," Chew repeated.

"He apparently hates frivolity," he remarked. "Apparently," Chew agreed, "DJ's unnerve him."

"Well, if dem DJ's can rattle my nerves so badly, what say what dem do to the nerves of a poor dog who don't have a voice to swear and curse?" Pappy observed. The dog seemed to be aware that they were talking about him. He eyed them warily, his ugly snout lain, out while his tail flapping up and down and sideways, made dull thuds on the carpet.

Pappy had been trying to befuddle the ice-dispenser by pushing and pulling away his glass under its ice-spout before the machine could dispense a cube of ice into it. He was unsuccessful after several attempts until he fell into a rhythm that mistimed the machine and it started to miss his glass. "You think you can't be caught, you wise ass yuh?" he shouted in triumph. Pluto pricked his ears, but did not raise his head nor did he growl. The other men observed Pappy's jubilation without commenting.

"Bat, how are things with you?" Chew asked.

"Fine," he replied. "Everything is just fine."

"Sorry about George's death," Chew continued. "I can't believe that your brother blew up himself in his cell by his own experimenting with making bombs. Why would he want to make bombs, anyhow?"

"Experiment!" He muttered. "But how did he come by the materials for his experiment?"

"I wouldn't know," Chew replied. "I am only repeating what I hear on the news. It's rather mysterious."

"Mysterious is a mild way of putting it," Pappy remarked. "The whole affair is downright damn funny! There is mystery to it. Life in this country is cheap!"

Pappy resumed tantalizing the ice-dispenser with his refilled glass of gin and water. Three cubes fell dully like a game of Cow and Chicken in rapid succession into his glass.

"Pappy, it is hard to beat that fella at his own game," he remarked.

"Life seems to be getting cheaper day by day," Chew remarked.

"Yes," said Pappy. "I don't t'ink we will ever have any decrease in crime until we begin to respect people's right to life once again. Nowadays, taking a life or losing one's life is no big t'ing."

"Well, a few months ago," said Chew. "The Prime Minister identified the root of the problem that we no longer appreciate the value of human life as seen not only in the heartlessness of trigger-happy, fast shooting gunmen, but in the way we drive, as well as in the attitude of the wealthy and the powerful, and in the treatment of women by men and in the neglect of children by the men who fathered them."

"I t'ink," Pappy added, "that the increase in crime is due to the fact that our penal system seem' not to know what to do wit' murderers. The Police is confused an' brutalize' by the attitude of the very people they tryin' to serve an' safeguard. They never seem to be doing anyt'ing right for some people. So dey don't seem to care whether they doin' somet'ing right or dey doin' somet'ing wrong. It is all the same to them. Some people don't seem to respect or love police. Many people don't trust none o' dem!"

"But," said Chew, "We shouldn't use the fat of the bad ones to fry all policemen. That wouldn't be fair. The majority of policeman are conscientiously good men. Bad eggs among them are comparatively few."

"A few is enough to give the entire force a bad name," he stated.

"That is true," Pappy said. "I have seen some pretty good and respectable policemen turned into brutal killers by the spate of violent crimes in the country today. It is very difficult for the police to act friendly under so much danger to their own lives and under so much stress."

"Is the problem due to economic stress?" he asked.

"Probably," Chew said. "But our preachers and moralists have been pointing out daily that a spiritual upliftment more than economic, social and political reform is what we need, and that reform in politics, economy and social life will be in vain without a return to recognizing the high value of human life in a national form of rearmament to go forward. We are badly off as far as respect for life goes in this country."

"Yes," said Pappy. "Think of what is 'appenin' in the inner-city and the garrisons or enclaves of Tivoli, Rema, Hannah Town, Denham Town and such like. The people in these communities are law-abiding, but there are criminals who care little or not'ing about life. The people in these communities have to bond themselves to clean up their areas. They cannot depend on the Police to do this. In fact, it seems to me that when the Police enter these areas sporadically on raids, on mobile patrol or to maintain the peace they become a part of the problem, as from time to time they are fired on. And as for the children in these communities, what future is there with guns barking day and night?"

"The guns that bark in those areas," Chew pointed out, "are the same ones that rob and murder helpless men and women in other communities. Business people, especially, are targeted. The people in Grant's Pen recently mounted a demonstration against crime in their area. I don't t'ink that di middle class is doing much about the problem other than talking about it. Too much talk, too much complaints against the Police, and too little action. Although we have organizations such as Jamaicans for Justice, such organizations are late. Recently, the casket of a man killed by the Police was shot up allegedly by JDF soldiers. Police patrols are shot at by gunmen on high-rise buildings and roads were blocked, while people coming from schools and work had to dive for cover. My heart grieves over what is 'appenin'. Life in the garrisons isn't easy. The security forces need to exercise restraint and good sense. But I agree with you that the people themselves must come forward to defend the safety of their communities."

"What are the garrisons like?" he asked.

"Garrisons!" Chew exclaimed. "Garrisons had to do with distribution of scarce benefits especially housing. Back-A-Wall for example was bulldozed to build one community. Those who were able to acquire apartments and homes became strong supporters of the party forming the government of the day. Thus, a 'garrison' was formed.

"A number of other such 'Political' enclaves development around Kingston. They created Dons who became community leaders and they became safe-seats for the candidates of the favoured political parties. It was believed that these places became the breeding grounds for all types of corruption, gun-feuds and crime, non-payment of mortgages and illegal access to water and electricity."

"But couldn't the government and non-governmental organizations seriously address this problem?" he asked.

"As a sociologist pointed out," Chew replied, "dismantling the garrisons by getting in the guns through some ineffective offer of an amnesty or the other, has never worked. If government and the private sector organize unsustained social work in these areas that will not work either. Means must be found-the sociologist said- to make the garrisons less effective as political strongholds or footholds. Some means must be found to remove or disperse the present residents and to ferret out the criminal core. Political and social abscesses is what these garrison communities are."

"Which government would dare to remove those people?" Pappy asked, rhetorically. "The politicians created the environment that breed community rulers called "dons". Nowadays when the dons crack a fart certain politicians-I not callin' any names-run after them to smell it. A snow ball stands a better chance in hell than a politician in a constituency where the don is unfriendly. I now notice that the politicians are now coming out to publicly admit their affiliation with dons. Politicians attendin' the funerals of dons, regardless of their criminal notoriety, is the usual t'ing for years. Police intelligence says there are over four hundred of these gangs and dons. A certain politician calls his alliance with dons a 'symbiotic relationship'. What I admire about him is that he hopes that the current debate on this relationship between politicians and dons, crime and politics, as well as on drugs and guns, will continue and eventually resolve some of our problems."

"Jamaica? No problem!" he muttered. He lifted his glass to Pappy and Chew, looked at Pluto, and said sardonically, "Cheers! The reward for trouble is more trouble. Probably we need some more trouble to bring us around."

"What?" shouted Pappy so loudly that Pluto lifted his ugly snout and growled.

"Down, Pluto!" Chew growled once more, back at him. "Some more trouble to turn us around," Chew exclaimed, a question of doubt passing across his forehead. Was he hearing rightly?

"Anansi seh' two trouble better than one," Pappy grumbled, returning to tease the ice-dispenser, "but, I wouldn't like to see more trouble in this country than we are havin' right now."

"I notice," he remarked," that despite the incontrollable violent and senseless crimes, people are as carefree as if they were in paradise."

"The colour of our flag bears the message," Pappy solemnly said, "that the sun shineth. There are difficulties to overcome, but the grass is green."

"Yes," said Chew, "that is a good message. The million dollar question is why can't our people in a land of so much fruits, rain and sunshine get the message?"

"The outside world won't let us," Pappy said in disgust. "Too much corruption, too much interference, too much drugs from outside."

"This week is Carnival," said Chew. "Nothing stops us from enjoying ourselves. Almost every day is Christmas for most of us. Why can't it be so for everybody?"

"Maybe the Creator doesn't wish everybody to be happy," Pappy suggested facetiously.

"As a rule, I don't make fun of the Creator," Chew gently admonished. "Every day or night there is rape, robbery, murder and yet our people go out at all hours to the dancehall, the theatre, to the beach, as if violent acts are not happening."

"Jamaica? No problem!" he announced, with a sardonic chortle, "See what I mean?"

"I love dis country," Pappy angrily said. "Despite everyt'ing. "I live abroad for many years, an' all dat while, my greates' desire was to come back here in my own country. But if I was a younger man I would ha' gone a'ready, for good dis time. What is goin' on in dis country is hell!"

He noted with slight amusement that whenever Pappy was deeply upset he resorted to expressing himself in a sort of quasi-patois.

Chew looked bored and seemed anxious to change the subject. "I went to Calypso Tent, last night," Chew said.

"What do you think about Amnesty International?" he asked Chew.

"I think," said Chew, "that in the global world, international censorship of our affairs is necessary and is unavoidable. I personally support their intervention. They claim that their aim is to urge the Jamaica government to devise and implement a national human rights plan of action that protect people from human violations and involving all sections of the society, including the security forces, human rights groups, and civil society, as well as the human rights movement of the United Nations and other international bodies."

He wondered if Chew would simply point his gadget at a panel in the wall and a table spread with goodies would appear. Chew however, rang a bell and a Chinese lad appeared. "Pizza for every-body?" Chew asked. He spoke to the lad in Chinese when they said that they weren't hungry. The young man bowed and with-drew.

"He is from Korea," Chew said. "He cooks and cleans."

"I don't like these people coming here and projecting their pro-colonial and imperialistic views on us, their so-called poor relatives. To hell with them!" Pappy angrily continued, offending Pluto once again.

"You ought to apologize to Pluto every time you shout, Pappy," he teased.

"Damn right!" Pappy said. "But who apologize in dis country when dey shout or make a whole 'eap o' noise in you' ea's, you can't sleep at night? Nobody! Is which government official dat Secretary General of Amnesty International present his credentials to? How we know he is not a fake? How we know if Amnesty International is not a money-making thing with some people jumpin' on di ban'wagon to earn a easy livin' like dem televangelist? Threatenin' to talk to nations that have association with us to get them to impose sanctions on us is downright aggressive, imperialis-tic and wicked. It would be better for them to ask those countries to assist us to improve. I have never heard of them assisting any-body. They only advocate and threaten. They are not an altruistic organization, an' they have enough problems in their own country not to interfere with other countries' business. Do we know on the inside anyt'ing about their movement?"

"I don't think I do," he replied, amused by Pappy's vehement eloquence. "I have been acting on the wrong side of that organiza-tion, if they knew anything about me."

"You? What do you mean?" Chew asked.

"I was a policeman," he replied.

"What are you now?" Chew asked.

"We will talk about that some time," he said.

Pappy grunted in a disgruntled manner. "Hope what you doin' is legitimate. I don't want another like you' brother, George, in di family."

"We have to do some drastic things in this country," he remarked, "to curb the wild and senseless killings going on. Amnesty International wouldn't approve of some of the drastic measures I have in mind."

The others in the room gravely looked at him, but none of them asked him what he had in mind. "Some organizations, I read, are calling for the removal of the head of the CMU from front-line duty, but that would be a crazy thing to do. The man impresses me as a fearless crime-fighter. A fearless and ruthless crime-fighter is needed to strike fear in those who are on the wrong side of the law. I make no bones about that! The human rights organizations ought not to go overboard in their sympathy for criminals. I sometimes think that these organizations do not think how nerve racking and traumatic it is to be a policeman in a country as this."

"Not even one, I am sure, of their members," Pappy interjected, "would be willing to expose himself, including that pompous Secretary General of AI, to be shot at by criminals almost daily, to undergo the daily stress of poor workin' conditions, long hours of dangerous work, and a society that is unfriendly, over-critical and non supportive."

"The Police have to be fearless and put fear in the criminals," he continued. "I think that the CMU is doing a terrific job. Mistakes are bound to be made, some innocent people as in wars, at the wrong place at the wrong time are bound to get killed, but this is one of the hazards of war. There are bound to be civilian casualties."

"Are you saying that the public should not protest police killings whether deliberate or accidental?" Chew asked, greatly perturbed. "In this country, the Police kill an average of one hundred and forty persons per year. It is hard to believe that in this tiny country of less than three million, over a hundred and forty people attack the Police, each year, with guns and other weapons."

"No, don't misunderstand me," he asserted. "I am quite in agreement that police action must be censured or a tendency to ruthless killing instead of capturing, could lead to a police state. I, personally, have no objections whatever against the killing of criminals."

"Do you support the due process of law?" Chew asked.

"Of course, I do," he coolly replied. "But where the due process appears to be failing, what alternatives do the Police have that will satisfy those they are employed to protect and at the same time satisfy public concern? You, tell me!"

"What I can't figure out," said Pappy jabbing his glass under the spout of the ice-dispenser, "is what causin' the youth to be so vicious. Jamaica is one of the most violent countries in the world. An' a lot of the violence is being carried on by young people. What could be the cause?"

"There are many reasons," Chew replied, "including post-school unemployment, frustration, lack of guidance and moral support within a strong family structure, child abuse and neglect, hopelessness, license, drugs and gang warfare. Jamaicans held as undesirables, many having served prison terms for drugs and other crimes including murder, deported to the country also add to the problems.

"Some people blame the political directorate," Pappy added. "If you associate with criminals and dons and attend their funerals and you hide your head in the sand like di proverbial ostrich from political violence, what kind o' message you sendin' to the nation? Thank God, I am not a politician!"

"I think that the rapid decline in family unit, with its strong belief in God, its loyalty and self-respectfulness, its strong moral code inculcated in children from day one of their childhood, its responsibility to see that the other man's child obeys the rules of the society and have manners, decline in school discipline of former days, too much sophistication including the immoral influences of television and crude sounds commercially claiming, to be music and the 'want-it-now-get-rich-quick-and-easy' syndrome are behind the violence. Too many youngsters are absconding from school or are leaving school without the vital or basic tools to find a useful place in society. Too many parents have given up on themselves and on their children, as well. Too many parents, many barely older than their own children and just as senseless, refuse to co-operate with teachers in the disciplining of their children."

"You are an expert on the subject," he said admiringly.

"Well, I was pursuing a course in sociology when I was at the Seminary," Chew replied. "I love the subject."

"Oh yes, I ought to have remembered that I heard that you had been studying to enter the priesthood, and that you left the Seminary when your father was murdered. I am sorry," he said.

"Yes. I left," Chew said sadly, "to look after my mother and the business. She was severely battered by the thugs that murdered my father and never recovered her health."

"I was very sad when I heard about it," said Pappy.

"It happened so long ago. I learnt to live with it. It is no longer a painful memory," Chew murmured, as if to himself.

"You used to be an altar boy at the Cathedral. Do you still go to church?" he asked.

"I was also an acolyte and later became a novice. Yes, I go to church. That is where I gain my weekly strength to face my daily challenges and renew my faith in the future." Chew solemnly replied and crossed himself.

"I think," said Pappy, "that the lack of hope and political misdirection among our young people by successive governments-no one government can be blamed for it-are the reasons our young people are violent. Moral values are bein' betrayed, instead of bein' instilled by their elders, especially older men. Too many men in our society are selling youth and the country short. This must disillusion young people. We seem to be movin' in opposite direction. Young people are not really bad. They are just terribly confused by what is 'appenin' around them. If our young people are fed on violence, on coarse sounds and noise, what do you expect? We goin' to hell! Where we goin' when young people claim 'Man fi dead so man can live'?"

"That's pretty close to what Christ said before he went to the cross. Ain't it?" he scoffed.

"Let's not make fun of the Crucifixion," Chew piously admonished. "Civil society in this country is threatened and endangered by the upsurge in violence."

"What is this civil society?" Pappy asked.

"The word, 'civil' refers to anything that has to deal with the welfare of citizens in common, such as laws," Chew set out to explain. "A civil society is a country or community that is united to achieve and maintain a good life for all by the cooperation of all the citizens in that country or community. But history shows that this unity is not possible, without some form of civil authority to formulate and enforce laws focused on the collective will of the society, in order to achieve what is called the common good of all members, of the society."

"Thanks, I get the point," Pappy said brusquely. But Chew didn't seem to have noticed.

"In a civil society like ours," Chew continued, "what has to hold our people, together is the juridical bond, in other words, a justice system to which all members are required to adhere."

"Pardon me," Pappy asked. "Juridical bond? What is dat?"

"Juridical bond," Chew explained, "involves the rights and duty of every citizen, as regulated by 'rule of law'."

"Rule of law," said Pappy examining the ice-dispenser running up and down the length of the counter top, on its rail, as if he was seeing it for the first time. "At least, I understan' dat!" he murmured.

"Well the ideal purpose of civil society such as ours in Jamaica should be to secure the happiness and prosperity of all citizens," Chew stated.

"What?" shouted Pappy. "Happiness an' prosperity of all citizens? Am I hearin' right? What you sayin', Mr. Chew? What about di citizen who don't want any happiness or prosperity? What about di citizen who don't want to see anybody happy or prosper or the citizen who won't work, but beg, rob or steal?"

"Those are a serious threat and a grave danger to civil society," Chew asserted.

"A threat to Utopia!" he exclaimed.

"Utopia?" asked a disgruntled Pappy. "What obscene word is that?"

"Utopia," he explained, 'is an imaginary and remote heaven-like place where everything is perfect, laws, government, social justice, name it. It is obscene in a sense. The people who yearn for it are very unrealistic day-dreamers."

"Putting Utopia aside," Chew said impatiently, "Peace and prosperity are the aims of a civil society. Prosperity is what supplies the needs and wants of citizens in a civil society, and depends a great deal on jobs, money, health care, church, schools, roads, water and electricity, free religious and political persuasions, free speech, free movement within the society and on other forms of securities. Since a civil government has the duty and the authority, as well as the responsibility to safeguard provision for the civil society, in accordance with a constitution, there is a sort of social contract between government and people wherein each citizen has an obligation to every citizen to behave in such a way as not to jeopardize another person's rights or that of the State or Community in general. A philosopher by the name of Hobbes said that human nature is basically depraved and that the only constants in his behaviour are aggressiveness and the urge to survive. Hobbes describes man's life as 'nasty, brutish and short', and that the best anyone could do is to give up so much of your so-called rights to others as you would expect them to give up to you. Some other philosopher, Rousseau I think, claims that man is naturally good and morally upright and that he has a natural urge to improve himself, which often causes conflicts. Therefore, man sets up organizations which he sometimes calls civil societies as necessary for preserving peace and generating prosperity, and in which every man is expected to subject himself to a code of behaviour or laws which are considered normally acceptable for the common good of everyone in the society. In a democracy, as most civil societies are, where there is a pretence of government for the people by the people, citizens are bound to obey the laws formulated by their representatives in a parliament which they may change from time to time by balloting."

"Do citizens lose the right to challenge civil authority in a civil society?" he asked.

"I hope to God not!" Chew replied. "But the fear of what is called civil disobedience which may hurt many citizens in a number of ways, including loss of property and life, may force citizens to resign their freedom to the State. There is always the danger of despotism or dictatorial action by civil authority. We should not overlook that in a civil society, the government has a moral duty to the people it governs to see to their common welfare. Of course, that moral duty can be violated by slackness, negligence, corruption, lawlessness and the inability or reluctance of government to enforce the laws."

"I was blind to all this. Now I see," said Pappy. "Thank you, Mr. Chew.

"I am sorry that I wasn't able to put it across better," Chew apologized.

"Oh, it was pretty good, couldn't be better. It was well done!" Pappy reassured.

"Let's change the subject," Chew said. "I am a Carnival buff, you know. I have been to carnival Las Vegas, Rio de Janeiro, and I attended the Brixton Carnival last year. Have you ever been to any of these, Bat?"

"Yeah, I have been," he replied. "Mardi Gras is celebrated on Shrove Tuesday, the day before Lent begins. The Mardi Gras Carnival in Rio de Janeiro is the biggest in the world. I went last year. Man, thousands of musicians and dancers in costumes, beautiful and fantastic floats, parade through the streets."

"I was in London, in August, last year," said Chew. "That was a marvelous event! Some streets were cordoned off for the Carnival and over a million people of every race and colour were on the streets daily for two days. And the floats and costumes! Magnificent is the word to describe it!" And the smell of food, jerked chicken, jerked pork, mannish water and the smell of ganja smoking filling the British air! Stupendous!"

"Did you find ganja smoking stupendous?" he mischievously asked. "Rather stupefying, I should think."

"I didn't mean it in that sense," Chew said, chuckling. "What I mean is that the British atmosphere was charged and the Police acted as if they were oblivious to it. That was stupendous!

"I agree with you that London Carnival is a stupendous event.

It was initially created by West Indians of Brixton, London. The British government recognizing its significance makes an annual grant of more that a million pounds, more or less per year towards organizing it, and it is usually held the Sunday before Bank Holiday and on the last Monday in August which is the Bank Holiday.

"The barriers are down for at least a day or two as people enjoy in a common exercise on common ground a brief period of abandonment. I think that people need occasions like these to let down their hair and discharge tension."

"Some let down more than hair," Pappy commented to the laughter of the others, "They let it all hang out! An' they discharge their tension only to load up again, renewing their energy to behave worse than before to one another."

"Don't be such a pessimist, Pappy," said Chew. "Look at the brighter side of things."

"I wasn't born yesterday to be told such t'ing," Pappy grumbled.

"I went to Chukka Cove in St. Ann, last Tuesday," Chew recounted. "Blast-off 2001 was really a blast off! There were about fifteen thousand people, men, women and children. I went to the Soca/Calypso Tent last night. The event started late, but it was scintillating with the lights and with the Mighty Sparrow and Beenie Man. Do you like carnival, Pappy?"

"No, sah!" Pappy exclaimed in disgust. "So much naked flesh make me sick!"

Chew hummed a few bars' of 'Dust In Your Face' from the calypsonian David Rudder.

Pluto rose and emitted a howl, presumably of boredom. Chew looked at the dog, with an enigmatic smile. "Gentlemen, it is time for Pluto to get some fresh air and exercise."

Chew stood up and patted the restless dog on the head. "Will soon be ready, Pluto," he said, and he hummed a few bars of another calypso, while the dog licked his hand and whined.

"What is that you' singin?" Pappy asked. "I am sure I heard it some place."

"That's 'Saltfish'," Chew replied.

"Saltfish of course!" Pappy exclaimed. "Now I know! I heard it a number of times on FM 107!"

"How about you guys going to the Road March on Easter Sunday with me?" Chew asked.

"No, sah!" Pappy said. "So much naked flesh, at one time, will destroy my appetite."

"Your appetite for what?" Chew asked.

"Meat!" Pappy said, to laughter. Pluto responded by changing his whining to an angry growl.

"Down, Pluto," said Chew sternly.

"I will go with you," he said.

"Alright," Chew replied. "I will pick you up at ten o' clock, and he pointed his gadget at the ornate double doors which slid apart with a soft hiss and rumble as it had done, two and a half hours before.

Chapter 7

THE SLEUTH LEARNS OF HIS FAMILY AND GETS A LEAD

*P*appy said, "Mr. Chew, you have taught me a lot. As I said before, you've opened my eyes to a lot of t'ings, today. Great talkin' wit' you."

"You're welcome anytime, Pappy," Chew replied.

"Come, Bats, Let's go." Pappy said.

Chew said, "One for the road?" Pluto started to fidget and whine again.

"No, thanks," said Pappy. "We will have it another time."

"See you tomorrow, Chew," he said.

As they pulled out of the parking lot, he said to Pappy. "I should have asked Chew if he had seen George at any time before he was detained."

"You could ask him on the phone," Pappy suggested. "We're stoppin' at somewhere to buy some chicken. I not cookin'."

❦

They had almost finished the bucket of chicken and chips, washing it down with cold Red Stripe, when Raymond appeared. "Why yuh didn't call me, Big Broddah? I been lookin' all over di place fi yuh. I phoned yuh at the hotel, no answer. I drive to the hotel, I don't see your car. Pappy is not at home neither. So I put two an' two togeddah an' check by the shop. Dey tell me that you was dere playin' domino, but nobody know where yuh gone. So I keep checking di house till you come."

"Yuh foot short, Ray," Pappy said, handing the bucket to Raymond. "Only two pieces o' chicken lef'. Beer in the fridge."

Raymond went to the refrigerator and called out, "Everytime I come here, the fridge empty. No beer is here."

"Next time yuh come, bring some," Pappy retorted. "Don't look for what you don't put down."

"But see yah! You invite me to look for beer, you know, Pappy. I didn't jus' get up so go look for any!" Raymond explained.

Pappy took some money from his pocket and handed it to Raymond, "Go buy half dozen," he said.

"It's alright," Raymond said, "I have money,"

"Eh, yuh have money?" Pappy teased. "Where yuh get it from?"

"Comin' Big Broddah?" Raymond asked, ignoring the question and signaling his brother meaningfully to accompany him.

"Yeah, I could stretch my legs, yes," he said, rising and arching his back and lifting his hands above his head.

Pappy merely grunted and turned his interest to the news on television.

"I locate de man," Raymond said, as they walked down the road toward the beer shop, "cool an' easy."

"Leave out the 'cool an' easy' and tell me what progress you made," he ordered. "How did it go?"

"Easy as cuttin' cheese! Di warders seh you're to come as the man' lawyer," Raymond explained.

"Is that safe? Are you sure?" he asked.

"Safe as church, cool as a cucumber!" Raymond replied.

"So when am I to play this dramatic role?" he asked. The love of adventure began to salivate his 'sleuth-hormones'.

"When?" he asked

"Next Tuesday at ten," Raymond replied. "We go to di prison.

The two warders will be on duty at the guard-house by the gate. One of dem will take us to the room where lawyers talk to their clients in prison. Yuh mus' take you' briefcase an' papers in it, like a real lawyer."

"Sounds good to me," he replied. "I'll buy the beer."

"Yes, Missa Price," Raymond mocked. "I have to get more dunny, I mean money."

"How much!" he asked.

"Six thousand dollars more," Raymond said, "real Jamaican money. Dey don't want no foreign money. Two for di prisoner an' four for the warders."

"Ah, ah! Four for the guards and two for the guarded, eh?" He said. "Alright, tell the warders I will bring the money with me Tuesday morning."

"But I did want to pay it before Tuesday," Raymond said.

"We will take the money with us, on Tuesday, They can take it or leave it."

Raymond took the money from him to buy the beer and they walked back to their grandfather's house in silence, each buried in his own thoughts.

"What keep you two so long?" Pappy queried. "I nearly had to come lookin' fo' you."

"Nothing really," he replied. "We just walked leisurely. Fooling around taking our time!"

Pappy snorted and returned to reading his paper. "I can't understand what is happenin' these days," he remarked. "Just listen to this!" He said stretching out his hand to receive a bottle of Red Stripe Raymond had opened, without taking his eyes from the page. *'Drugs, Shipriders and U.S. Caribbean Relations.'* It says here that the Caribbean has become the trans-shipment point for *forty* percent of all cocaine and heroin destined for the United States. President Clinton added Aruba and the Netherlands Antilles as 'major drug producing trans-shipment countries'. The Bahamas, Belize, The Dominican Republic, Haiti and Jamaica are also listed; U. S. Virgin Islands and Puerto Rico are all classified as 'high intensity areas'."

"You don't seem to read any other part of the newspaper, Pappy, only about crime an' cricket," Raymond complained.

"Right now, what else is there to read about?" Pappy angrily retorted. "They are the most vital issues affecting us in Jamaica today. If it's not crime it is Sports! If it's not crime or Sports, it's politics! You realize that drugs and politics cause most of di violence in the world today?"

"I don't fully agree with you that drugs and politics are causing most of the violence. There are other factors such as desire to acquire wealth and power. As I understand it, there is co-operation between the U.S. Coast Guard and those of the Caribbean, and there is a shiprider's agreement between the U.S. and several Caribbean countries."

"What is this Shiprider's Agreement?" Pappy asked.

" It is an agreement," he explained, "which allows the United States unlimited access to our air space and territorial waters in pursuit of drug dealers."

"But," said Raymond, "the drug dealers have faster boats dan di Coas' Guard. The drugs comin' Jamaica an' reachin' *America*. Dem can't stop di trade wit' all dey don."

Was Ray defending the drug dealers or was he commenting on the inefficiency of the authorities responsible for frustrating the drug trade? he asked himself. He gave Raymond the benefit of the doubt and listened silently to the exchange between the two men while he was relaxing and enjoying his beer. At last, Pappy said, "I gettin' old. I can't keep up all night wit' yuh young people. I goin' to bed." Raymond left shortly after.

While watching the television on and off, and dozing in between, he thought that being the only known survivors of George, Pappy, Raymond and himself, if there be any estate of George worth seeking about, Pappy should see to it. Pappy probably would have to retain a lawyer and apply to the Administrator General. Lawyers were notoriously clever at eating away large portions of an estate when a settlement was being made by litigation, not to overlook death tax and administration fees. He recalled that a lord in England had to sell an estate he inherited from his mother in order to pay litigation and death tax in the settlement of his father's estate, thus paradoxically becoming bankrupt from the exercise. The Police, he learnt from Pappy, had sealed the premises leased by George pending the completion of their investigation. Now that the inquest was over and it was established by the Police that George blew up himself, he would advise Pappy to apply to the Police to release the premises. He needed access to the building as soon as possible. He might have to break his cover if the Police took their own time about it. He would discuss the matter of applying to the police authorities with Pappy.

He was surprised when Pappy returned after mid-day the next day and informed him that the Police, on finding nothing irregular on the premises, had agreed to hand it over to Pappy, on Tuesday of the coming week. "A sergeant said," Pappy reported, "that George's rooms and office had been ransacked and cleaned by an unknown person or persons, before the Police got there. Not a document, not a piece of paper, no passport, no cheque book, nothing was there except the furniture!"

"They clean out the place? Some mystery that!" he exclaimed. "Who was it and why did he do it?"

"Don't ask me!" Pappy shouted. "It wasn't me! One t'ing I am sure of, if you lie down wit' mongrel dawg, yuh ketch flea! Dat was what 'appen to George!"

He woke on Sunday morning to the ringing of church bells all over the city, and he could not resist the urge to go to church. Pappy was still asleep, and he did not wish to disturb him, therefore, he left the house as quietly as possible. He smelt the familiar aromas of Pappy's cooking as he returned. Pappy had eaten and was scanning the Sunday Gleaner. The Sunday Observer and the Sunday Herald lay untidily scattered about his feet.

"Hey, so, you t'ief away as soon as I shut mi eye to night-life and day ketch yuh." Pappy bantered. "Which dancehall yuh guh?"

"I went to mass at the Cathedral," he said. "It is just like old times. Only the songs are new."

"Wash yuh hands and have some breakfast," Pappy invited.

"What for breakfast?" he casually asked.

"Roas' breadfruit, ackee and saltfish, steam' callaloo wit' coffee an' fruits," Pappy replied.

"Mmm! It smells good! You're a good chef! Thank you," he complimented and sat at the table.

Pappy threw down the paper beside the others and sat at the table. Pappy was unusually quiet in a sort of absent-minded manner, and then suddenly he burst out, "Have I ever told yuh about my mad uncle, Laban? I think George was mad like him."

"Welcome back from wherever you went, Pappy," he quipped. "I thought you were lost and could not find your way back. Did you see your Uncle Laban? Who is he and how is he?"

"Come on, it couldn't have been as bad as that, unless you were lost too," Pappy retorted. "Uncle Laban was my mother's half-brother and he use' to complain that he had no name because his father did not own him. He lived in a two-room house on little rise opposite the St. Michael's an' St. George, the Anglican church-school. He was the beadle and when he was too old to ring the bell, his nephew, Simon, took his place. But every Sunday morning, Uncle Laban stood in his white flour-bag underpants and red undershirt, and shout, Simon, gimme back mi ten poun - ten Pounds, shillin'; an pence was the currency in those days."

He laughed because Pappy appeared very droll as he imitated Uncle Laban's, 'Gimme back mi ten poun' ten'.

"Why was he saying that?" he asked.

"Uncle Laban's ram goat had been stolen. Simon had announced that he was going to Bellas gate to 'obeah the t'ief' if the ramgoat was not returned. As a result of Simon's threat, the ram-goat mysteriously re-appear'. Uncle Laban claim' dat he gave the money to Simon to go to Bellas Gate an' Simon refuse' to refund it. Uncle Laban reminded him every Sunday at the ringin' of di church bell. Simon protested that it was not true that Uncle Laban gave him any money —not even one brass farthin', but he had no peace up to the week Uncle Laban died."

"What do you think? Do you think that he gave Simon the money?" he asked in merriment.

Pappy laughed dryly. "I have nutten to go by. There was no

witness. What is certain was dat Simon did go aroun' announcin' dat he was goin' to Bellas Gate, whether he meant it or not, an' the ram-goat did come back. I was a young man at the time." Pappy was wondering how the story of his uncle came to his mind on such a morning. Then he recalled that his uncle had lent him the money for his fare when he first went to England. He thought of telling his grandson the story, but decided against it. He recalled, with amusement, the battle he had with his uncle. He thought that Uncle Laban was compromising him as he had fallen out of grace by his wild behaviour in Trench Town when his father went to live with another woman. He had made a girl pregnant and he was considered a nuisance in the community. Uncle Laban who raised him, was a churchman and he was being castigated for 'letting loose his nephew to run wild'. It spread about the community that Uncle Laban was paying his fare to England to get rid of him. The gossip wounded his pride and he decided to have a show down with his uncle. He shored up his courage by a full morning of drinking white rum with his cronies and then encouraged by them, he declared. "I am goin' to tell that——where to get off. What I do wit' my life is my—— business!"

"I don't want to see you. Yuh a' disgrace di fambily!" Uncle Laban angrily shouted back. "Go a Englan'! Dem wi know weh fi do wit' yuh up deh!"

"I won't go nowhere a ——!" He shouted at his uncle, his voice slurred with drunkenness and he was barely able to stand on his feet. "An' dat Alvin plannin' wit' you."

"Come, come! Don't curse any nasty words in mi ears! I am a Christian," his uncle admonished and drove him and his friends from his gate.

"I not plottin' wit' anybody fi get rid o' yuh," Alvin said to him, next day, when he became sober. "Uncle Laban say him wi' pay yuh fare fi go a Englan' fi get rid a' yuh. If I was you I woud ha' go. I wouldn't miss dat chance. An' sen' fi me when you reach and wuk some money." Alvin was Pappy's cousin and he believed him. He never saw Alvin alive again. He had hopped on to a truck, lost his grip, fell under the rear wheel and the truck crushed him. He was so shaken up that he accepted his uncle's money and went to the mother country. "Yuh know yuh had a cousin who was killed by a truck?" Pappy asked.

"No, you never told me! " he asked.

"He was dead when we found him. I was really unhappy when Alvin died. He was de only person who understood me."

"Is this a sort of confession?" he mischievously asked.

"Not really!" Pappy replied. "But I am sort of reminiscing an' feel dat you would probably like to share on memories an' sentiments."

"OK, thank you!" he replied. "Spill the beans!"

"It's more like raisin' ghosts and diggin' up skeletons," Pappy said. They both chuckled.

"Ugh! You are morbid today Pappy," he remarked.

Pappy chuckled at his grandson's suggestion of morbidity on his part. He rebelled, at first, when he discovered what he regarded as Uncle Laban's intrusion of his rights. He decided not to tell his nephew that he had eaten humble pie and went the next day after Alvin's funeral to tell his uncle that he would accept the fare and go away.

Uncle Laban was eating his breakfast of yellow yam, ackee and saltfish which he washed down with a large mug of homemade chocolate. "Want some breakfus?" Uncle Laban asked, eyeing him suspiciously, his mouth full of yam which he was chomping with nearly toothless gums.

The sight of his uncle's cavernous mouth and shriveled lips turned him off. In addition, his stomach wasn't feeling too good, after that drinking spree. "Uncle, I decide to go Englan'," he started. "Please lend me the fare. I will pay you back"

Unde Laban had wiped the crumbs from his mouth with the back of his hand, and belched loudly, before he replied. "Alvin gone," Uncle Laban said. He noticed that there was no deep feeling of sadness in his uncle's voice. "I know yuh nuh have no money, bwoy. You never did a hones' day' work since I know yuh. Only walk up an' down an' make trouble. I try to be a good uncle to you. My mother never know who is mi father.

"You don't know yuh' father neither. I help mi sister raise you an' yuh tu'n roun' come cuss me. Dis is how yuh show yuh gratitude. You run 'bout an' drunk. Yuh ruin you'self. Yuh is a disgrace!"

He needed no lecture. He only wanted to get away, to escape the community which was becoming claustrophobic and stifling. He had pride. If Uncle Laban lent him the money, he would surely repay.

"Dis generation," his uncle continued, "give dem a yard an' dey take a mile. Fi me generation never did stay so. When I was forty-big big man-I say somet'ing dat my father thought was rude, an' he lick me down wit' him coco-macca stick! You know how ol' he was? Him was eighty! Yuh can't do dat to dis force-ripe generation, Dey would lick yuh back. Da's why dis generation bad so. You can't talk to dem! If me take mi supple-jack an' lick you right now, yuh would a lick me back!"

Pappy denied that he would do such a thing. He would run away from punishment. The long and short of it, was that his uncle lent him the fare and went to Kingston Harbour to see him off on the S.S. Irpinia.

He broke the silence into which Pappy had fallen with his secret thoughts and reflections. "It has never occurred to me to ask you why you gave up your job and returned to Jamaica the time you did," he said.

Pappy smiled with a far-away look in his eyes. "I got tired of cartin' people day after day across London, I guess." he replied. "So I decided to come an' transport garbage. I thought there would have been less worries."

"And you haven't found it so?" he teased.

"Well, I have not been complainin' to anyone, have I? Nor stirrin' any waves neither. Now they disturb my peace of mind," Pappy truculently replied.

He looked at Pappy incredulously, and Pappy laughed. "Don't look at me like dat," Pappy admonished him. "I am not Uncle Laban! It wasn't like that. After your grandmother, Merrie, died, Mother Country felt kind of cold, so cold and lonely dat I yearn' for the warmth of my own country. I had to come 'ome." Pappy stood up to turn up the volume of the television and he was humming, 'The Green Grass of Home'.

He told Pappy that he understood, Pappy looked grateful.

"It has just occurred to me, Pappy, that you have never told me about our family — our foreparents and relatives you know about," he said. "How is that?"

"You have never asked!" Pappy countered. "There ain't much to tell." He began to tell him the history of his own parents and the uncles and aunts he knew of. It was quite ineresting that, he thought that someone like Pappy had such a mixed heritage. *Ain't much to tell* he had said.

Pappy paused to observe a moment of silence, and perhaps to reflect on their happy days of marriage. Letting out a deep sigh, he resumed his account. "I guess you realized that my only son, Bateman Carter, was your father, You're the splittin' image of him! He named you Bateman Carter Jr. He was a stray shot, the result of a little wild-oats I sowed before I went to Mother Country. Pity he didn't stay alive to see you grow up into the man you is today! He didn't marry your mother. I loved your mother, Beryl Taylor. I don't know anything about her. People accept that she was from Oracabessa and she was nice to look at, had nice ways and I loved her as if she was my own daughter. I kept tellin' your father to marry her. He kept saying he was savin' money for a big weddin' because he had plenty friends to invite. I offered to help him. He said he wasn't ready. I had to come home to bury him."

Pappy suddenly stopped talking, slouched his shoulders and it seemed as if all the burdens and wear-and-tear of sorrowful years had suddenly rested on them in a load too heavy to bear. He rested a reassuring hand on Pappy's shoulder, "I am sorry, Pappy, so sorry! But never mind. Fate is so unkind, but we cannot surrender while we have a little strength left."

Pappy looked up, threw back his shoulders, shook his head and softly laughed. "I ought to be braver!" he said. "I am not a weakling! I am a fighter from way back! Our family has had a fair share of good things and a fair share of tragedies. I suppose all families get crosses in different ways to test their faith and stamina."

"Of course, Pappy! Different strokes for different folks! And as people often say, if you think you have worries, listen to the troubles of another man, and see yourself as still lucky that you're no way worse than you are!"

"Yeah! I agree. We still have a lot to be thankful. I did not want to tell you de truth why I came home from Mother Country for good, but I may as well tell you. I do not care to keep any secret from you. Not anymore! About a year after I returned to Mother Country from burying your father, I heard that your mother became pregnant for some man or di oddah who never came forward. She didn't seem to know who made her pregnant, and I was mad about it, for I was sendin' her money to look after my dead son's children. The nex' t'ing I heard was that your mother died at Jubilee in child-birth."

He became numb with shock and disappointment. "Died at the Jubilee Hospital in childbirth? Oh my God!" he exclaimed.

"Yeah!" said Pappy. "That's life, when you fail to control it. It is sure to mess you up! If you spread yuh bed in a sardine can, you 'ave to lie down in a it. I came home from Mother Country to bury her, and I stayed to look after my three grandchildren, George, you and Raymond! Your mother's relatives wanted to share the three of you among them — one of you to go one way, an' another of you to go elsewhere. I said to them 'Sorry my grandchildren are not pup-pies to give away here and there, dem staying with me!'"

"Sorry, Pappy, I am really sorry that you had to make such a sacrifice!" he said, "How can I make it up to you?"

"You 'aven't got to do a damn thing!" Pappy replied. "I am grateful that I was able to do it! It could have been worse! Now that I have told you the trut' why I came home, I wish I hadn't told you!"

"Thanks, Pappy," he said. "As they say in Britain, you're solid like the Rock of Gibraltar." He took up the paper. "Pappy did you see this?" he asked thumbing a page of the paper.

"What is it?" Pappy asked.

"Listen to this. *A quantity of arms was seized by the Police at Norman Manley International Airport on Friday. The Police also found three illegal guns in Kingston, St. Catherine and St. James. The firearms and several rounds of ammunition at the Customs Department at the airport were hidden in a barrel containing foodstuff, clothing and other items. The arms found were a M-l Enforcer machine gun, an AK-47 assault rifle, a 9mm Roger sub-machine gun and a 36 calibre hand gun. Detectives have held a man for questioning.* Listen to this! *A 9 mm pistol can cost as much as ten thousand to twenty-five thousand dollars on the street.*"

Pappy sadly shook his head. "Just last week some big Director was shot to death on his driveway. And it didn't look like the motive is robbery."

"There are people, I believe, who must have some information to help the Police," he asserted.

"True," Pappy replied, "but nowadays, the Police have to buy the information. Hardly anyone is giving it to them for free. People 'fraid. Dey just won't talk for fear of reprisal. Some are distrustful of the Police dat information will be let out on the identity of informers by the Police themselves. Of course, there is no foundation for such distrust. I don't believe it. It's a coincidence that exactly a month to date, a bag of rice was being unloaded at Port Bustamante when it burst and nuff 9 mm semi-automatic guns fell out. Others were in other bags. Dey say dat de security guards were bribed not to look while the guns were being unloaded and collected. Dem all seh dat it was for a certain don."

"This is rather startling," he commented, not forgetting that he also had an illegal gun hidden in the hotel.

"Listen to what I am sayin'," Pappy continued. "It was rumoured that the said don presumably gave some guns to his henchman to do a hit job. De man failed an' him never come back wid di gun dem. Dead men turned up in crocus bags, and the henchman ran away to New York. The don arranged for him to be received. The don, so I heard, get a e-mail few days later, saying that de goods were refrigerated."

"Ah, ah! Refrigerated, indeed! So what is the arm of the law doing about this don?" he lightly asked.

"Gettin' amputated, I suppose," Pappy bantered.

"The Police appear more likely to be in danger of emasculation, from what I gather of the hostility of some people against them," he sardonically said.

"Damn sad, ain't it? If yuh get your good arm amputated at the expense of your bad arm?" Pappy observed. "The Commissioner an' the country fightin' a losin' battle agains' crime, if hones' policemen an' the public don't want to come forward an' give information to the crime authorities, an' evidence in court."

Their conversation was interrupted by a car-horn and he looked at his watch. "That could be Chew," he said. "He's on time."

"Most business men are usually punctual. Time means money to them," Pappy observed. "When I use' to drive for London Transport, I had to stick to a timetable and if I don't obey the Company schedule and run my bus on time, I had no job. Out here, if a man has an appointment to meet with you at ten o'clock today, hope to see him at eleven if you're lucky or better still eleven tomorrow or the next day. Nobody, even in *High Places*, cares about hours an' minutes wasted. People are inconvenienced and stressed out by the tardiness of the people we have to deal with. Lateness at the workplace is a national syndrome. You better hurry!"

They got in the car one by one and were silent for about five minutes. "Carnival has really taken root in this country," said Chew as he drove. "When it started in 1990, by Byron Lee, not many people felt that it could become a part of our culture, as we already have National Festival and Independence Celebration. But it has caught on like a bush fire. For this year, Jamaica Carnival launched Carnival City at the Market Place, their new home. It also is the home for such carnival groups as D'Masqueraders, Goodyear, Socarobics and the Junior Carnival. Carnival this year started off with Fire On the Water Front, an affair at Mahogany Beach at Ocho Rios. I went. There was a Beach J' Ouvert last Sunday, but I couldn't make it."

"What is this J' Ouvert?" he asked.

"It is a traditional carnival event in which participants paint their bodies. This year it was held at Oracabessa on James Bond beach. Last year, I took Raymond with me. There was a huge bonfire on the beach and hundreds of gallons of body paint were used. People went wild to the soca music." Chew explained.

"Where are we going now," he asked.

"We are going up to Liguanea where the action begins," Chew replied. "Here is a map of the Road March route. There will be two Carnival Camps, Byron Lee's camp called Jamaica Carnival and Bacchanal. I think I will find a parking space right here," said Chew. "That's King's House up there. Remember?"

"King's House! Yeah, I remember," he replied

Chew managed to manoeuvre an awkward parking space on Hope Road which was already overflowing with parked and moving vehicles, and locked the car. A tiny street kid looking less than seven years old appeared at once and offered to watch the car until they returned.

"There they are!" Chew exclaimed excitedly. "Here comes the *D'masqueraders*. Look at those floats and music trucks. There goes Byron Lee and the Dragonnaires! The music is fantastic! Jamaican women are the most beautiful in the world! My Gawd, look at those effigies and the Mokojombies!"

"Correct that!" said he, greatly amused. "Let's say, Caribbean women are the most beautiful in the world."

"Right!" Chew replied. "Caribbean women! Let's join the March."

They went along Lady Musgrave Road, Trafalgar Road, along the lower section of Constant Spring Road, past Ruthven Road to Liguanea Park. Soaked with sweat and the fire of the soca-reggae beat, he was too exhilarated to care that he was tired and that his feet were aching.

"This is great!" Chew exclaimed, his features more yellow and bonier than ever.

"The grand finale is the Last Hurrah at Cinema 2 in New Kingston. But we won't bother with that. The bacchanal will go on until mid-night. Let's take a taxi back to the car."

"How was the Road March?" asked Pappy.

"It was great!" he replied.

"Yeah," said Pappy. "I saw a little of it on the tele. I still feel that people shouldn't get so wild, goin' half-naked, wrigglin' up themselves and goin' on bad. An' to be doin' it in di Easter at dat! It immoral an' ungodly to me! Is sacrilege!"

"Different strokes for different folks, Pappy. Some find satisfaction in going to church. Others find satisfaction in sport. We all got to have our kicks. There is little harm in carnival. It is a lot of clean fun."

"I don't agree," Pappy objected. "Is modern madness! Dem all goin' to hell!"

⊰ℐℒ⊱

Tuesday morning, Raymond came early and drove the Datsun to the prison. He had borrowed Pappy's old briefcase and placed some note paper, a pen and a pencil in it. In the guard-room, one of the guards pretended to examine his briefcase and asked him if he had a weapon. The other guard advised his companion not to make an entry of the visit in the Log Book, then the guard beckoned him and Raymond to follow. Their feet sounded ghoulishly hollow on a metal walkway that led towards a cell block. The guard opened a door, ushered them inside and asked for the rest of the money. He handed the guard an envelop and said. "I prefer to pay the prisoner myself." The guard shrugged his shoulder and muttered, "As yuh say, Boss. I goin' for di prisoner."

He examined the room in the meantime. In the centre of the room was a long table, its legs screwed onto the concrete floor. Two backless benches on either side of the table were also firmly bolted to the floor. The warder reappeared, in a short while accompanied by a burly man who announced himself as a innocent murderer serving life sentence. The prisoner was eager to tell his story, but he dissuaded him by promising to listen another time.

"Dis is you' lawyer," the warder explained, "Talk to di man." Looking directly at Raymond, he said, "I standin' near di door. Call out if any trouble, an' when yuh done."

The prisoner swiftly snatched the two five hundred notes proffered to him and without asking for more, thanked them effusively and licked his lips greedily as he folded them and furtively tucked them in a hole inside his waistband.

"Your name is Basil Power?" he asked, as he opened the briefcase and took out a sheet of paper and the pen.

"Yes sah. Is mi same one. Dem call mi Big Bird."

"Did you know Mr. Carter?" he asked,

"Sar? Mi know him like how mi know misself. Him nuh was ha' make any bomb. Dem kill him!" Power cried.

"Hold on! Take it easy!" he tried to calm Power. "Who killed him?"

"Dem people outside who nuh want him fi live. I don't know who kill him, but is not him kill himself!" said Power. "I use' to carry his food for him twice a day, everyday, from de gate when Miss Ida bring it. She cook fi him, She bring 'im food two times a day, mawnin' an' evenin'."

"Did anybody visit him when he was here?" he asked,

"A man Mass George call Diamond Toot," Power said. "Him 'ave a stone in him teet' and when him open him mout' to the sun, it flash. Da's why dem call him Diamond Toot. Him come often, for Missa Carter say is him frien' an' dat who look after him business while him deh inna prison."

"His friend!" he exclaimed. "Did Mass George tell you what business he was in?"

"Yes, he say bus and taxi busines," Power replied.

"Diamond Toot'!" he muttered, turning to Raymond who seemed uncomfortable. "Ray, do you know anything about this man?"

"No," said Ray, "I know not'ing,"

He turned to Power, "Tell me Mr. Power, did anyone else visit Mr. Carter?"

"Dis young gentleman here come one or two times," Power replied, pointing at Raymond.

"Did he talk with you about anybody else?"

"Mass George," Power answered, "he say he 'ave annodda fren' name Mr. Chow or Mr. Choy, I don't remember."

"Has Mr. Chow or Choy ever visited?" he asked.

"No sah," said Power. "I never seen him an' I would ha' know if him come. Him sen' t'ings for Missa Power all di while, milk, soap, ovaltine, cigarettes an' those t'ings."

"Mr. Chow or Mr. Choy!" he murmured. "What did he tell you about Mr. Chow or Mr. Choy?" he asked.

"Yes sah, Missa Chow, him 'ave big supermarket ah Allman Town. He 'ave fishin' boat too," Power replied.

Just then the guard looked in and signaled that the time was up. He looked queryingly at his brother, but said nothing to him. He told himself that he had a few questions to ask Raymond. "That is all for now, Mr. Powers. I will come again as soon as I process the first stage of your appeal," he snapped his briefcase shut. "Tell me, Mr. Power, about the bomb. What really happened?"

"Well, Diamond Toot' take all sort of wire an' t'ings to make radio. All sort of wire an' battery."

"How did those things pass the guards at the gate?" he asked.

"Well, after a while, the warders stop lookin' in what come fo' Mr. Carter. So he 'ave television an' eletric fan an' gas stove an' cellular an' dem t'ings deh."

"Gas stove!" He exclaimed in disbelief. "No wonder his cell blew up! What happened on that day?"

"I took the dinner basket from di lady an' take it to Mass George. Well, I just take the basket to him and he say to put it down. Him not ready to eat yet."

"What was he doing?" he eagerly asked.

"He was watchin' di TV. Him was not makin' anyt'ing." Power declared. "An' as I leave an' turn di corner of di block, I hear whump! An' it look like di whole a' di prison fall dung pon me an' throw me ah groun'. Mi know nutten more. When I wake up, I hear say Missa Carter bomb up in a di cell an' dead. Him nuh was ha' make no bomb!"

"Did you say the blast happened after you took the basket to him?" he asked.

"Yes sah! Mi sure a' dat. Right after mi put down di basket an' turn di corner, di place broke down an' fire start."

"You said Diamond Toot was here earlier that day?" he asked.

"Yes sah, I remember him now. He was leavin' when I tek di basket to Missa Carter," Power replied.

"Are you sure of this?" he asked excitedly.

"Yes! Mi sure, sure, sah."

"Oh, I see! So the bomb was probably not in the basket then! Did you see when Diamond Toot' come in? Did he bring anything for George that day?"

"I never said any bomb was deh in di basket, sah!" Power angrily protested, "You want mi fi tell lie pon mi self now. I don't see nutten', sah. I don't remember seein' anyt'ing."

"Try an' remember, Mr. Power," he pleaded.

"Sorry sah, I seen nutten'," Power apologized. "Can I go now sah? Di warder ready."

Chapter 8

FROM ROAD-WOES TO
DRUGS–DIAMOND TOOT'

"*R*ay, I am thinking that we need to talk with Miss Ida," he said, as they drove from the prison. "We need to find her."

"Findin' her is small matters," Raymond replied, "But gettin' her to talk is another matter. Everybody 'fraid to talk, dese days."

"Well, when she sees our money, she will talk, if she knows anything." Wrapped in their own thoughts, the rest of the way to Pappy's house was done in silence. He told himself again that he wasn't ready to apply 'the thumbscrew' to Raymond.

Pappy looked up from the evening paper he was browsing, when he and Raymond walked in. "What you two been up to?" Pappy bantered, "I hope you didn't get into trouble. Look at this Bat," he said, thrusting the paper into his hand.

The headline leapt at him from the page. '*Cache Of Arms Uncovered*,' he read softly. Below he glanced at: '*Cache of arms and approximately a million dollars of cocaine sized by the Police at Rocky Point*'.

"What the hell?" he swore. "We were reading about the Ship-rider's Agreement and the trans-shipment of drugs a few hours ago. These drug-dealers are very persistent. How about going to Rocky

Point, tomorrow?" he asked.

Raymond said that he couldn't go as he had to collect fish from the fishermen on the Cays and take them supplies. "What for?" Pappy asked. "To get ourselves arrested as druggis' an' gunmen?"

"I am here on holiday. Remember? I plan to visit a number of places I have never had the opportunity to visit. Rocky Point is one of them. The Police can't arrest us for anything as legitimate as a pure and harmless holiday. We won't be doing anything outrageous as breaking the law," he declared.

"OK!" said Pappy, shoving the newspaper of the day before, into his back pocket. "I goin' to play a game of dominoes. Want to come?"

"No, thanks," he replied. "I think I will have a snooze,"

"Good!" Pappy said. "Dinner is there. You an' Raymond help yourself."

"Raymond said that he couldn't stay," Bateman replied. Pappy took up his hat and, followed by Raymond, went through the door. Stretched on the new bed in his old room, he smoked and wrote *DIAMOND TOOT*'and *CHEW* on a sheet of note paper. He deduced from Power's description that Chow or Choy was the same person known to him as *Chew. Vincent Tenn Chew!* Chew and he had gone to school together. Hours after school were spent playing illicit football with other boys on the grounds of the Polo Club. They had cut a hole in the metal fencing of the Polo Club and the caretaker was in collusion with them. Chew regularly bribed him with goods he stole from his father's shop. Chew and he, urged on by the other boys, once got into a fight. He couldn't recall what the fight was about. He didn't know then that Chinese people could fight. Chew's eyes seemed excellent for driveling a ball, but they didn't seem right for throwing a punch.

He painfully found out since Chew did not only use his fists, but his head and foot, to give him a sound beating. The following day, Chew brought a peace offering of a whole bag of bullas. He refused, at first, to sign a treaty of peace , but coerced by the bunch of hungry and greedy boys who had instigated the fight, he accepted the bullas. They became the best of friends, until Pappy took George, him and Ray to England. Chew and George were not friends in their boyhood, George being four or five years older. He was now wondering what brought and held Chew and George together as friends. He lit another cigarette, crushed out the butt of the former into the body of the satyr and added a tail to it. He wasn't succeeding in forming a theory on the relationship between the three men, George, Diamond Toot' and Chew. But from his talk with Power, there was a relationship, and within that relationship lay the mystery of his brother's death. Making no headway, he gave up, tore the paper into shreds, flushed the pieces in the toilet and had his dinner. "One thing is certain, there is no prison security in this world that is efficient and fool-proof enough to protect those inside from those who are outside. The obscurity surrounding the mysterious death of persons in prison all over the world is bound to cause speculation, fear and distrust of prison systems and authorities everywhere. Just think of it! The mysterious death of some prisoners, I heard, caused children to stay from school. Some people stayed away from work for fear of reprisals and repercussions. My brother's death did not stir even a wave –Donkey says the world's not level."

When he woke, the stumbling and bustling around the house indicated that Pappy was up early, as usual. When he emerged from the bathroom, Pappy was already dressed and breakfast was ready.

"Not much of a breakfas' this mornin'," Pappy quipped. "We are travelling light to make faster time. When we reach Old Harbour, we can catch up on fried fish and bammy." Pappy stretched his hand towards him, "Car key," he said. "Nobody drive me nowhere on dat Ol' Harbour Road. Is a cemetery dat! I don't t'ink di Creator ready fo' me, yet, and I'm into no hurry to go."

Pappy enjoyed joking about religion. "He wouldn't be caught alive in a church," he used to say.

"Well, Pappy, like Mr. Chew, religion is not a joke to me, but the Great Builder, if he has gone to prepare a place, as he says, then you will be here a long time to come, since he needs a long time to erect a strong room or steel vault to keep you permanently."

"I have a problem," Pappy hinted with a sly and infectious grin.

"What is it?" he asked suspiciously

"I am allergic to milk and I don't eat or drink honey! I don't think I could learn to dance to a harp either."

He almost doubled up with laughter trying to envisage Pappy dancing. He didn't think that, though Pappy loved music, he had ever danced in his mortal life.

"More than that, I wouldn't want to meet certain individuals up there. I want to be around to see them go first so as to know where they are. I intend to stay on Mother Earth as long as I am able."

"Pappy, I don't normally joke about religion," he explained. "I respect every man's religion, whether he is Catholic, Hindu or Jew. Any belief that satisfies a man's idealistic and spiritual views of making himself and his brothers and sisters better, and serves to give him hope for life on a better plane, so long he compromises and does not endanger my beliefs, my dignity and my freedom is good enough for me and useful, in my estimation."

"Ugh! You 'ave said quite a mouthful," Pappy replied. "But I am followin' what you're sayin' that every man should be allowed to do his own good t'ing so long it is good."

"I wish I could express it as simply as you do, Pappy," he said.

"Experience, my Son! Experience comes wid ol' age!" Pappy bantered. "Though I know some people, the older dey get, de more stupid dey become."

"Quite right! What I truly believe in, is that a man or woman must understand and believe strongly in his concepts and ideals, so that he is able to defend them."

"I have no quarrel with that," Pappy muttered, as he backed the Datsun past the mango tree. "But I find what you're sayin' a little tough to digest. Good thing we had breakfas'." Pappy drove west along Spanish Town Road. "This part of the road is now called Mandela Highway," Pappy explained, after driving a few miles out of Kingston. Skirting Spanish Town, they soon took to the Old Harbour Road. He involuntarily ducked almost under the dashboard as an approaching bus appearing from behind a slower vehicle, roared seemingly on a collision path towards them.

"For the life of me!" Pappy exclaimed in horror, easing his fingers from the horn of the Datsun. "I wouldn't want to travel on one of those. Just look at the smoke dat bus left behind. An' some o' di drivers an' conductors is a force to reckon with! Dey endanger the lives of passengers an' di public at large."

"You're bearing down too thickly on them, aint 'it' ?" he suggested.

"No, no" Pappy replied. "Listen to me. Dey can't be worse! I have seen conductors on West Street where the country buses park, grab passengers an' shove them on buses. I seen a 'ductor grab a woman an' push her into a packed minibus. At the same time, another 'ductor had gone with her baggage an' her baby screamin' like hell onto another bus. You don't know what I'm talkin' about! You 'ave to travel aroun' an' see mad drivers on di road."

He couldn't help laughing, regardless of the seriousness and disgust of his grandfather, "When they sort' t'ings out, the lady was going to Cave Valley. She was abducted an' pushed on a bus bound for Bonny Gate. Her poor little infant an' her luggage were put on a bus to Morant Bay. One conductor said he had asked her where she was going an' she said Bonny Gate. The other impudently asked her why she had changed her mind about goin' to Morant Bay. When she insisted that she had not mentioned where she was going, he said, 'Lady, yuh nuh know weh yuh ha' go. Yuh is a cavewoman!'"

"Is this one of your corny jokes? That dolt of a conductor was acting more like a caveman than the lady with her baby and her baggage," he commented.

"No," answered Pappy, "it 'appen. Commuters are also at fault. No better herrin' no better barrel! I wouldn't allow myself to be packed like sardine or banana in any public transport. Or be shoveled into buses an' taxi like garbage. Some passengers get what dem deserve. Dey climb into buses where dere is not even breathin' space left. Some passengers refuse to budge from entrance an' exits on buses. Some refuse to pay di fare. Some abuse drivers, conductors an' passengers. An' I grieve to know how dey treat school-children. Some passengers are uncouth brutes. Dey are t'ieves, cut-throats an' louts who attack passengers, drivers an' conductors with knives, guns an' acid. Some brave policemen who accost these rascals on the buses have lost their lives."

"The situation is really ugly," he empathized. "A special transport security system is needed to be organized to protect commuters, as well as to train drivers and conductors. A public education propaganda is also necessary to educate commuters how to relate to bus-drivers and conductors. Do the conductors and drivers wear uniform?"

"Some do. Some don't," said Pappy.

"Has it never occurred to commuters to protest the treatment meted out to them by withdrawing their patronage for a week or a day at a time?" he asked.

"Come to t'ink of it!" Pappy exclaimed, greatly amused. "I have never thought of it. You see, in dis country, only about three percent of the population own their own vehicles. A demonstration of such magnitude is impossible to organize, an' di operators know it."

"The disruption would probably be as effective as when the operators withdraw their service – the shoe would be on the other foot." Bateman defended.

"Well," Pappy said, "a philosopher says that we often get what we deserve. The Transport Ministry has taken over urban transportation an' it look like there has been great improvements since. The city has been sufferin' for long years from what a journalist call 'run-down relics and motorized shells'. It was real chaos when the conductor, called a 'ducta', rule' the roos' an' dispense injury, insults an' familiarity to passengers, school girls an' young women especially."

"It's as bad as that?" he asked in dismay.

"Bad?" shouted Pappy above the blaring horn and roar of a fast truck passing in the opposite direction. "Bad is a mild word to describe it!"

"I tell you, transportation was in shambles. The latest t'ing I am hearin' is dat di ductas organize sessions on the buses called 'no panty days'."

"Eh, what're you telling me?" he exclaimed.

"Yeah. On such days, those school girls who bare their little tails an' left their underwear behind, presumably at home, get free rides on the buses. I leave di res' to your imagination!"

"Free rides, indeed!" he murmured sardonically. "A far cry from the well run JOS. Those were golden days, halcyon days, in this country. What did we do to mess it up?"

By then, they had reached the Old Harbour roadway. "Dis road is a graveyard. It worse dan Devil's Racecourse. Once upon a time, there was an average of two deaths on dis road per month. Drivers use' to think it was a racetrack," Pappy related.

"How is the accident rate today?" he asked.

"Oh, drivers have out-grown their fascination for fas' drivin' on dis road, an' of course, there are daily Police speed-traps," Pappy answered. "I tell you what I'm puckish. Let's stop for a roast fish an' bammy an' perhaps a beer."

They drew up near one of the food-stalls on the left side of the road after passing the Old Harbour clock tower. The bammy and fish, wrapped in aluminum foil, was served hot by a jolly and buxom woman.

"Pappy, how about going through May Pen?" he asked.

"What?" quipped Pappy. "You hear seh di fish an' bammy better up dere?"

"I should think not, but I haven't been there a long while, and I like that little town."

They had almost gone two miles from Sandy Bay. Pappy shouted. "Look out! Fasten your seat-belt!" Pappy began to swing the steering wheel wildly from left to right as if he was searching for a place to dump the car, while he fumbled with the belt which he had not re-latched when they left Old Harbour. The Datsun skidded off a smooth patch of macadam with a frenetic squealing of tyres and headed across the white line, as Pappy alternatively feathered accelerator and brake to get free of the skid. The zigzagging car came to a stop on the right soft-shoulder of the road.

"Gawd! Did you see dat?" Pappy angrily shouted. "An' you forgot to refasten you' seat-belt! Dat car-door fly open an' di driver fell out an' I nea'ly ran over him! I have told dem damn fools, over an' over not to lean on di car-door when drivin'. I'm sure dat one dead! Some even keep dere hand hangin' outside waitin' for a passin' vehicle to 'lick' it off!"

"It looks like he was pushed from the car!" he said. "He came out waving his hands in the air, and then he fell. There was gunfire from the car. He was probably hit!"

While Pappy was fighting to regain control of the Datsun, they did not see the man was trying to rise, and that a policeman was rushing towards him with his revolver cocked. Three or four policemen alighted from a jeep and were approaching the car that had upended in a ditch, its battered front facing the direction from which it was proceeding. There was a brief fusillade of gunshots from the car and the policemen fanned out and returned the fire, their bullets hitting the overturned car with dull, whumping sounds. If there was an innocent person in that car, it was just too bad for him. He did not stand a chance of being rescued alive.

"Jesus! Are those gunshots?" Pappy asked, resting his throbbing head on the steering wheel, his brow dripping cold sweat. "Is who dey shootin' at?"

"They're shooting up the overturned car," he replied in horror. "There can't be anyone left alive in it!"

"It's safer to drive a garbage truck, anyday," Pappy said, groaning.

"If you were driving a truck, I doubt that you could have avoided colliding with that car."

"If I was drivin' a truck, I wouldn't bother to get out of the way," Pappy angrily shouted.

"It seems as if the Police shot those people," he remarked. "A crowd is gathering around the car."

"You know, believe me, I didn't hear a thing when I was tryin' to prevent dis car from killin' us." Pappy said. "What were you screamin' at me?"

"I can't recall screaming," he replied. "Everything was happening so fast. Thank you for reminding me to fasten my seatbelt."

"Don't move," a policeman truculently ordered, and they stared into the barrel of a pistol. Another policeman, his orange coloured bulletproof vest over his shirt (though bulletproof jackets are normally worn beneath a shirt), sub-machine gun on the alert stood a little distance covering for the one who was accosting them.

"Driver's licence," the one armed with a pistol brusquely ordered, stretching out his free hand.

Pappy produced his licence which the officer examined. Seemingly satisfied, the policeman, pistol still in hand, peered through the car window to ask, "You folks awright?"

"Bat, you alright?" Pappy asked.

"Yeah, only a bit shaken up," he replied.

"I 'ave a mind arres'in' you for dangerous drivin'," the policeman threatened, opening his eyes to view the drag marks of the Datsun.

"Me?" an irate Pappy shouted. "Arres' me for dangerous driving? I been drivin' a bus in Mother Country before you was born, an' for twenty years I drive a garbage truck in dis country fo' government, a policeman never write me up yet!"

The officer became amiable, "Don't drive away. I comin' back to take a statement from the two o' you."

"We were too busy saving our lives an' tryin' not to hit anyt'ing to see what happened," Pappy said.

"I still want a statement from you," the officer insisted, as he holstered his gun and walked away towards the crowd. "Every bit of evidence is important."

"We were lucky, very lucky," Pappy sarcastically said, as they stepped from the car and stood looking in the direction of the crowd. "We nearly got ourselves killed an' arrested fo' dangerous driving."

"Dead and arrested!" He exclaimed, merriment playing around his mouth and eyes. "Do you really mean that the Police would arrest a corpse?"

"I think I did read some place dat a English prince, when he became king dug up his enemies, try dem and hang' dem. One of those corpse was taken out of Mother Country and secretly buried in Jamaica so as not to get dat dead man arrested, tried an' hanged. This is Jamaica! If it happen abroad, it could 'appen here, I not swearin' dat it couldn't 'appen!" Pappy replied.

He came from his side of the Datsun and joined his grandfather.

"Excellent driving," he commended, squeezing his grandfather's hand. "You could win the Grand Prix, anyday!"

"Let's see what is happenin' down dere," Pappy said, looking at the increasingly long lines of traffic that had come to a standstill. They could not get through the thickness of the crowd. A squad of policemen attempted repeatedly to clear the street to restore the flow of traffic. There was a mile-long pile-up of cars, buses and trucks. The honking of horns by impatient motorists added to the confusion. They asked a policeman what had happened. The officer indifferently shrugged his shoulder, twisted his lips and grunted, "Don't know. Look like some gunmen get shot."

Noticing that the traffic started to move again, Pappy walked around the car, kicked the tyres and opened the doors. "Let's get out o' here," Pappy said.

"What about the officer who ordered us to stay put until he returned?" he asked.

"Ugh!" replied Pappy. "He isn't comin' back. "Pappy manoeuvred the Datsun past a decorated handcart with a slogan, 'TRY LIFE', painted on its side in red against a yellow background, then across the nose of an ancient Toyota, and passing a Toyota Camry nearly as close as the thickness of its paint and chrome trimmings would permit, he put the Datsun back on the road.

"We lost a whole hour," Pappy said. "We will hear it on the news, tonight." Pappy drove gingerly and silently until they began to climb the sombre and tranquil hills. Pappy then began to clip away the miles and soon the panorama of Carlisle Bay basking in the sunlight, unfolded before them. The fishermen had returned with their catch, and women, children and dogs formed a noisy crowd around the boat, and the village of Rocky Point sleepily and peacefully overlooked the sea. He commented on the stillness of the settlement.

"Still river run deep in Jamaica," Pappy remarked. "Now that we here, what we do now? Jus' sit on di beach, roll up wi pants an' dip our feet?"

"I have my swimming trunks," he replied. "What about yours?"

"Me?" Pappy replied. "Never own one in my life as I don't

plan to drown. I will watch for sharks while you swim."

"You're not coming in, Pappy?" he teased.

"Me, go in dere? You don't answer my question. What do we do now that we are here?"

"I tell you what? Relax! Think of something, anything, while I take a dip."

"If there is anyt'ing I hate, is not to 'ave a plan," Pappy grumbled.

"Let's play it by ear," he suggested.

"Hurry an' take your dip. I feel for a beer," Pappy said, leaning on the Datsun, having crossed his arms and legs and looking seaward.

He dropped his pants and peeled off his T-shirt with a picture design of sea and coconut tree and a slogan, 'JAMROC' hand-painted on it. He threw his clothes on the backseat of the car, and waded into the water. He sank his head and with powerful thrusts of legs, he sent himself into a dive toward a pile of black rocks that barely protruded out of the water. When he surfaced, he turned on his back and lay still. He was exhilarated by the clinging warmth of the tropical water and the sun and breeze sucking at the drops of water sticking to the hair on his chest. After a while, he spun around and swam parallel to the coast, made a couple of somersaults and pulled himself with a rapidly executed crawl towards the beach.

"Good!" he exclaimed, as he walked back towards the Datsun. The sun and breeze were still licking at his skin. There was salt in his eyes and mouth and a horse-like vitality was suffusing him.

"You didn't see any sharks?" he teased as Pappy handed him a towel.

"Have you missed a part of your body?" Pappy asked gazing at his crotch.

"No, why" he asked laughing.

"If you haven't missed anyt'ing, it means that I did not see any shark," Pappy straight-facedly explained. "I didn't know you could swim."

He did not comment. He would not like his grandfather to know that when he was a boy, he used to compete with his peers, diving from Victoria Pier to recover coins thrown into the sea by tourists.

"What next?" said Pappy.

"You said that you wanted a beer," he replied. "Come on, let's go get it!" he drew on his pants over his wet trunks and pulled on his T-shirt. Pappy locked the Datsun, and they walked along a narrow lane under a forest of coconut trees, until they came out on to the single street of the village. Coming out of the vibrant sunshine, they entered a dark little bar. The solitary quietness had an eerie effect on him.

Pappy muttered, "Seems as if no one is here," and he rapped loudly on the counter top with the flat of his hand.

A thin, yet paunched man past middle-age, wearing a huge green, yellow and black woolen cap, leisurely came from a backroom. He placed his outstretched hands on the counter top and stared at them, a query in his eyes and on his brow.

"Two cold Red Stripe", Pappy said.

The man twisted his body around and opened the battered refrigerator behind him. He took out two bottles of beer and banged them on the counter. Then he reached for an opener tied to a string and removed the bottle caps, pushing the bottles simultaneously close to their hands on the counter top.

"How much?" Pappy asked.

The man did not reply. Pappy put two hundred dollar Jamaican notes on the counter. The man twisted his body around again, put the note into a drawer and loudly slapped down fifty dollars on the counter. Pappy did not take up the coin. The bar-tender, obviously that was what he was, his hands as rigid as at first, stood on his side of the counter and stared outside. He felt that the bartender was actually scrutinizing them. He glanced at the man while drinking his beer, but he couldn't discern the outline of the man's face because of his thick and heavy growth of beard from which peeped a bumpy, greasy looking nose and thick heavy black and red lips. He shifted his eyes to the fridge noting where the pale blue paint had peeled exposing what was once white enamel.

Pappy crossed his lips with a forefinger, when the bartender wasn't looking, signaling him to keep silent. Pappy cleared his throat.

"How are t'ings aroun' dese parts?" Pappy asked.

"Cool, Man! Jus' cool!" the bartender answered.

Pappy was seeking a conversation opener. Pappy wanted the man to talk. "What are you? Rasta or Dread Locks?"

The man smiled for the first time and he noticed that the man's eyes were jaundiced, but he was revealing strong white teeth from the gap in his beard. "Jah Rastafari" The man replied.

He was aware that there was a difference between Dreads and Rastas, but he wasn't familiar with it. He made a mental note to learn, at some other time, what was the difference.

"So yuh bu'n di collie?" Pappy genially asked.

"You is Babylon?" the bar-tender replied. "Babylon know say I an' I bredrin penetrate."

"Babylon wicked!" Pappy said.

"Jah, true wo'd!" the bartender said, "Dat is wisdom. Respec'!"

He silently congratulated his grandfather. He didn't think that he himself could do so well to win the man's confidence. He would wait an opportunity to intervene in the dialogue to ask a few questions. Pappy was making headway and enjoying it. Pappy beckoned the man to draw closer. "I bet you deal wid somet'ing mo' powerful dan collie?"

"No, Boss! Like what so?" asked the bartender warily.

Pappy spoke in a lower voice. "Crack," he said.

"I man, don't like trouble!" the man suspiciously whined. "I man don't trouble what don't trouble me."

"No trouble, at all. This man is a touris'. He is my frien'. He want jus' a little fix. Know where he can get it?" Pappy tried to reassure the man in a convincing voice.

"Oh, you is a touris'!" exclaimed the bartender, greatly relieved. "Den dat no diff'rant business? Why yuh never say so long time? Ah weh unnu come from?"

"He, not me," replied Pappy, pointing at his grandson. "He is from New York."

He was a little startled that Pappy had not said Mother Country.

"He is lookin' a little fun," Pappy explained. "I jus' come wid him as his frien'. You can tell us where to look?"

The bartender answered, "Man funny roun' dese parts. Dey don't like man who talk too much or fast wid dem business. You can go down Negril, it a walk street down deh! An' yuh don't ha' fi ask any question. Dem bring it come ask yuh."

"Not dat kind a high," Pappy replied. "We know where to get dat. You know what I mean!"

"I don't deal," replied the bartender. "But I can put you on to a man."

"What is your name?" Pappy asked.

"Peter Lyons, but dey call me Ras Lion," the bartender replied. "Lion like di lion of Judah! Some people jus' say Lion."

"OK, Ras Lion, put mi bredrin on. Him want it bad."

"See 'ow it go now," Ras Lion explained. "Go 'pon di beach. Crack yuh fingers so, when you see anybody ha' pass." The Lion demonstrated by cracking his fingers like fire burning dry wood. Pappy cracked his hand by using his right hand to pull and press the finger joints of his left hand. Crack! Crack! Went the fingers of Pappy and the Lion.

Bateman's fingers refused to crack. Ras Lion's face became bigger and rounder as he laughed and repeatedly demonstrated. "It's easy," Pappy demonstrated, alternately cracking the fingers of both hands.

"Hol' you' han' so, pull di joint so," Ras Lion instructed. "Is as easy as cheese!"

"Not so easy!" he protested, "My fingers simply refuse to crack!"

"You must be a dunce!" Pappy said, giving up in feigned disgust.

"Is more practice di fingers dem want," said the Lion. "See deh, it easy!"

"Let's suspend the class for another day," he said dryly.

Ras Lion clapped an empty Pepsi bottle on the counter. "Look out fi Babylon when you doin' dis one. Babylon deh bout dese days. Since you can't crack you' finger, hol' dis bottle so an' di drug man dem will know that you lookin' a stick or you can ax the canejuice man on di beach fo' some ice. He wi' put a man 'pon yuh to fix yuh up."

Pappy told him to practise saying, "May I get some ice?" He practised several times with Pappy and the Lion correcting and improving until they were satisfied that he was word perfect and convincing. Ras Lion thought it was great fun. Their uproarious laughter attracted three men who were standing outside. They came in, hoping to join the fun. Pappy bought each man a Red Stripe.

Ras Lion said rather arrogantly to the men, after serving them, "I discussin' a little business wid dese gentlemen here. Kinda private."

The men got the hint, apologized, said thanks for the beer and went outside.

"Two more Red Stripe and have one on us," he said, slapping three one hundred dollar notes on the counter. The Lion slammed three bottles of beer on the counter, but opened two. Then, he pulled the till, deposited the notes in it and slapped down some coins on the counter top. When the bartender twisted his body around to get the beer from the fridge, he touched Pappy and whispered. "Ask Ras Lion if he knows a man called Diamond Toot'."

The bartender again became cautious. "Strangers don't ask fo' dat man aroun' dese parts," he said almost in a whisper, "I man mind I business. If yuh open yuh mout', dem will shut it fi yuh! You is Police?"

"We told you before that he is a visitor and I am his friend," Pappy reaffirmed. Pappy rose. "We leavin' now. Thanks fo' di beer an' di line-up".

The bartender gave them two empty Pepsi bottles and charged Pappy two dollars for them. "Jah peace," he said, bidding them goodbye.

On their way back to the beach, Pappy threw the bottles in a clump of shrubs and asked. "Who is dis Diamond Toot'?"

"George's friend," he replied.

"Well you heard what the Lion said. It dangerous. Don't go askin' for no frien' of George!" Pappy vehemently shouted.

"No more dangerous than Old Harbour Road," he quipped.

"Let's play it by ear."

"Playin' it by ear wasn't my idea," Pappy grumbled. "You come here wit' out a plan. You can't even crack you' fingers. I hope you can crack a fart. We better get out of here before we get in trouble."

"There is the cane-juice man. Let's have a bottle of juice," he said. "We may even ask for some ice." They went in the direction of a neat looking cart painted yellow with 'CANE JUICE' daubed in red on its sides, and with a green and white striped beach umbrella perched atop of it. He paid for two bottles of cane-juice which looked sickly green and venomous in the clear pint bottles. Pappy upturned his bottle to his mouth and drank deeply. To his great horror, Pappy slyly asked, "Any ice?"

The cane-juice vendor silently stared at them. "Want some ice?" someone quietly asked behind them. He turned to see a young man behind him. Pappy cracked his fingers and the cane-juice vendor nodded to the young man.

"You is Police?" the young man asked.

"You 'ave to watch fo' Babylon aroun' here?" Pappy asked.

"No," said the cane-juice-vendor. "I don't 'fraid fi Babylon. Dey don't trouble we small fish, if we don't trouble dem. An' I know Police when I see dem."

"How yuh know them?" he asked.

"Dat easy," the cane-juice vendor replied. "Babylon walk like if you shout, 'Halt!' him woulda stop 'brap!' an' stamp him foot. When Babylon look 'pon yuh, look him in di eye. If him is Babylan any at all, you can know. For Babylan always look 'pon yuh like everybody is criminal! I know dem as I see dem!" The cane-juice vendor looked towards the sea and pointed. "Dey 'ave bigger fish out deh! Di police ketch a big load what day. I hear seh is fi a big man."

By then, the young man had disappeared. "He gone fo' di ice," the cane-juice vendor explained."

"How long will it take?" Pappy asked.

"Not long, the cane-vendor replied, pointing to his left, "Is jus' roun' di corner dere so."

"You know di name of di big man whose load of fish Babylon

tek weh?" Pappy asked.

"Dem call 'im Diamond Toot, but Boss, don't tell anybody dat I tell yuh. Is a dangerous man. Him don't like anybody ax question 'bout him."

He was wondering how Pappy was going to get them out of the deal with the young man who had gone for the crack-cocaine. Pappy looked at him and blinked an eye. Then Pappy said to the cane-juice-vendor, "We will sit in dat car over dere until your friend come back."

When they reached the car, Pappy said, "Let's get di hell outta here!"

They did not exchange another word until they reached Alley. "Dat was playin' it by ear," Pappy grinned.

"You could make a good detective, Pappy," he complimented his grandfather.

"Naw," Pappy replied, "Too dangerous!"

"When did you learn such excellent patois?" he asked. "I remember a time when you wouldn't allow us to speak it nor did you either."

Pappy pressed the accelerator harder and grinned. "Patois in de blood," he slyly said. "You don't 'ave to go to school fi learn it. I learn it tryin' to get Raymond to speak English."

They stopped at Old Harbour to eat a second serving of bammy and fish before arriving in Kingston. "I goin' to bed right away," Pappy said. "When man reach my age, too much excitement in one day is not good."

Chapter 9

FR. CHEW, DIAMOND TOOT', GEORGE – STRANGE BEDFELLOWS

*H*e was dozing in front of the television when Pappy, dressed in scarlet satin pyjamas, returned to the living room. "News coming on now," he said. "I nea'ly forgot. I'm so tired!" Soon, an attractive young lady with a melodious voice began to read the news with exuberance, as if she relished it. *Three gunmen abducted a taximan and his Toyota motorcar at Porus, today. The car overturned on the Bustamante Highway near to May Pen. The three gunmen were killed. The taximan escaped with severe injuries and was admitted to the Spanish Town Hospital. According to the police report, a white Toyota Corolla motorcar overturned at about 11.30 pm today on the Bustamante Highway. When some policemen who were traveling in a policejeep to Spanish Town alighted from their vehicle and approached to assist the occupants, they were greeted with gunfire. Fortunately, none of the policemen were shot. The Police returned the fire. All three gunmen were killed. The driver of the car whose name has been withheld pending investigations, was admitted to the Spanish Town Hospital with severe injuries, but is in a stable condition. The injured driver* *reported that three men hired his taxi to go from Porus to Rocky Point. On the way, one of the men pointed a gun and ordered him to proceed to Sligoville in St. Catherine. When a police jeep drew up behind him on the Bustamante highway, he decided to jump from the car. The three gunmen suffering gunshot wounds were taken to the Spanish Town Hospital where they were pronounced dead. Up to newstime, they had not been identified. Two 9mm automatic pistols, their serial numbers erased, and fifteen rounds of ammunition were recovered."*

"An' we were there! An' a policeman unlawfully threatened to arres' me fo' dangerous driving!" Pappy shouted at the television. "I tired an' I goin' to bed!"

After they exchanged goodnight, he got out his notepad and wrote *Diamond Toot', George, Chew.* Then he drew a circle around the three names. Beneath 'George', he wrote, 'Exit the prince in flames'. Beneath 'Diamond Toot' he redrew the satyr and wrote 'Dangerous'. Above 'Chew,' he drew an angel and a large question sign. Below the circle, he scrawled, *What is the relationship between these three men,* Diamond Toot' and George knew each other; George told a prisoner that Diamond Toot' was his friend. Chew knew George and sent him presents regularly. Diamond Toot' and Chew were involved with George. Did it mean that all three were involved in an unholy alliance with one another? If all three were involved, what was the nature of their involvement? Who killed George? Why was he killed?

He mulled over his notes for some time, tore the notepaper into shreds, and rose. He had to talk to Chew. He muttered, "I think I will call him right now and inform him that I wish to visit him on Thursday."

⁂

Chew was happy to see him. He had phoned the day before. "How is Pappy?" Chew asked. He explained that his grandfather complained that he was tired and had decided to rest at home. When Chew opened the side door, his dog, Pluto, growled menacingly at him. "Down, Pluto," Chew ordered. The dog persisted in growling and snarling. Chew patted the brute's head, "He is very temperamental. He doesn't seem to be in a good mood today or he doesn't like you. Pluto is trained to kill. Down Pluto! This is my friend!"

"Ah, I see!" he exclaimed. "Trained to kill!" Should he tell Chew that he also was trained how to subdue and kill killer-dogs? The procedure was simple. He rapidly rehashed it in his mind like a cooking recipe as they walked to the saloon. "I could give Pluto a dose of his own medicine," he said.

Chew laughed. "Do you hate dogs?" he asked.

"No," he replied. "On the contrary, I love dogs! I have two French pink poodles. I named them Poo and Pooch. I also have an old bull-dog. I call him Bellows because he looks like a bag full of wind."

Chew laughed again and led the way to his psychedelic bar and the automated ice-dispenser. "I never carry a gun," Chew said, as he opened a Red Stripe and a Pepsi. "It's a damn nuisance. Pluto is my bodyguard."

"Is he? Are you telling me that Pluto carries a gun?" he quipped.

Chew smiled enigmatically. "No! Come off it! Pluto is reliable. Last year in august, I was held up in broad daylight in Hannah Town. I had just parked the car when a gun was poked into my ear. 'Police,' the gunman growled, 'come out di car!'

"As I slipped out I left the door open and shouted, 'Sic' 'im Pluto.' He sprang out immediately and seized the gunman. The other man ran down the street as if he had seen a ghost."

"Did you allow Pluto to kill him?" he asked

"No. I was tempted to do it," Chew replied, "but I didn't have the heart to do it. If I had shouted 'Kill him, Pluto,' he would have torn him to pieces! I could not prevent the people of Hannah Town from beating and stabbing him to death before the Police arrived."

"Hannah Town?" he asked. "Has it become a bad place now?"

"Hannah Town, nowadays," Chew related, "is a place where people live in fear. Political tribalism has infected it. Hannah Town people don't cross Blunt Street and Drummond Street without risking their lives. Some weeks ago, I heard that a man whom I know very well we used to call him Hi-Jack – came home front New York to bury his father who lived in West Kingston. Some friends of his sisters who live in Hannah Town attended the funeral. After the funeral, Hi-Jack accompanied his sister and their friends to Hannah Town. On his way back, he was held up by some young men who accused him of inviting Comrades to his father's funeral. They robbed him of his wallet, watch, shoes, rings and chains and shot him."

"When we were young men, it wasn't like that."

"Things have changed," Chew replied. "People once could move safely about and socialize even in the darkest night. Nowadays, they can't do that freely even in the brightest daylight. Unlike Tivoli Gardens, Hannah Town is wide open and gunmen defend their turf. I am told by people that armed men might come anytime, night or day and shot up the place."

"So what do the Police do about it?" he asked.

"They doubtlessly try. They usually turn up after the shooting."

"That is not the way to remedy the problem," he remarked. "Prevention is better than cure."

"Cure often becomes part of the problem," Chew replied. "The Police are often frustrated and there are public outcries against Police brutality, and politicians are blamed as the cause of the trouble."

"Such tense and restive communities need constant and vigilant policing," he suggested.

"The problem is too subtle and deep-seated to be handled solely by policing since it involves the craving for power and the inequitable distribution of scarce benefits along political party lines."

"Ah, I see! A *bread an' butter affair!*" he exclaimed.

"Yes," said Chew. "There are more dogs than bones and water more than flour! Hannah Town people have had to be on the alert, for doors may be kicked off without threat or notice and gunshots may shatter the stillness of the night."

"There must be a sore point that the authorities ought to identify and work from there," he said. "Intense and sustainable social action, as well as political restructuring is the key?" he said.

"Political restructuring?" Chew asked, "What do you mean?"

"A non-political agency invested with statutory powers and with judicial support could work with the community to rectify social injustices and to promote tolerance among people of different persuasions."

"Good! I see your point clearly," Chew responded. "The Hannah Town folk claim that the residents of West Kingston visit Hannah Town regularly without being molested, while the Hannah Town folks cannot visit some parts of the West End. Hannah Town people are also affected by the bad publicity they have been getting. They complain that the Drummond Street gate through which they more easily enter KPH has been locked for years, because Hannah Town folk were accused of harassing the hospital with criminal activities. The hospital authorities have avoided employing anyone from Hannah Town, although the hospital lies in its vicinity."

"How do you know so much about the problems of these people?" Bateman asked quizzically.

"You see," Chew replied, smiling enigmatically. "My parents lived their lives among these poor people and were sustained by them, by every pound of sugar or ounce of salt these poor people bought. You could call me a rich man, today, but I was a poor boy once, growing up among the poor. You know all about that. Today, I can move out of this area, from among the poor and live in Cherry Gardens or in Rock Hall, or in Canada or Miami, but I would feel that I have abandoned and betrayed the poor who made me what I am today. I am not a politician, but I listen to the complaints of my people and help them in their distress in whatever way I can."

"Are you a don?" he facetiously asked.

"No, I have no axe to grind. I do not crave for power. The character of a don is rotten. People have asked me again and again to be a don, but I don't have the guts for it. I love a quiet life with my music and Pluto here." Chew paused to whistle at Pluto, then pointed his remote gadget and filled the saloon with Bob Marley's 'One Love'.

"What are social conditions like, nowadays, Fr. Chew?" he asked.

"Hey, no one has called me by that nickname since you went

away!" Chew exclaimed. They broke out into laughter.

"Those were wonderful childhood days. Remember when we fought and made up?" Chew said

"Yeah. We became better friends after that fight, and then we lost track of each other when Pappy took George, myself and Raymond away to England."

"Memories never die," Chew sadly murmured, pouring him another Red Stripe, without asking, "They just keep floating around waiting to be picked up occasionally."

"I agree with you," he replied while he pensively viewed the ice-dispenser running up and down its rail and squawking, "Ice, ice, ice."

"Ice, ice, ice! And Rocky Point!" kept reverberating in his mind. He needed an opening to approach Fr. Chew with some questions. "But seriously, what are the social conditions like?" he asked.

"In Hannah Town," Chew replied pausing to whistle at Pluto, "unemployment among the poor is nowhere worse than anywhere else in the city. There are lots of tradesmen, cabinetmakers, carpenters and masons, electricians, plumbers, hairdressers, higglers, household helps and casual workers. Many work at their own small businesses, selling to larger manufacturers and to local stores. Some, mostly women, work in the garment industry and as store-clerks. Housing is none the worst than in other parts of Kingston. Quite a large number of dwellings contain extended families and are over-crowded."

"What I understand," he commented, "is that housing allotments are made on the *scratch my back or parson christen him picni first principle.* How about crime in Hannah Town?"

"It's too obvious," Chew replied, "crime, however, is no worse than anywhere else in West Kingston. The Police find most of the residents co-operate with them. Most of the recreational activities, a vital interest of life in West Kingston, take place at the Dalton James Complex. The Mel Nathan's institute which has been operating quietly in Hannah Town for over a century helps with social and cultural development. It provides training in skills. I am always impressed by its objective of *teaching a man to fish instead of giving him a fish.* There is also a community centre in an old building on Upper Oxford Road. You see, I try to do as much as I possibly can to assist people in need, particularly in Jones Town and in Hannah Town."

"You have not altogether abandoned your priestly mission," he observed.

"I hate a selfish, useless and unforgiving life," Chew responded, his enigmatic smile playing on his features."

"Ice, ice, ice!" the ice-dispenser squawked incessantly. Chew pointed his gadget at it and it silently retracted to rest at one end of the counter top. "Enough of that little nuisance," he remarked. "I hate to see anyone in need. I hate poverty. I hate injustice. My urgent desire, as I said before, is to assist anyone who needs help."

"Where I come from, they call that altruism or philanthropy," he murmured, looking at Pluto, idly estimating his weight and strength. "Have you ever been conned?" he asked Chew, a grin widening his mouth.

"No, why?" Chew answered a query furrowing his brow.

"Nothing," he replied. He took a long sip from his glass, then began to trace hieroglyphics with a forefinger in the moisture that formed on the side. "I was thinking of a notorious character, when we were boys, who lived in Hannah Town. He once sold Race Course to a country man, for a hundred pounds, diagram, title and all. Remember him?"

"Oh, yes!" Chew exclaimed. "Samfie, the three-card who used to tell people on his seasonal return from prison, in an American accent that he went to Harlem in New Jersey to visit relatives and friends. He never seemed to remember that Harlem is not in New Jersey."

A brief silence as if in a minute of silence in respect to the dead, followed their outburst of laughter. "Race Course is now National Heroes Park," Chew said.

"Yeah," I know," he responded. "And Victoria Park became Sir William Grant's Park, thought I don' recall who he was. And that statue of Bowerbank! You remember how we used to stick out our tongues at him, and run weh?"

"Yes," said Chew. "It's now at the Bellevue Mental Hospital."

He laughed. "Know something?" he remarked. "I used to think that he looked a bit mad. I was a bit afraid of his pompous look."

"Proud and arrogant, perhaps, but he must have been a good man for the government of the time to erect a statue to his memory."

"I used to admire Queen Victoria's statue, although I thought that she was too proud, too fat and smug," he commented.

"Queens have to be fat and smug," Chew said humourously, "or they wouldn't look like queens."

"As Beauty Queens," he lasciviously asked. "They wouldn't stand a chance on the cat-walk with the judges, would they?"

"We are talking about sovereign queens," Chew reminded. "They don't have to be beauties or have brains. Queen Victoria is still revered in Jamaica as the great giver of freedom to Negro slaves."

"What happened to her statue? Is it still in the park?" he asked.

"Come to think of it! I have no idea," Chew replied. "It is bound to be some place."

"Do you know I was conned once," he asked, "by none other than the notorious Samfie?"

"No, tell me about it!" Chew requested.

"One day, I was coming from school and was doing some window shopping on King Street when a little brown man stopped me by Woolworth and called me by name. I didn't know that he was Samfie, the prince of conmen. I did not know him at all! He acted surprised when I asked him who he was. "Wait, Bat, you don't remember me? Hopwood, Man! Mi is Hopwood. Mi an' Pappy is frien. Dem call mi Fleetfoot. 'Membah 'ow mi use' to run like lightnin' an tackle yuh?' He showed me four dollars in his hand. 'Di man, mi jockey fren, jus' put mi on a hot tip. Him say Bouncin' Baby sure to win dis Satiday. Him gwine sweep street an' lane an' lef' every oddah 'orse standin'! Him gwine pay thirty dollar!'

"Samfie shoved his four dollars into my hand and pleaded with me to make it up to a ten dollar bet on the understanding that we would split the winnings fifty-fifty. 'Bat, we will 'ave money to buy out Victoria Park an' Ward Theatre an Sabina Park an di whole o'

Kingston,' Samfie said to me."

Chew filled the saloon with laughter. Pluto rose and angrily joined in.

"He invited me to go to a betting shop on East Queen Street with him to buy the horse," he continued. "When I pointed out the sign, 'Watson's Betting Shop' on Kings Street just a little ahead of us, he looked at me in scorn.

"A fool yuh fool-fool, Man? Yuh want spwile wi luck? The jockey say you musn' carry yuh tip a dem big place dey! Dem wi buy off di tip wit' big money an' miss you chance fi win some big money fi yusself.' So we went shoulder to shoulder to East Queen Street. 'See di shap deh,' Samfie pointed to the sign. 'Watsons' Betting Shop'. 'Make up di money quick!'"

I took out the ten dollars I had in my pocket for my bus-fare. Samfie grabbed the ten dollars plus the four dollars he had given me to hold. 'Di shap full a people. Wait here, till I come back,' Samfie said. I had to beg money to get home."

Chew almost fell from his stool with laughter. Pluto, this time, raised his head and ominously growled. "Down, Pluto!" Chew said. "And you never see him again?" Chew exclaimed.

"Yes, I saw him again," he continued. "The story did not end there. When I reached home, I saw Pappy with his eyes close to the TV. He was watching the races. 'Evening Pappy', I said. 'What's happening?' He confessed that he was watching for a horse named Fleetfoot to win. 'Fleetfoot!' I shrieked. 'What happen?' Pappy asked. 'Fleetfoot tek weh mi bus fare an' run weh!' I cried. 'What yuh mean?' Pappy shouted. When I told him the story, he told me that a man whom he knew as Samfie met him down town that very morning and borrowed ten dollars from him to make up a twenty dollar bet on Fleetfoot who was sure to win that day, and that he would share the winnings fifty-fifty. Pappy told him he wanted only his money back, whether the horse won or lost. I said to Pappy, 'Well he won't be back!' Pappy said that Samfie had borrowed from him before and never paid back. 'We won't wait for him to come,' said Pappy. 'We shall go lookin' for him.' I said to Pappy, 'So you know that he cons people?' Pappy grinned and said, 'It's none a my business. I only want our money back!' Samfie almost sank into the ground when we found him downtown and he paid up quickly when Pappy threatened to call the police."

Pluto started to growl again at his master's laughter.

"Samfie! I must ask Pappy what became of him," he said. "He ought to have retired by now or he probably died in jail or became converted and took over where you left off," he mischievously suggested.

"Why me?" Chew asked. "For some people, it's not easy to change from old habits. He is likely conning, if there is anyone for him to con, wherever he might be," Chew harshly said, with a bitter laugh.

"Tell me something, Chew," he suddenly asked. "Since I came, I have seen the type of housing development in and around Kingston, the magnificence of the hotels, the type of shopping complexes and entertainment centres. The million dollar motorcars. Are these signs of a vibrant economy? Not many metropolitan countries enjoy this quality of life. Yet, we are talking of an economy that is in deep trouble. Many people are suffering in abject poverty. Many roads are in bad condition, some communities are lacking in amenities. Yet, there is a lot of money being flaunted around. The drug trade may be one source. Could it be that dirty money is being laundered here as well?"

"I must confess," Chew replied, "I don't understand the term, 'money-laundering'. How does it work?"

"Usually, what drug dealers do, is transfer money earned by illegitimate activities to another country and invest it in legitimate businesses such as real estate, industry and sports. American based offenders have been practising this to get away from investigations by the United States revenue departments into their wealth and possible prosecution and seizure of their assets, if proven guilty."

"So that's it!" Chew said. "I have been hearing rumours, though I have not given it any attention, that monies are brought here from Colombia and invested here thus feeding a sort of informal economy. But there had never been concretely reported that it is so."

"Money laundering can cause inflation of the economy and price increases," he explained, "since businessmen cannot compete with people who have the money and are prepared to clean it at any cost. There is also the temptation which could head to political corruption and violent crimes. It is a simple possibility that money laundering could be creating and supporting the lifestyles I see around. All that is needed is banks, preferably 'off-shore' ones, that are willing to accept deposits. These 'dirty' banks invest the money in banks in New York and London off-shore banks and major banking systems, as well as in Swiss banks. In the Caribbean, for instance, anyone in the financial circle can set up a bank. It is that easy I think. I think we have a proliferation of banks right here in Jamaica. Some have merged, others went bust. Money laundering is so subtle that it is difficult to detect. It can take many years to break open a fool-proof system."

"You seem to be an expert," Chew observed.

"I keep looking at it," he replied.

"Higglers and Informal Commercial Investors seem to get an easy and constant supply at dollars for their business, when at the banks there always is a limited supply and you need a license," Chew stated. "They buy and sell dollars, of course, on the black market. Even when it is illegal to buy or sell dollars, on the black market, foreign currency never runs short on the street. I often wonder how all that enormous amount of foreign currency get on the street. Some businessmen who bought on the black market sometimes get carried down by thousands of dollars of counterfeit money."

"And they didn't make much outcry, did they?" he asked.

"Not many did," Chew replied.

"Abroad, they don't squeal," he remarked. "They find the man who swindles them and hit him hard!"

"A few have been killed here under mysterious circumstances," Chew replied, "the Police often fail to find motives for the killings."

"According to a recent report of the United States Department of Justice, billions of dollars have been taken out of the United States by drug traffickers and others for fear of forfeiture of their profits. But according to the report, money laundering is not practised by drug traffickers alone. It is suspected by U.S. authorities that a billion dollars from illegal businesses is being cleaned around the world. I have also been hearing some veiled warnings about an influx of counterfeit money floating in the island."

"You seem to know a lot about money." Chew said excitedly. "What business are you in? Money laundering?"

He told himself that he needed time to decide whether to expose himself or not. "You don't mind me smoking, do you?" he asked.

"No, not at all, though I don't smoke!" Chew replied.

He pulled a slim *Craven A* from a packet, tapped an end leisurely against the packet, and slowly closed his lips around the filter, lit the cigarette with his silver Roneo lighter and exhaled even more slowly. "I am a detective, a sort of private eye. I do work for an International firm of investigators – a sort of secret service. We sometimes do work for Interpol," he casually announced.

Chew laughed uneasily. "Don't think I am prying," Chew said. "I am a little curious. Do you make much money?"

"Well, I manage to keep the wolf from the door, as we say in England," he replied, mildly smiling at his own modest boast.

"You haven't changed much," Chew remarked. "You hardly ever gave a straight answer. I remember when Miss Hartley asked you what was the sum of x and y, when x equals 2 and y equals 3, you said it was the same as the sum of y and x."

They both laughed aloud, discomfiting Pluto.

"Did I say that?" he mildly protested.

"Yes, you did!" Chew insisted.

"Probably, I did. I can't recall," he said.

"Well, you ought to remember your experience with the cane in the Principal's office." Chew retorted. "So Mr. Bateman Carter, you're a big time detective! Congratulations! Why are you here? To investigate money laundering, the drug trade or your brother's death?"

"Seriously, Chew," he gravely replied. "I am not here to investigate neither money laundering nor any trafficking. I mean to get at the truth of George's death. I shall need all the help I can get. I am privately investigating George's death. I ask you to keep it a secret." He made a mental note that having blown his cover, he had to inform Pappy, at once, before someone else did.

"That's alright, I won't say a word to anyone. I believe that Carter's death was an accident," Chew said.

"The evidence points in that direction," he said, "but there are unanswered questions. I should like to see the police report, but since I am working incognito, I cannot request it. Assume that he was making a bomb, someone brought the materials to him, and taught him how to put the materials together or brought him written or printed instructions. How did that person get explosives through the prison gates? Why was he making a bomb? Were there people inside the prison working with him? If so, what was their motive? Did certain people want to break him out of custody? If so who are such people? Why was it so important to get him out? Did someone want him dead? There are many questions."

"It is serious," Chew said. "My theory is that your brother and whoever was helping him, planned to set off the bomb to cause a distraction. In the confusion, he would be spirited away. It was rumoured that just about the time of the explosion, a car was seen near the prison wall at a spot where prisoners have been known to make their escape. There had to be people working inside and outside the prison as George's accomplices. The bomb must have accidentally gone off and put an untimely end to George. May his soul rest in peace." Chew solemnly crossed himself.

"You sent things to George when he was confined, I hear. Thanks! That was mighty fine of you!" he said.

"How did you know of that? Raymond told you?" Chew asked, seemingly alarmed.

"Raymond didn't tell me anything," he replied. "I don't think he knew about it. It doesn't matter how I heard. Detectives have ways of knowing things. When we were all at school, George was our senior and did not associate with us. How did you both become friends after so many years?"

"When he came home from America to live," Chew related, "he came to see me. I assisted him to set up 'SERV-U TAXI AND BUS SERVICE'. I leased him my premises at Dunoon Road and helped him to settle in."

"Did he tell you why he was hiding here under an assumed name?" he asked

"Yes. I asked him and he told me that he was wanted in the States for tax evasion. It was when he was arrested that I learnt that he was wanted as a suspect of several murders."

"His rooms and his office were cleaned out by some unknown person or persons," he said.

"Yes." Chew replied. "I discovered that, when I went to re-claim the premises"

I wasn't aware that you had recovered the premises," he calmly said. "Does Pappy or Raymond know?"

"The Police gave me permission to do so. I didn't think it was necessary to inform anybody. Are you annoyed?"

"Oh, no, no! It is your premises, ain't it? I don't think the Police have the right to give you permission, but we won't fight over such small matters!" he said. "Do you have any idea what happened to the cars and buses?"

"I have no idea. I saw none at Dunoon Road. The Police say they know nothing. I can find no one who knows anything," Chew replied.

"George had a friend by the nickname of Diamond Toot'. Do you know anything about him?"

Chew obviously wasn't betraying what he was thinking, "He hired my boat, *The Sea Bird,* once or twice to go fishing with his friends."

"Fishing? Are you sure of that?" he incredulously asked

"I never ask my clients for what purpose they intend to use my boat. It is insured that if anything should happen to it, I would be compensated. I know nothing about Diamond Toot'."

"Have you met him?" he queried.

"Yes a number of times. George brought him here. That's how I met him."

"I have nothing tangible on him, but I hear that he deals in drugs."

"I have never been curious about his business." Chew replied. "I hope that you finish your investigation soon. You will tell the

Police what you find, I suppose"

"If I find anything that smells bad enough, I will surely shove it under their noses," he replied, laughing harshly enough to elicit a growl from Pluto.

Chew continued to smile. "Down, Pluto," he ordered his dog.

"Well, I've overstayed. I better be going," he said.

"We will keep in touch." Chew said, as he conducted him to the door.

"Thanks, Fr. Chew, it was a damn nice session with you – for old time's sake."

Chapter 10

FLOGGING, HANGING OR REHABILITATION?

*W*hen he returned from visiting with Chew, he found Pappy dozing before the television. He had not bothered to close the front doors.

"Pappy, what's cooking?" he lightly greeted his grandfather.

"I have been waiting for you to get home for dinner." Pappy dryly replied. "I said to myself that after watching all dat naked flesh promenading on the street, you wouldn't want to eat meat for a couple of weeks, so I went out and bought some fresh fish an' cook' it for dinner."

"Thanks," he said. "It smells good!"

"Yeah! It smells better than British fish. Taste' better too," Pappy replied. "You hardly get fresh fish in Mother Country. I find frozen hake an' haddock rather unpalatable, though I like salmon. An' herrin', too."

As they worked through the steamed fish, Pappy asked, "How was the day?"

"Good," he replied.

"Happy to hear," Pappy glumly said, noisily sucking away at a fish backbone. "Don't bother to tell me about it."

"Why?" he lightly asked. "You had a bad day?"

"It came over the tele, today that vandals destroyed Hon. Norman Manley's statue. It was found on the ground torn from its pedestal and with its hands severed! Why dey do a t'ing like dat?" Pappy shouted in disgust. "Have some reverence for our heritage nuh!"

"They did it in protest," he suggested. "They know why they did it. Sometimes they don't know why. People all over the world protest. When you were in England, women protested by burning their bras in public. Remember?"

"Yeah, I remember. What were they protesting? I don't seem to remember. They were fed up wit' bein' women?" Pappy quipped.

"Probably, we should have a beer."

"Yeah! That's a good idea!" he replied.

"Look into the fridge." Pappy said. "There usually is, when Raymond is not around."

Pappy went back to sit before the television. He went to the fridge and found two bottles of Heineken.

He found the opener and opened the bottles, offering one to Pappy, then threw himself on to the couch opposite Pappy. "Pappy, I want to tell you something about myself, before you hear from anywhere else. Prepare yourself to hear."

"Nutten you tell me can surprise me at this time of my life! You hear me?" Pappy said in a disgruntled tone. "I thought you said that you came for a surprise holiday with me. There has not been a moment of peace since you came!"

"What happened, Pappy?" he teased. "They gave you six-love?"

"I hope what you have to tell me is not worse," Pappy grumbled.

Bateman took a deep breath and continued.

"I have three things to tell you. Firstly, I am a secret service man. Secondly, I am not here on holiday. I am here to investigate George's death. Thirdly, I am here incognito. I have not entered the island under my real name. I have false papers. My assumed name is Edmund Price. Until my investigation is complete, I ask you to call me by that name. I have to swear you to absolute secrecy."

"I be damned if I call you Mr. Price!" Pappy angrily swore. "I am resignin'! I have retired! I want nutten to raise my blood pressure!"

"Calm down, Pappy," he pleaded. "Take it easy! Nothing is going to happen to you," he tried to mollify his grandfather.

"Nutten is goin' to 'apppen? It done happen a'ready!" Pappy moaned, dropping his head into the palms of his hands, and covering his eyes with them.

He placed his hands on his grandfather's shoulders, looked in his eyes and gently shook him re-assuredly, but Pappy ignored him. He felt helpless and uncertain about what else to do. "Pappy, I think I shall go to bed." He said, tiredly.

"Suits me!" Pappy groaned. "You can go to hell an' don't come back!"

Instead of going to bed, he collapsed into the couch and clasped his hand behind his neck and allowed his mind to go blank.

After a while, Pappy called out, "Bat, we didn't finish discussing why dey tore down Mr. Manley's statue. Is sick dem sick, those people who did it?

"I wonder what is de motive?" Pappy asked. The question was addressed more to himself than to his grandson.

"Iconoclasts don't have to have any motive," he replied.

"I was t'inking dat their motive was to stir up political strife between the two major parties, to get the political factions at each other's t'roat, killin' one another," Pappy suggested.

"If that was the design, then it was diabolical," he replied.

"According to what I heard on the tele," Pappy informed him, "The Prime Minister an' the leader of the Opposition have decried the act and defused the tension. The Prime Minister has assured the nation that di statue would be repaired and replaced within a month."

"Are you telling me that no one saw what was happening and could have reported to the Police?" he asked.

"It said on the news," Pappy related, "that some motorists passing by North Parade saw the vandals cutting away at di statue at about 4.00 a.m. but did not intervene even by callin' di Police, because they feared for their lives. A motorist said over the news that he saw a group of men an' women sittin' an' standin' around eatin' chicken from lunch boxes an' drinkin' box-juice, while some men cut away the feet of the statue. What I am happy about is dat both political parties have strongly condemned the act."

"What is that about, 'No Cat o' Nine tails in Jamaica'? Please pass me that paper, Pappy. Do we flog offenders in this country?" he asked in disbelief.

"We stopped the practice of beating culprits some twenty or thirty years ago. Some judges have been recently sentencing convicted felons to be flogged. Last week, a judge created excitement by ordering, for the first time in many years, a man who stabbed a woman in the neck with an ice-pick to be given six strokes of a tamarind switch. No prison or police officer would be willing to do de honours." Pappy concluded, chuckling.

"There was a report in the papers, a year or so ago, of an American who got the cat in Singapore, for desecrating a statue. I believe," he recalled

"Yeah!" said Pappy. "I read it! But here we have stopped using the cat so long, we cannot locate it. So a culprit may be saved, after all, especially if the bleeders cry out loudly and fierce enough against it."

"Is flogging really effective as a deterrent to crime?" he asked.

"In my opinion," replied Pappy, "no punishment is effective, nowadays, as a deterrent to crime. Nowadays, when a man come from prison, he act as if he went on a vacation. When the prison use' to cut ass along wit' di prison term on de way in an' on de way out, convicts rarely return to where people know dem. They felt humiliated an' ashame' dat dey got floggin'. It usually had a salutary and permanent effect. A man who went to prison hardly ever commit' any more crime for fear of gettin' another floggin'. Everytime a man who was flogged was tempted to commit an offence — I was told — the whip marks on his backside began to 'itch an' burn an' his blood run cold as ice an' he become' as soft as butter."

"Flogging was a horrible practice in England, long, long ago. Sailors who were mutinous or failed to carry out orders were ordered by the captain to be publicly and mercilessly flogged aboard ship. It happened in the army as well. The object, as I understood it, was not to torture nor to dehumanize the victim. To inflict a good hiding on the tail or back, stripping away a layer or two of skin tissue was intended to associate a degree of pain with the offence, so that next time when an act of similar nature was being thought of, the unpleasant memory of the punishment would deter the person."

"We use' to be a friendly and simple fun-loving people-probably most of us still are," Pappy said. "What happen' to us? What has changed us? Look on what today' paper say in di 'eadline: 'Murder, suicide by acid and fire!' Read further down: 'Forty-three killed in ten days!' Most appalling! Dat don't sound like we are a civilize' society. I don't believe dat happenin' in di jungle of Africa or in Sadam' country! I seh ketch dem an' cat dem! Yuh hear what I seh? Cat dem! An' tell Amnesty International fi go weh! Dem a interfere in wi business!"

"Pappy, you're mad," he said, chuckling to himself.

"Nowadays, killing is the order of di day! Two a day, three a day an' we not havin' any civil war. What kind o' genocide we havin'? Tell me! Daylight robbery, shootouts between criminal an' police, bodies found in trash cans, sister killin' sister over fifty cents, man killin' his whole family, wife an' pickney over domestic affairs! To add to our troubles dis whole heap o' deportees America let go 'pon us! Drugs is big heart-ache! Prisons are finishing schools for first offenders! Some of us is blamin' it on the drug culture that is overtakin' di whole world." Pappy took the papers from him and angrily crushed them as he turned them. "Look on dis!" he growled. "I seh, ketch dem an' cat dem! Let us read further on: *the Police have solved only two hundred and six of these cases. Two hundred an' ten of these murders were due to domestic feuds. Ninety-nine were due to robbery and seventy-eight to gang wars. Forty-three were due to reprisals and the murder of witnesses. Eight were drug or homosexual related. Motives for the rest of murders were unknown, not to mention police killings and suicide. Most of the murders was by shooting. The Police have recovered over three hundred guns since January.'* Good God! Where *all dese guns* comin' from? Anybody would think we have a gun factory here!"

"Something drastic has to be done about the guns," he said.

"What can we do wid dat asshole Amnesty International holdin' us by di neck an' threatin' to strangle us?" Pappy shouted. "We can't even break wind an' dey don't smell it an' bawl out dat dem smell it! We slippin' under gun rule an' don't matter to dem one bit so long we give every murderer two meals a day. An' dey not offerin' to pay di food bill and boardin' fi dem neither."

"Pappy, what we need is speedier justice," he explained. "Over the years, governments spend lots and lots of money on programmes, yet we are failing to achieve security, adequate educational facilities, adequate employment opportunities and realistic alleviation of poverty, particularly in the so-called third world countries. I think that governments with their preoccupation with political power have been consciously or unconsciously destroying the natural independent spirit of people. It is happening in the Americas. It is happening in Europe. It is happening everywhere. We have become a world of suckers, creditors and debtors, parasites, beggars, swindlers and thieves. There is nothing altruistic about powerful nations. Beneath their philanthropy lies a price, their own axe to grind. Our people need to see the way to better their own condition. They need to pull up themselves by their own bootstrap, so to speak.

"You read George Orwell's Animal Farm?" Pappy excitedly questioned

"No, sir, I have never read the book," he replied. "Why?"

"Well, what you said soun' like the gist of that book," Pappy said.

"I must read him, one of these days," he said. "You are painting a good picture of the situation, Pappy."

"We know that people afraid," Pappy said. "They are afraid of the level of violence in dis country, chiefly the murders, the gunmen, the manslaughter and mayhem on the roads, but what they ought to bear in mind is that there is crime wherever they are and in any place they may choose to find themselves. They need to reassure themselves that we not being complacent about crime. It is being combated." He paused and continued.

"Floggin' use' to be effective in Jamaica, data or no data," Pappy stated. "It can work again. As I said before, prisoners are afraid of floggin'. Men prefer to be shot or hang' than to be flogged, anyday!"

"That is backward," he remarked.

"This is not Mother Country," Pappy retorted. "When I was a boy, youngsters got their bottoms whipped an' it made respectable men out of them. I use to whip yours! My headmaster had two leather straps — Dog to keep you on the straight and narrow way, an' Bees to make you industrious. He kept them soaked in linseed oil an' when you got two or three strokes from Dog or Bees you walk straight, upright an' smart many a day."

"My, my!" he groaned and shook his head. "Flogging," he said, "as far as I know has no proven merit. We believe, in Britain, that one of the reasons for violence is what parents an' adults do to children, and a nation's tendency to apply violence to the young will develop an attitude of violence in the nation. Parents are liable to believe that violence and abuse inflicted on children will make them brighter and better citizens. That is not true if George is a sample of the product."

"George was incorrigible. Nothing could change him. A few strokes did make me a better person. I am sure, an' not one of those scroungers you see wanderin' around di place as if dey can't find nutten to do. Dey mus' t'ief an' beg!"

"What evidence do you have that flogging helped you?" he asked, "You are likely to be the product of careful nurturing and good example by your parents, your teachers and other friendly factors in the favourable environment in which you grew."

"You're probably right," Pappy replied. "My parents were in-telligent and stric'. They were circumspec' an' didn't spare di rod either. I had to go to church an' Sunday school every Sunday whether I want to go or not. I had work at home to do after school an' at weekends an' Trench Town a beautiful an' happy, quiet place."

"Flogging in your case, I am almost sure, was punishment judi-ciously applied," he suggested.

"Not on every occasion," Pappy replied." It was sometimes unwarranted, but it helped to make me a man jus' di same."

"All the more for you to object to it, if at times it was unwarranted," he contended. "The use of physical pain by parents is positively related to the amount of aggression in children. I was reading a report, some time ago, that as many as half the number of boys in the USA, who were rated as highly violent came from homes where parents applied physical punishment to children."

"We gettin' technical here," Pappy complained.

"Sorry, I didn't realize that I was getting technical," he replied apologetically. "But the subject of punishment and child abuse is of great interest to me. I did a bit of study on it. People in the western world new form of punishment as barbaric and dehumanizing."

"Dat may be so," Pappy interrupted, "but people like me consider floggin' as appropriate for such acts of violence as felonious woundin', rape, robbery with aggravation. I go beyond that an' recommend it for murder, as well. Floggin' even for women should be mandatory to go with a prison sentence."

"Crazy, perhaps," said he, a broad grin widening his face. "Here, in the paper, another judge has ordered three men to be flogged for holding-up and robbing three Italian tourists of over US$6000, cameras and jewellery. Their women friends wept when they heard the sentence."

"Dat was a magnificent haul," Pappy ruefully said. "Sorry fo' those ladies. Sometimes tourists take large sums of money to buy coke. If dat was what dey was doin', den dey are probably lucky to be alive! Yet dey have a right to carry their money an' to be safe an' unmolested. Nobody should rob them. Cat di t'ieves an' cut dem rump!"

He laughed with vehemence and fury. The heat and vigour of their discussion had driven away their earlier desire to sleep, as well as Pappy's doldrums. "You are naïve Pappy," he teased.

"Naive!" shouted Pappy. "Blimey! I was picked of my wallet only once in my life an' dat was when I was livin' in London an' di only valuable t'ing I had in it was a picture of Merrie, your grandmother! My money was safe in another pocket. Since den, I don't carry a wallet." Pappy took a sip of beer and continued, "I t'ink we doin' di right t'ing to set up our own Caribbean Court of Appeal an'

I hope dat Court will recommend every time, 'Don't hang di murderers. Cat dem'!"

"I wouldn't say, nay, to a Caribbean Court to supplant the Court in Britain," he replied, "but I am not too enthused with the idea of catting. Catting is just as barbaric as hanging."

"Hear what I say?" Pappy concluded. "Jamaican man 'fraid o' di cat more dan 'ow him 'fraid o' di mouse."

"The Cat and the Mouse, not the Cat and the Noose?" he asked in merriment.

Pappy paused to watch his grandson in awe, then burst out laughing himself. "I hadn't thought of it. Di Cat an' di Noose. Man 'fraid o' di Cat like 'ow mouse 'fraid fi puss. In China an' in Saudi Arabia, countries thousands of times bigger dan our little island, crime is rare, for accordin' to what I read, in Saudi Arabia, dey cut off the hand of a t'ief. In Japan, dem cut off your head if you're caught drug traffickin'. In China, dey shoot corrupted civil an' public servants in the back of di head, within twenty-four hours after you've been convicted. Is jus' your bad luck if you're innocent as there is no Court of Appeal. We need some summary justice in this country."

"Pappy, you have been saying all night that you're against capital punishment," he argued. "Are you aware that summary justice would tip the scale of injustice against the poor, the disadvantaged and the unrepresented who are the main offenders in the society? Executing a man who is innocent, or even cutting off his hand, is an appalling thought."

"The senseless an' brutal killin' of helpless ol' people is no less appalling," Pappy retorted. "And talkin' about capital punishment, a priest once described the gory details of a hangin' he witnessed in Spanish Town Distric' Prison. Di condemn' man was put away a few days in a special cell 'to fatten him up' for his final big day. At the appointed hour, he was escorted, accompanied by the priest an' di prison Superintendent, to the gallows room. He put up a hell of a fight wid di warders, even wid his hands bound an shoutin' dat he didn't kill anybody. In di end, they had to carry him. Most men, the priest said, havin' been seen an' prayed wit' by minister, an' havin' made peace wit' God, dey believe, go docilely. Some condem' man even make fun of it, callin' out to others on Death Row, dat dey gone an' soon come back. Some take cigarettes in their pocket an' dress in good clothes, sayin' dem will need a smoke for the long drop an' di journey. The warders help di man to stand on di trap-door. Dem tie him ankles to prevent him kickin' an de' put a black hood over his head. Den di hangman pass' di noose over di hood an adjust the knot behind the man's left ear. By dat time, di man ha' bawl under di hood beggin' fi mercy, say him innocent an' every-body, includin' di priest an' di Superintendent an di hangman was tremblin' an' breathin' loud an' hard. Dat was it! Don't dem was about to butcher a man like how you butcher a goat? You heng up di goat first, then you cut di t t'roat. The priest said the warders have to hold up di man on di trapdoor. The Superintendent keep lookin' at his watch while he hol' a white kerchief in his hand. Di priest keep chantin' from a little black book. Den di Superintendent drop his hand an' di hangman pull di handle releasin' di trapdoor. An' some of the warders an' di priest groaned and let out a sigh. Di Superintendent an' di hangman wear dark glasses so nobody could see dem eye."

"As simple as that?" he asked in a horrified voice.

"Not as simple as dat!" Pappy exclaimed.

"It sounds like fast dirty work!" he continued.

"It is dirty work!" Pappy swore.

"I think I understand," he solemnly said. "Horror of horrors. Horrible!"

"It is horrible!" Pappy wrathfully said. "A bullet in di back of di head is cleaner, quicker an' more humane. But those bleedin' hearts! Dey don't bleed for the woman raped an' di father shot in front of his four-year old child, an' dey tell me dat di society is makin' sav-ages out o' some people by treatin' dem badly."

"The problem is more fundamental than that, Pappy," he re-marked. "it has to do more with modern thinking on psychoses and human rights."

"Meanin' what?" Pappy said, letting forth a weary yawn.

It is deeprooted in severe human factors such as child and substance abuse, effects of domestic violence on children, hate, greed and envy, contempt for humanity, disrespect for life and property, psychotic and homicidal tendencies and homophobia, megalomania and moral disorder, social injustices, poverty and the inequitable distribution of wealth and we could go on and on?"

"You're gettin' technical again," Pappy accused, "but you need not apologize again. I find what you' sayin' to me rather too interestin' to be true. Are you implying that a murderer has right to kill because he is some sort of nut an' dat the State has no right to punish him? That is jargon!" Pappy shouted. "What is seriously wrong, an' I will say it again an' again, too many modern day people are being allowed to do their own t'ing. Too much license!"

"What do you mean by too much license?" he asked.

"Well take di dancehall culture," Pappy replied. "Dat mashin' down di country! When young people should be home resting and sleeping at night to renew their bodies to work harder next day at useful an' gainful activities, where are they? Spendin' and wastin' energy. When conscience prick dem dey call it culture. Yes the word culture is a bag for carrying a lot o' undesirable t'ings and activities such as smokin' pot, ratchet knives, barking to a reggae beat instead of singing, disrespect for womanhood, guns, dancehall lingo an' safe-sex! It is downright madness an' it helps to create criminals and bums. We now have a generation that no sane person can appeal to, to change their ways. Dey say yuh fightin' dem down if you dare talk to dem, an' you fi dead! We sow di wind an reapin' di whirlwin'. An' t'ings look like dey goin' to get worse. We have a generation now dat glorifies in dons and gun. They sing lewd songs about body parts, that are degradin' an' disgustin'. Dey block roads an' litter gullies an' expect government to do everyt'ing fo' dem. And, those institutions and what dey stand for are daily t'reatened, assaulted an' eroded by those fatuous elements that are drawing young people, away from solid values. Dis dancehall culture is taking us nowhere dan di tile dey are told by di DJ to hold, gyratin', wrigglin' and twistin' to di reggae music."

"What you mean by the dancehall culture is taking us nowhere?" he sleepily asked, yawning.

"I don't know anyt'ing about it," Pappy replied. "You know what?" When you see Raymond, ask him about it. Di dancehall is where 'im live."

"OK, Pappy! When I see him I will ask him," he said.

Pappy let loose another sleepy yawn. "We shouldn't spend di whole night discussin' depressin' matters, especially those we can't do anyt' ing about. It is past my sleepin' hours. I can't sleep again di rest of di night. I goin' to watch di BBC news. The soothin' BBC music may just put me to sleep."

"It is almost morning," he remarked, "I may as well watch with you, Pappy."

When he woke and looked at his watch, it was 7:00 a.m. his normal waking time. He was alone in the living room. He heard Pappy snoring gently in his room. Pappy had awakened, or probably had not slept until the wee hours of the morning and retired without disturbing him.

Chapter 11

DAMNATION; DOMINION AND DANCEHALL

"*I* am hungry, I don't think I shall wait on the Ol' Man to make breakfast, this morning," he murmured. "I shall see what is in the kitchen and knock together a bite." In the refrigerator, he found all the commodities he required — bacon, eggs, half-litre of orange juice and a jar of margarine. Seasonings of many kinds were neatly arranged in labeled canisters on a tiny metal wall rack near to the towel rack and the electric stove. Pappy was always proud of his housekeeping. Should he pry, he'd be sure to find a small Accounts Book in which Pappy was prone to enter every cent of his domestic and personal expenses, including every gram of salt he bought. Pappy was in good practice as a bachelor, husband, grandfather and widower in England who used to cook for his family. Like Pappy, he enjoyed cooking. In the twinkling of an eye, he had hashed an appetizing breakfast. From Pappy's bedroom, gentle snores had developed into stertorous breathing which could be construed either way that Pappy had changed gears to fall into deep slumber or that he would soon awake. He decided to breakfast alone. While he was putting the food on the table, the news-vendor called out, "Gleaner" and he heard a dull 'twack' as the vendor threw a bundled newspaper into the yard. Pappy was one of the vendor's regular customers, and he would knock on the gate to collect his money, at the end of the week.

He opened the double doors, picked up and unfolded the newspaper. "My Gawd!" he cried, as the headline devilishly shrieked at him, '*Death runs awry again and again.*' He was tough and ruthless by nature and training, but his hands trembled and a chill ran up his spine in horror, as he read and read again, his breakfast forgotten nor was he consoled by the deplorable news that *violence had resurged* in downtown Kingston, sparked off by a feud between the opposite political factions. "Well, at least," he muttered sardonically, "It is giving the churchmen something tangible and positive to do."

'*On Saturday,*' he browsed. *There will be a special church service at the St. John's United Church in Hannah Town to bring people together.*'

When he returned to the kitchen, paper in hand, Pappy was standing barefooted at the dinning table, in his tousled scarlet pyjamas, looking innocent and querulous like a little boy who was still drowsy with sleep. "That food smells good an' I am hungry as a shark! If I didn't smell it, I would still be asleep!" he bantered." The smell woke me up. Hunger and food go well together." Pappy went to the kitchen sink and returned with a plate and a fork.

"I simply just knocked together whatever I was able to find. You run your kitchen on a tight shoe-string. I hope it can be eaten," he quipped.

"No big thing!" Pappy roguishly remarked. "We can fire di cook! When hungry worms start bite, hungry man doesn't care if food taste good or bad! You can make coffee?"

"I am not too sure. There is coffee more than coffee. Some people like it bitter, some like it sweet, strong, medium or weak. Some like it black some like it white. Some like it brewed, some like it boiled. Some like it hot. Some like it cold. What's your order?"

"Just a hot cup, a teaspoonful of Blue Mountain Peak, no milk and absolutely no sugar!" Pappy said, as he picked up the paper from the table. "Kiss me ass!" he shouted as he looked at the paper. "More murder on top o' murder! Murder, suicide by acid and fire! Bat, did you see dis?"

"Yeah, it is the most gruesome act I have ever heard of and I have had to come all this distance, over five thousand miles, to know that it can happen!" he replied. "What you said last night, that crime is likely to get worse is no longer a speculation, I thought, last night, that you were over-reacting, and I was tempted to pooh-pooh your fears as over-cynical and misanthropic. I count myself lucky that I did not voice my sentiments about you last night or I would have to retract and apologize to you this morning."

"Dat would have been alright! "Pappy replied. "People are callin' one anadah worse names in Jamaica, today. Ever 'ear di name *chi-chi*?"

"No, I am afraid not! What is *chi-chi*?"

"Whenever you find out, tell me, but dere is a song about burnin' wood in a *chi-chi yard*. T'ings getting worse!" Pappy wrathfully replied. "Trouble has started in Hannah Town!"

"Yeah," he replied. "The only redeeming feature is that the United Church is trying to defuse the feud, and the politicians have committed themselves to restore normality to the area."

"We were talking about Hannah Town, last night," Pappy remarked. "The Editor is damn right!" Pappy angrily swore. "But dis story of dat man who tortured his own three-year old child an' killed her by pourin' acid down her t'roat! Dat man has taken us to the lowest level that any human being can descend. We can't go any lower!"

"Do you think, Pappy, of the possibility of some evil force contaminating the world with rot?"

"You mean something like global warming, the Green House effect?" Pappy asked. "I am no scientist, so I can't answer dat. But it possible. I have seen it happen in a chicken house where di birds overcome wit' di heat, an' overcrowdin', start to cannibalize one annodah, like dey gone mad! An imbalance in nature could possibly cause us to behave irrationally, yes! But wouldn't it affect di animals an' di birds an' di bees too? I don't t'ink I see any o' dem actin' abnormal!"

"I am just idly fantasizing," he said apologetically.

Pappy laughed, spluttering and spilling his coffee. "Dis coffee is cold. Have you any more hot water? You could be right. Probably those astronauts disturb di space demons an' dey impregnatin' di planet wid evil."

"I am just being facetious, Pappy," he said, laughing. "There were appalling evil forces at work before space exploration began."

Pappy held up the paper for his grandson to see a photograph juxtaposed next to an Afghan report. "Now look at dis picture of human misery!" he read, jabbing a forefinger at the photograph. His coffee had gone cold again.

"Good God! How could that be?" he exclaimed. "I didn't see that!"

"I t'ink you callin' on di wrong god," Pappy slyly said. "You should ask di Japanese god how such a t'ing could happen. There are too many other distressin' t'ings to see," Pappy ruefully remarked. "Dis worl' gone mad it is a sad an' tired ol' worl'! When will we 'ave peace an' happiness? A man can only die, but women an' children suffer so much, unspeakable terror an' misery. We are blessed in dis land. Look what 'appenin' in Afghanistan. We don't know what real starvation is. People have to eat grasshoppers for supper!" Pappy said.

They both sat silently over the remains of the breakfast, each immersed in his own private thoughts, the crumpled newspaper lying on the floor where it was untidily thrown by Pappy, and the wall clock in the living room softly ticked away the minutes with an occasional and intermittent bang! After what seemed like an eternity of silence, Pappy said, "We don' have answers for di ills an' pains of di worl'. It don't seem dat those who claim dey are more qualified by God dan us 'ave any answers either. Dey 'ave volumes of empty an' fruitless words. We spend almos' all di night until morning; light, lookin' at di problems of di worl', an in Jamaica, wat do we find? No answers! Absolutely nutten!"

"If we had," he interrupted his grandfather, laughing sardonically, "you and I would become rich and famous. Our formula for saving the world would sell faster than hot bread. It would be the hottest commodity on earth!"

"You might be right about dat cosmic contamination, after all," Pappy said, "What other explanation is dere? I am not a religious man, as I mention before, but I repeat dat probably only di Church can save us from utter destruction!"

"Pappy, from what little history I learnt at school, when Church had absolute power over Europe, Northern Africa and the Western World, they, Church authorities, committed cruel atrocities against the human race, in their great and holy zeal to transform the world and get the world to conform. Should Church assume earthly power again, what guarantees are there that it would not perpetrate similar errors or even worse?"

"Enlightenment, My dear fellow!" Pappy replied. "Enlightenment is the guarantee. We are more liberal in our t'inkin' dese days, an' more difficult to govern in modern times. The church wouldn't stand a chance to impose anyt'ing on us, wit'out some bright guy questionin' an' protestin'. Dese guys would overturn statues, burn Bibles an' climb church steeples as a show of protest."

"Pappy, you say you are not religious but you have great faith in the Church that it can cure the world's troubles. Why?"

"Faith?" Pappy responded with derision "Faith, as we know it, is a cover-up for a lot o' doubts, uncertainties, disillusions, pain an' sorrow, confusion an' unanswered questions about di universe. Whenever you seek enlightenment on dark and vague issues, you're told, 'Have faith, my brother. If it is to be revealed to you, it will be revealed'. Faith an' belief are di same t'ing, ain't it?"

"*O vain man, thy faith without works is dead,* not to overlook that metaphysical fillip to our ego and confidence: *Faith can move mountains.*"

"Dey also say: *Ignorance is bliss,*" a disgruntled Pappy remarked. "All I know is dat belief can breed disillusionment an' become part of di problem instead of the solution to di problem, an' give people a false sense of security. It can be an escape for those who doubt or fear di unknown universe in which we are destined to live tragically an' to flee from our own shadows."

"Pappy, I told myself that I shouldn't brand you as a cynic. But I am now convinced that you are one of them," he teased.

Pappy looked dumbstruck at his grandson for a moment. "Cynic!" he shouted. "It is di first time anybody ever call me dat! I t'ought you said you'd change' your mind about callin' me cynic! It could be worse! What 'appenin' in dis country is bad enough to make a cynic out o' anybody. You know what? You an' me can't change di worl'. An' I don't t'ink it healthy to spen' di whole of di day wallowin' hopelessly in di metaphysics of t'ings we don't understand, let us go play a game of dominoes wit' those men down by di shop. We can learn a lot from dem. Take dat ol' man, Ferdie, who I take di paper to. He wouldn't buy one fo' himself, but every time he see' me he ask' if I bring him di paper, an' vex too, if I forgot. He reads a page, spellin' an' guessin' di words an' when he starts readin' di nex page, he soon forget' what he read on di previous page. I sometimes wish I could do di same, forget di past, live di present only, unmindful dat di future soon to be di present, is just anoddah dimension of measured time. An' dat young man, quiet an' silent, pleasant, always intently listenin' to di radio on his shoulder. All he want is to listen DJ, cricket an' football all day, to work if he can get wok or if he feel' like it, to wish fo' a office job, dough he can hardly sign his name an' to beg money to buy drop-pan or di lotto. Whenever he has money, life for him is cool. If he has none, life is still cool. Him have no care in di worl'. An' for those men playin' dominoes an' t'rowing dice? Dey all have opposite political views, but dey are friends. Dey don't fight wit' one annodah. Dey buy one annodah a beer an' willingly pass a dollar or two if any o' dem need it. Dey have no grudge agains' one annodah. Dey would not t'ink of liftin' a knife or gun agains' annodah man. I ask myself di same question again an' again. Why can't di worl' be simple an' wonderful like dese men?"

"Any attempt at answering that question is over-simplifying matters to no useful purpose," he replied. "Come on, get on your clothes. Let's go play some dominoes!"

Arriving at the haunt, he noticed the unusual quietness under the guango tree, as he stepped from the Datsun. "Nothing seems to be going on here," he said to his grandfather.

Pappy noticed at once that the young man with his radio-cassette player was missing. "Where is Bert?" Pappy asked. "Gone to work, at last?"

One of the dice-players squatting in the dust replied, "Dunno," and nodded in the direction of Ferdie who was sitting dejectedly on a low bench. He noticed that only three men were playing dominoes. Pappy went over to Ferdie and handed him the newspaper of the day before.

"What tek you so long to bring the paper?" Ferdie asked. "Didn't you think I want to read it? You're not bringing the paper regular."

"But see 'ere! Don't I 'ave to read it first?" Pappy responded, pretending to be annoyed.

"But that was yesterday," the old man grumbled. "You are not reliable."

"Ferdie, you damn ramgoat, what a piece of forwardness!" Pappy shouted.

Ferdie ignored Pappy's outburst and started to spread out the newspaper on the ground.

"Who is this gentleman reprimanding you, this morning?" he mischievously asked. "Your friend or your boss?"

"He use' to work as an accounts clerk at KSAC. He says dat he is a retired man who wid a tiny pension is down on his luck, but it doesn't seem to bodder him. He spends day after day by the shop readin' newspaper an' occasionally playin' a game of wily domino." Pappy stood over Ferdie and asked, "Where is Bert?"

"The Police arrested him," Ferdie replied. "He stabbed his girlfriend several times with a knife."

"Good Gawd!" Pappy cried. "Why can't dese young people stay out o' trouble? Di leas' little t'ing an' is beat-up, cut-up, box-down an' kick-down! He got two years, some time ago, for stabbin' his own friend over domino. Luckily, di man didn' die,"

"He is a nice boy!" Ferdie sadly explained, "but he won't control his temper."

"Where is he?" Pappy asked. "At Denham Town? I will bail him, if he can get bail."

"The Police said that he has to go before a judge to get bail," Ferdie said.

"OK," Pappy said. "Let me know if he can get bail. I will bail him."

"Aren't you runnin' a risk to bail him? Suppose he absconds?" he spoke in a low voice close to his grandfather's ear.

"I don't t'ink he will," Pappy said. "As his grandfather said, he is a good boy. He has a weakness for knife-wieldin'. He won't run away. Anyhow we are here to play a game o' domino let us not get involve' in other people's business. I will bail him, but di law mus' take its course. He mus' pay for his stupidity."

They approached the three men who were half-heartedly playing a game of French dominos, and the tallest of them rose. "Want a game, Pappy?" he jovially invited. "Play dese two novice'."

"Who yuh callin' novice?" the smaller of the men shouted in pretended anger, jumping up and pressing a thumb into his own chest, "Where yuh was when I did a play domino? Yuh know who dis? A Parish Champion dis!"

"Ah, cut out di crap an' play!" drawled the tall man. "Stop run yuh mout'. We will take on di winner when Big Mac come. Pappy, I hope yuh 'ave money fi buy di beer!"

After an half-hour or so, he got into the rhythm of the game and they won their second six-love. The thin little man, the most vociferous of their opponents, got up and shouted to his partner, "Yuh nah do nutt'n fi pass di man an' yuh deh 'pon top o' him! Yuh ha' joke wit' him! Yuh fi pass di man! Change place wit' me, make mi show 'im if 'im badder dan mi!"

To wrap up the third set, Pappy said, pointing a finger at each of their opponents, "Yuh have dat an' him 'ave dat! Which means you don't have dat! He looked at the thin little man and slammed down three dominoes he was holding close to his chest. "Game block!" he shouted, displaying double-blank in the palm of his right hand for all to see. He threw the blank piece at the thin little man. "Take dat an' study it fo' you' homework an' eat it fo' you' super," he playfully advised.

The thin little man shook his head and rose, "Jerry, is not fi wi day," he ruefully said to his partner.

"No, sah," Jerry agreed. "Nuh fi wi day at all! Nex' time ah fi wi!"

"Winners buy di beer," the thin little man slyly announced.

"Not a damn!" Pappy retorted. "Better yuh say yuh beggin' a beer."

The thin little man boastfully pulled a bundle of notes from his pocket and gave one or two to the tallest of the group. "Is how much man deh yah? Buy fi everybody what dey want," he said.

The tallest man counted aloud, pointing a curved and wagging forefinger at each person. The number had increased to nine, including everybody. "Membah fi bring back mi change, yuh hear sah?" the thin little man shouted after the tall man.

While they were having their drinks, the tall man asked him if he was interested in drop-pan. Bateman said that he had heard that there is such a game, but he knew nothing about it.

"It easy!" said the tall man. "I got a rake dat dey gwine play 'cock' dis week"

"What do you mean?" he asked.

"It easy!" the tall man repeated. "Di drap-pan now. See how it goh?" the tall man explained. "Di drap-pan 'ave t'irty-six numbers. One o' those numbahs is di winnah each week, but di bankah, he keep it a secret to 'imself. Him one know di number dat gwine play. Nobody else know' it. Him naw tell nobady! Make me show yuh supp'n. Look ovah deh so."

He allowed his eyes to follow the pointing forefinger of the tall man.

"Yuh see dat little piece of cardboard nail 'pon dat tree?" the tall man asked.

"Yeah, I see," he replied.

"It 'ave a numbah write on it. Dat is di winnin' numbah las' week. Dey stuck di winnin' numbah every week over town, an' di people who buy drap-pan know where fi go collec' when dem win."

"What do you mean by *cock* is a rake?" Bateman persisted.

"Di rake is a clue yuh get in a dream or somet'ing strange dat you notice. A rake could be some word dat you hear or somebody say to you. Every numbah has a name "Dead is numbah three; Dawg is numbah eleven; Big House is t'irty-t'ree and Cock is numbah five or numbah ten."

The tall man took a dirty sheet of paper from his shirt pocke. "See dis paper?" he said. "It call a Kent. On it I 'ave all di winnin' numbah dat play dis year. I work from it how di bankah suppose to move, an' I ketch him almos' every week. I ketch all di time."

"I see!" he exclaimed, greatly impressed. "Do you share your rakes with your friends?"

"No, sah!" the tall man vehemently said. "If you tell one frien', he will pass it to is frien' an' dat frien' will pass it to anoddah frien' an' de bank will burs', an' yuh don't get anyt'ing. I keep mi rake to myself. Mek di man dem go look rake fi demself!"

"But you told me that cock will play this week," he reminded the tall man. The tall man grinned broadly. "A ketch yuh for I didn' tell yuh if is cock 'pon roos' or cook 'a crow' or is 'black cock' or 'red cock' ha play. An' besides yuh don't know drap-pan, so yuh couldn't tell anybody wha' ah play."

"So you win me there," he laughingly suggested. "And so you trust me."

"Yes, Boss, I trus' yuh," he replied. "To tell yuh di trut', Boss, t'ings kinda t'in wid me dis week. I axin' you to drap a money 'pon mi fi buy di rake. I sure to win, Boss!"

He gave the tall man a twenty dollar Jamaican bill. "T'anks, Boss," the tall man said. "You is a nice man, Boss any time yuh want a rake, Boss, jus' tell mi. Irie!" No sooner than he got the money, he went away.

Pappy was very proud and elated that they had won the domino. "Yuh play like a worl' champion, Bat," he commended his grandson.

"I hate losing," he teased, recalling how Pappy had reacted the first time they played as domino partners under the guango tree. Pappy grinned, "I am a poor loser too," he admitted. "Da's why I stop playin' domino wit' Ferdie. He is a worse player dan you. He won't learn to read di cards an' he don't like anybody, but himself to win, an' he get' angry at di leas' joke made at his expense. He is a poor loser."

"Pappy, let's buy KFC on the way home, so that you won't have to cook," he suggested. "I will pay for it."

"Fine!" Pappy jovially replied. "How did you know dat the cook was goin' on strike today?"

"Intuition or instinct or self-preservation, I guess," he bantered. They had almost finished the chicken and fried potatoes straight from the red and white bucket when Raymond came whistling through the gate.

"Raymond, yuh foot short again," Pappy shouted. "Yuh miss it by inches dis time! An' dere is no beer neither! Everyday bucket go a well, bottom mus' drop out!"

"Yuh listen to too much reggae, Pappy," Raymond teased.

"You mus' listen to di message, an' listen good," Pappy retorted.

"Oh, that reminds me to ask you, Ray, about the dancehall culture. I heard that you're an exponent," he said, a wide grin spreading across his face.

"Who tell you, Big Breddah, dat I am a' exponent?" Raymond asked, looking suspiciously at his grandfather.

"Forget who told him. Tell us about it," Pappy said, lazily bringing the paper container of fruit punch to his chin and noisily sucking at the drinking straw.

"How did you spend the day, Big Breddah?" Raymond asked.

"Oh! So and so," he replied. "We gave a couple of six-loves today."

"Yuh mean yuh was playin' wid novice!" Raymond gibed.

"Go-away! Take dat back!" Pappy irritably shouted. "I don' play wit' novices! Don't take dose feisty chances wid me!"

"But I wasn't talkin' 'bout you, Pappy dear?" Raymond affectionately replied. "You not a novice."

"Don't listen to him, Bat! Let him tell yuh 'bout dancehall. Da's all he knows!" Pappy shouted.

"Yes, Ray, tell us about it," he urged.

"Dancehall? What yuh want to know 'bout it?'" Raymond somberly asked.

"Pappy is claiming that dancehall culture is destroying this generation. I want to get a clear picture of this dancehall culture, in order to form my own opinion," he explained.

"Di bes' way to know is to go yourself. Want me to set you up? Pappy prejudice'," Raymond said.

"I am not!" Pappy objected.

"Yes, you prejudice," Raymond insisted.

"I wont listen to anymore of your cheek!" Pappy furiously said, rising to his feet.

"What a piece of audacity!"

He induced their grandfather to sit. "He only teasing, Pappy. Don't mind him," he soothingly said in an effort to mollify Pappy. "Ray means no harm."

"Go ahead, Ray, dancehall culture!" he urged his brother once again.

"Dancehall culture!" Raymond drawled. "Now dat bigger dan wi. Dancehall culture is a cultural t'ing. It technical. It big! Pappy don't understan' what ha' gwaan. Him blind!"

"Ray, leave Pappy out of it. Just talk." he impatiently admonished.

"OK, Bredda. I don't think dancehall is a culture. Is a anti-culcha thing," Raymond explained. "What a mean is dat it a free up di culture fi everybody fi become one people-uptown-downtown. Yuh know out o' many, one people? Yuh ha' fi upfront, Yuh ha' fi groove an bubble wit' di music or yuh can't understan'. Is a big t'ing, Irie!" Raymond paused for a while. There was a faraway look in his eyes. He was picturing himself in a large hall flashing multi-coloured lights and stars and the smell of herbs.

His could hear the beat of the drum and the acoustic guitar in his head. Di music loud, sweet. Di bubblin' an' di groovin'. Di aroma of the herbs fillin' his nostrils, an' he was thirstin' for a beer. Dere was wrigglin' an' bubblin' semi-nude women all over him. Betty, dat rich lesbian, big-bodie' big-mouth' bitch wit' har woman posse an har coke! She was always dere, like she live'nowhere. Da's dancehall! Culcha!

Raymond used to go up to the mike to ask the disk jockey for a 'bligh'. He used to hold the microphone like a huge phallus between the damp palms of his hands and 'shield' his lips over the mouth-piece. He used to feel the electric power flowing from himself into the microphone and spreading out into the crowd. He was Elvis Presley, Bob Marley, Peter Tosh, Dennis Brown, Buju Banton, Beenie Man, Red Rat and Tiger. He could be anyone he wanted to he responding to the vibe of the crowd.

He used to move the crowd and had them bubbling and grooving, eating from his hands. He could call them anything, and it was a great feeling. He didn't know from where the lyrics were coming, but they used to fill his brain, and he was glad to get them out of his head. All he had to do was sing, keeping time with the reggae beat of the drums and the acoustic bass guitar. The crowd loved his lyrics. They asked for more and he gave them. Yet he never made it, because the recording studio said that he lacked stamina, resonance, stance, consistence and such like. He couldn't keep time with the beat, the studio-man said, but he wasn't going to tell his brother anything about that.

"Dey say dat a DJ by di name of Big Yout' start' dancehall," Raymond heard himself saying in a hoarse voice.

"How did Big Youth get into the act?" he asked.

"He use' to float aroun' a dance in Town, an' he use' to beg to spit in di mike. Den one night the singer didn't turn up an' Big Yout' ax fi di bligh."

"Ask fi di bligh?" he asked. "What in heaven's name is that ?" he asked.

"A bligh is a chance, an opportunity dat you beg or give to some- body." Raymond replied, mischievously lapsing into some semblance of Standard English.

"See now, him can talk properly," said Pappy in disgust. "He is talkin' patois to annoy me!"

"Ah, come off it, Pappy, I not annoyin' yuh," Raymond retorted. "Yuh annoyin' yuhself!"

"Alright, alright!" he said. "Go on Raymond and stop the bickering, Pappy!"

"Big Yout' got a bligh dat night an' he never look back!" Raymond said. "Den odders come after him, like U-Roy an di Ugly One an' Yellah Man."

"What do you mean when you say that dancehall is anti-culture?" he asked.

"Yeah, groovin' di music an' all di people dem lovin' it." Raymond explained. "One time only ghetto people an' low class people did was grooving. Uptown, downtown, di massive groovin'."

"Groovin'? What do you mean?" he asked.

"Yeah, it mean say di artiste was makin' up some class a lyrics, an' di people was lovin' it, singin' an' dancin' it. It was life music, true to life. DJ's was promotin' lyrics dat di radio couldn' play on di air. Some a di music dey call nastiness. Nowadays, di station dey playin' dem. DJ like Buju Banton, Lady Saw, Shabba Ranks, Ninja Man, Beenie Man, dey become international name in di music business. Dancehall even 'ave queen."

"Yes," Pappy interrupted. "Dey 'ave a queen who go aroun' showin' plenty o' skin in little bit o' clot'. I wonder why she boddah wear any! She nuh cover nutt'n!"

He laughed at Pappy's gaucherie while Raymond glowered uncomfortably as if gearing himself for a stream of vitriol from their grandfather.

"I notice," he remarked, "that even in England, in the dancehall the DJ's bark out lyrics that are crude, coarse; humorous, suggestive and most of them offering serious comments against the ills and evils of the society, such as drugs and guns."

"I don't t'ink you 'ave been hearin' di real obscene ones in Mother Country, in which the DJ's deal in female private parts!" Pappy growled. "What baffles me, dere are women who enjoy dese lewd songs about demselves. Dey even wear clothes designed to fit di lyrics!"

Raymond pictured himself shouting into the mike at the crowd, "Are you ready?" He pictured himself shouting, wriggling his buttocks, pushing forward his genitals and shrugging his shoulders like

Michael Jackson. "Plenty power out deh! Gimme more power!" he silently hear himself shouting to an imaginary crowd gone wild and groaned with the reality of an unfulfilled dream. "Dancehall is a big t'ing! Understan'?" he said too loudly. "It powerful more dan we! You ever listen' to Buju Banton an' Ninja Man?"

He said that he hadn't listened, since he couldn't understand the shouting and the ranting and the raving in what they said was the music.

"Da's a counter-culture problem," Raymond asserted. "You can't understan' di music if yuh prejudice. One big t'ing 'bout di music. Di music is free an' powerful. It nuh obey nuh rules weh fi cramp it. Is big soun'! Dem is freedom people. Bob seh emancipate yuh self fram mental slavery! Dancehall is emancipation! Dancehall say you fi big up yuh self an' big up you' breddah and sistren dem! It full o' power! It need space fi explode!"

Pappy exploded with anger. "Emancipate you' self? Dat is how we fi emancipate wiself? Raymon' you really believe dat is what Bob mean? Dat woman mus' tek off dem clothes an' men mus' smoke weed all night bussin' dem ear-drum an' keepin' decent people awake all night who wan' res' fi go back a' work nex' day? Bob mus' be turnin' in his'grave! I see! Yuh mean yuh need space to go on bad! To roar an' rant! To cuss an' swear an smoke an' sniff an' suck coke!"

"So Pappy," Raymond sneered, getting warm under his collar, "So decent people nuh go a dancehall to? Well, a big crowd o' massive fallaw dancehall. Di music is pullin' lock stock an' barrel, people of all class', an' it spreadin' all over di worl'."

"If it so powerful," Pappy bitterly asked, "why it is sayin' degradin' t'ings 'bout women? Why is it shoutin' bu'n dis bu'n dat, eeh? Lick dung, shot im up, eeh, eeh?"

"Di music is telling trut', Pappy. Babylan fi bu'n! Down wit' downpressers!" Raymond vehemently expressed. "Big Broddah, Di music! It hiding nutten. It has nutten to hide! It don't mean to 'ide nuttin either. It's like a mirror dat show you di pimples an' di blackheads on you' face an di warts on you' backside, you know what I mean."

"Be careful of your language!" Pappy growled. "Dis is my house!"

He asked himself whether or not Raymond was putting on an act to irritate Pappy, and satisfied himself that it was so.

"I see!" he said. "I suppose the music means to let it all hang out in the raw. How do women and the public feel about that?"

"What di public feel don't make much difference, since is majority count dese days. But di women t'ink it is di greates'. Even ol' ladies! Is di ol' 'oman dem irie! Dey like di music bad!" Raymond replied animatedly.

"Di nastier, di better!" Pappy sourly scoffed. "What kind a woman yuh talkin' 'bout?"

"Women are gettin' active," Raymond replied. "Mos' o' di 'oman dem come fram downtown, an' some o' dem like di big lesbian, are 'igglers. Some o' dem...let's say...dem in private business. A few 'ave dem don an' dey all dress expensive. Dey go dancehall in posse an' pay dem own bills an' even treat di man dem to drinks an' food. If dey like a man, dey will tell 'im dey want him. Dey don't joke' when dey want a man! Dey don't beat roun' di bush! Dey tell yuh dat dey like yuh an' dey want yuh!"

"You mean several women ask one man, all o' dem at di same time?" an agitated Pappy asked.

"Yes, Pappy," Raymond replied. "All a dem at one time an' dey don't jealous an' fight an' quarrel neither!"

"Dat couldn' be true. A lie yuh ha' talk, Ray," an unbelieving Pappy said softly.

"No, Pappy, it's not a lie. Dey do it, an' when dey tiad o' dat man, dey drive him 'way an' look anaddah!"

"Have these women ever asked you to be their ah... ah...how should I say it?" He was searching his mind for a word. "Have they ever asked you to be their escort?"

"No" Raymond replied laughing uncomfortably." I nevvah been so lucky! You have to 'ave a good car!"

He was tempted to ask Raymond what would he have done, if he was asked, but decided to let the question pass.

"Dere is a lot o' uptown massive. You can't know di difference, if dey is uptown or downtown when dey meet in a di dancehall!" Raymond continued to explain.

"It would appear that the dancehall culture has some startling implications," he remarked. "I think I begin to understand why you say it is counter-culture."

"Yeah, I agree," said Pappy. "Di women are strippin' sex raw an' callin' it safe-sex. Naked ass is di name of di game! Dey cut up dem clothes to show dem private parts an' use nettin' to hol' togeddah what lef'! Dis country is goin' to hell! One day it gwine sink like Port Royal!"

Raymond laughingly said, "I agree wit' you, Pappy. Some o' di P-printers an' di Batty-riders dem absolutely out o' dis worl'! Dey crazy! Man, dey leave nutten' fo' you to imagine."

"Yeah," growled Pappy, "I seen Batty-rider, but what is a P-printers?"

"I leave dat to you' imagination, Pappy," Raymond teased. "Whenever you see it, yuh will know dat dat is a P-printer."

"When I see it, I will know it?" Pappy growled irritably. "What the hell, yuh ha' seh bwoy?" Pappy did not insist on an answer. He seemed to have got the message that Raymond did not want to tell. "Dat dancehall madness is gettin' us nowhere!" Pappy scoffed. "I t'ink we goin' backward!"

"Pappy, you can't say dat!" Raymond hotly objected. "We gettin' somewhere. Everybody goin' places. Yuh nuh see it?"

Pappy and Raymond were always disagreeing, he wondered how it has taken so long in this debate for one or the other or both to explode into shouting and hurling insults. He remained neutral, amused and passively listening, and when he had had enough, he succeeded in calling a truce. When his fury had subsided, Pappy calmly said, "What about di gun-salute? What about di t'rowin' of bottles at artistes? What about di crack cocaine? I notice dat while di women are openin' an' revealin', di men are coverin' up in woman clothes an' gowns an' earring. Look like di women give up dem frock to di men an' di women wear what di men suppose fi wear. Di men all ha' earring an' woman hairstyle an' nail polish! Dis generation goin' to hell, I tell yuh! An' it doesn't matter one bit to you an' you' friends!'"

"Pappy, it matters, only dat we not going to hell," Ray calmly replied. "Why mus' ol' man t'ink di worse 'bout young people? Pappy, in di dancehall is where ghetto yout' get fi socialize, when him not playing cricket or football on di street. You musn' say dis generation is goin' to hell. Di music supply a need. It big! It bigger dan all a we, an' dat naw say much 'bout it? Dat deh music is power!"

"Dat is what I am complaining about!" Pappy declared. "Dis generation needs direction to pave di road of progress. Dey need somet'ing to 'app'n to dem like what 'app'n to dat preacher on di road to Damascus! He t'ink he was doin' a good t'ing till he got struck blind, then he began to see the proper t'ing what to do. If dis generation t'ink dey can turn di worl' round only by singin' an' dancin', dey in for a big surprise! Dey mus' plan well an' work di plan well, den sing an' dance after dey get di plan to work! Bat, what you t'ink goin' to happ'n when people like you an' mi gone?"

"Come on, Pappy," Raymond scoffed, affectionately placing his hand on his grandfather's shoulder. "Don't leave me out."

"Jus' take you' hand off my shoulder!" Pappy sneered. "Me an' you not any frien'! Leave di dancehall alone. If you inten' to make somet'ing out o' you' life."

"Pappy, dancehall music is fast changin'. It is becomin' sober. Listen to di message. I 'ave to leave now. I goin' to work. Den after work, I goin' to dancehall to watch Karlene, tonight. Want to come Big Breddah?"

"Not tonight, Ray," he replied. "I plan to go to Negril, tomorrow. I would like an early start, in the morning. Say, Pappy! How about goin' to Negril tomorrow?

"OK, by me, so long as I am drivin'." Pappy replied. "Nobody drive me on Ol' Harbour Road. Over mi dead body!"

"What about you, Ray?" he asked. "Coming?"

"Irie! I will drive," Raymond said.

Pappy did not protest Raymond's offer.

Chapter 12

TO NEGRIL:
AN IMPORTANT ENLIGHTENMENT

*A*s soon as they settled in the car, Pappy asked, "I wonder which road is shorter, nort' coast or' sout' coast?"

"I t'ink sout'-coast is shorter," Raymond replied. "Let me see! All di way from Black River by di sea, through Bluefields, to Sav, Little London, then Negril. Dat's about a hundrid an' t'irty miles. Along di sea-coas' to Negril is di mos' beautiful place. Scenery fi kill!"

"How big is the difference?" he asked.

"I would say a hundrid an' fifty-three miles as agains' a undrid an' seventy-five along the nort'," Raymond replied.

"You are a road map, Raymond!" Pappy quipped. "I haven't gone dat way for a long time. Let us go sout'. Do you know di road? If you don't I will drive. I don't trust you young boys, these days wit' motorcar. Life rough but it still sweet."

Raymond ignored Pappy's jibe. "I travel dis road pretty often," he boasted, "I can travel it wit' my eyes close."

"What?" Pappy shouted. "You got somet'ing stuck in you' head, at las'! Dat is a miracle. How long it take yuh to achieve such a remarkable feat? Well, no matter how good you are, you wont drive me wid yuh eyes shut! Hear mi?"

Raymond did not ignore this jibe, he shot Pappy a mean and angry look.

"Cut you' yeye, till dem drap out!" Pappy taunted. "Cut you' yeye an' screw up you mout', as much as yuh like. Take yuh yeye offah mi! Bad yeye an' tough look cyaan tear mi shirt!"

"Cut it out, Pappy. Remember seh I drivin'," Raymond bantered. "If you get me out, I might jus' crash di car or jus' nuh boddah goh no weh!"

"All right, I will ease you up dis time, but if you goin' to shut you' eye an' drive, tell mi from now, so dat I can come out o' di car!" Pappy grumbled.

"OK, Pappy, cool it!" Raymond said. "A only jokin'."

"Well bullfrog say, what is joke to yuh is deat' to me!" Pappy retorted. "When yuh go to places like Newmarket, yuh don't want to leave an' go anywhere else."

"Newmarket, Pappy? Is what yuh say? Newmarket is in St. James. Da's Montego Bay direction. We not goin' dat way?"

"Who said we goin' dat way? Yuh hear mi seh so?" Pappy sneered. "Yuh can't tell me nutten 'bout those places! Shut up yuh mout' an' drive! Yuh know Duppy Gate? Toll Gate? You know Lottery? Gimmemibit, Folly an' Pepper an' Shiloh, PollyGroun', Red Groun', Refuge, Time n' Patience, Wait-a-bit, Cumsee, Big Bottom, John Crow Gully an' Bellas Gate? Yuh nuh did born yet when I go to those places. Yuh can't tell me 'bout any place in Jamaica dat I don't know!"

"Pappy, yuh win!" Raymond said. "Big Breddah, yuh know any a dem place Pappy a talk 'bout?"

They had to admit to Pappy that they had not heard of some of those places. "So yuh a t'ink say I make some o' dem up!" Pappy cried.

By then, Raymond had swiftly and deftly pulled the Datsun out of the heavy traffic of Kingston and entered the busy Old Harbour Road. Pappy kept up a running commentary on the places they were passing through. "I know all o' dese places," he boasted, "Freetown, Milk River, Little London. I use' to go cockfight at Toll Gate. I once had a girlfrien' in a place called Rat Trap."

"Cockfight?" Raymond and he exclaimed in unison. "Tell us 'bout it!"

"If Raymon' promise to keep his eye on di road, I will tell you 'bout it," Pappy promised. "Da's how people get in accident. Dey drivin' in one direction an' lookin' in di opposite direction. Accidents don't happ'n. Dey are caused!"

"OK, Pappy," Raymond said, pressing his foot harder on the accelerator to pass a laden and noisily protesting truck.

"Ugh!" grunted Pappy. "Turn up di windows tight. Dat truck nearly kill us wit' smoke an' fumes. Di police should take dat truck off di road for pollution."

"Tell us 'bout di cockfight," Raymond urged.

"Some men in Tivoli, Allman Town an' Jones Town use' to 'ave cockfight in Cockbourne Pen. Dey held tournaments on weekends. In those days, there wasn't much war as now to speak or worry about. People were just friendly. You could go anywhere you want. People hardly trouble you."

"So how you get interested?" Raymond asked.

"Their was a superb Indian gamecock trainer by di name of Coolie Man. I was not really interested, at first, but Coolie Man had fallen out of luck. He drank too much, an' pawn' out his favourite gamecock called Blue Murdah to me. He promise' to bring back my money di followin' week an' redeem his cock. He instruc' me 'ow to exercise an' care dis cock. Coolie Man never gave me back mi money, he induce' me, instead, to become part-owner of di cock. He invited me to see a fight between a cock name' Murdock from Tivoli an' Blue Murdah. Blue Murdah knock' Murdock out in one minute and fifty seconds! From dat day, I atten' every fight involvin' Blue Murdah, from Negril to Morant P'int! Dat's how I get to know places. At Negril, cockfightin' was once like boxin' in Las Vegas. Cockfightin' is still popular in Kingston. On Saturdays an' Sundays, if you know where to go, you will find a crowd of men an' women go to cockfight too-'round a cockpit, an' some bet t'ousands of dollars on which cock will win."

"Did you make any money," he asked.

"No," Pappy replied. "Coolie Man probably did. Whatever

we made was never enough to buy feed an' tonic fi di cock. Coolie Man was always comin' to me for money."

"An' yuh give him?" Raymond exclaimed, pressing his foot harder on the accelerator to pass a pretty woman driving a swift looking red sports-car.

"Careful now, Raymon'. Don't look back," Pappy warned. "Is who sell yuh license? Well, what could I do? I didn't 'ave any money neither, but I was part-owner of dat cock. I couldn't make him starve. I had to find money to feed him. Some days, I go without food an' beg a cigarette to make sure dat cock eat ! I jus' couldn't make him starve, he was a champion!"

The laughter of the two exploded above the purring of the Datsun. "So what did you learn about cockfighting?" he jovially asked, winking mischievously at Raymond.

"Well, I learn a lot! What 'appens at a cockfight is dat dere is a square dat is fence wit' mesh wire. Each cocksman stand inside the square wit' his cock under his arm."

"What?" Raymond gleefully shouted, "Cocksman wit' him cock under him arm? Pappy, him cyawn do dat?"

"You fool!" Pappy angrily retorted," I mean di gamecock an' di man who handle 'im!"

Both managed to mollify an angry Pappy, and urged him to continue.

"Di cocks are shaven free of neck an' back feathers so dat dere is nutten' for de opponents to hold onto." Pappy explained. "Di fight begin as soon as di referee give di signal, the handlers let them go an di two cocks go at each oddah, wid beak an' spur. It is jus' like a bloomin' boxin' or wrestlin' match, only more bloody an' dere is only one roun' which end' when one cock can fight no longer or lay down dead. Di bettin' goes on durin' di fight, for at times it look like one cock will win an' di oddah lose, then the nex' moment, it look' like di oddah would win, an' di oddah lose, an so di fight go on back an' forward, until one o' di cock can't fight anymore."

"How long does a fight last?" he asked.

"Five an' up to fifteen minutes," Pappy answered. "Blue Murdah kill' very fast, he was what yuh call a rebeldo."

"A fight seems rather brief to me," he remarked.

"Well, it adds to the excitement of the spoil," Pappy explained. "It is usually a series of fights wid di oddah pairs o' cocks goin' into the pit. If a cock is still standin' in good condition after a fight, he is match' wit' anoddah, if di stakes are high."

"Did Blue Murdah fight like that?" he asked.

"Oh, yes! Several times. Dat was de only time we made a little money. Dere is hardly any t'ing about cockfightin' dat I don't know," Pappy asserted.

His grandsons laughed. "Pappy, you sound like a professional bookie," Raymond remarked.

"Yeah, cockfightin'," Pappy replied, "is sort of professional. There are promoters who arrange di matches, weigh di cocks an' pair off di fighters dat 'ave di same weight an size. Breedin' an' trainin' demand experience an' skill. Di trainer 'ave to know what to look for in a young bird. Bantams or game cocks are imported from Cuba or Puerto Rico. Dey 'ave to delice dem an depip dem. Den you feed dem corn, callaloo, tomato an tonic. Yuh 'ave to give dem sparrin' practice every day."

"How do you get gaming cocks to spar?" he asked. "Don't they hurt each other?"

"Yeah, if you allow dem." Pappy explained. "Gamecocks fight the moment yuh t'row dem at each oddah. It's natural. You 'ave to cover di spurs. At dat stage of di trainin', dey cut off di comb, ear lobes an' gills of di birds, so dat annodah cock won't 'ave anyt'ing to hold onto."

"Doesn't all that cutting hurt?" he asked.

"I t'ink so, but it heal quickly," Pappy said. "Next you trim his neck, his back an' his legs. Dat is a rule of di game. At dat stage, you feed you' bird on liver, mince' meat, milk, bread, corn an' vitamin. I learn' everyt'ing about di business."

"Yuh seh dat yuh didn't make nuh dunny, I mean money," Raymond reminded his grandfather.

Pappy acted as if he had not heard the remark. "Gamecocks," Pappy continued, "are bantams weighin' between two an'a half pounds. Dey come originally from di Guinea Coast of Africa an' dey come in different colours an' trainers give dem names such as 'Green Hornet', 'Pinto' and 'Blue'. Cockfightin' take place from December to July, an' although di sport is illegal, dere is a lot of fans."

"Where can you get birds?" Raymond asked.

"Most trainers breed dem own. Eggs can be imported from Miami. Raisin' a gamecock is a lot o' work! It takes fourteen weeks to grow di bird. Den you have to train 'im to fight! Yuh 'ave to train him like a boxer. You even have to keep 'im from hens!"

"What?" shouted Raymond. "Kiss mi back foot!"

"Yeah, some handlers fit steel spurs to di birds," Pappy said.

"Wait deh! You mean spurs fi ride 'orse?" Raymond exclaimed.

Once again, Pappy coldly ignored him. "Coolie Man would nevvah put any spur on Blue Murdah! An' he would nevvah put Blue Murdah into di pit against any bird dat fight wid false spur."

"How long does a fighter last?" he asked.

"Cocks receive injuries in every fighter. A cock could las' a minute or up to five years," Pappy replied.

"So what 'apppen to Blue Murdah?" Raymond asked.

"He died like a good warrior who had los' his last battle on di battlefiel' in di pit," Pappy replied. "Coolie Man buried him an' a mad 'oman use' to sing a verse or two of *Peace, perfect peace in dis dark worl' of sin.* daily over his grave, until she got tired of it. Coolie Man wasn't so lucky. He nevvah train anaddah cock an' died at KPH from too much drink an' too little food. He had no one to bury him," Pappy sadly related.

They remained solemnly silent, until Raymond laughed uncomfortably. "I hear say doctah did tell a dead man say him die' from not enough blood in 'im rum an' doctah did tell a man say, 'You' body is embalm' an' well preserve' by Wray 'n Nephew'. Yuh sure seh is not Coolie Man doctah did talk to?" he remarked.

"Mek we don't talk anyt'ing bad 'bout di dead. I don't joke about deat' for none of us can tell 'ow we goin' to leave dis worl'. You lucky if you die in you' bed," Pappy quietly admonished.

This apparently had a sobering effect on all, for they remained silent until they arrived at Middle Quarters where they each had two hot patties and a Red Stripe Beer.

"If it wasn't for the seaview," Pappy remarked, "We could cut through Darliston to Petersfield to Sav. We could save a couple of miles dat way."

"I am for the seaview," he said. "Let us go on to Black River. I have never been there."

"Have never?" Pappy asked in surprise.

"No! Never been this far south-west," he replied.

It took about an hour from Black River to Negril. "I remember," Pappy related, "when Negril was bush and swamp. It was a fishin' village. Dey drained mos' of di swamp lands an' now it is like a town."

"Look, a mongoose runnin' cross di road! Slide mongoose!" Raymond shouted.

"Did you see aneddah one?" Pappy shouted, looking mischievously at Bat.

"You're not calling me a mongoose are you?" he asked, amused. They all laughed .

Raymond parked the Datsun in the parking lot of the Sundowner. They took off their shoes and walked along the beach. "My, my!" Bateman exclaimed. "I have never seen so much white sand in my life and I have been around!"

"Yeah, the best in di world!" Pappy proudly exclaimed. "About seven miles of it!"

"It's heaven here with all these hotels and restaurants," he murmured.

"There is a lot of dream cottages too, behind those high walls," Raymond added.

"What happen' to di Rent-a-Dread business? Pappy asked.

"It seem' to peter out wit' di AIDS scare," Raymond answered.

"Drugs still strong though," Pappy stated.

"And Hedonism and Springbreak, nude weddings being the last feature of entertainment," he dryly added.

"Bat do you know how di place got its name?" Pappy asked.

"No, do you?" he replied.

"The Spaniards," Pappy related, "use' to trap di black conger eels in di swamps an' rivers here. Dey call di eels, *'negrille'*. After a while, di name stuck to dis place. Negril use' to be an area of over six t'ousan' acres of morass an' water."

"How did it get started as tourist resort?" he asked.

"It wasn't di swamp dat attracted di touris'," Pappy mischievously explained. "Dey was attracted to di white beaches when a group of foreigners who were called "hippies" discovered dat it was an ideal place, a sort of haven for smokin' pot, for free sex an' other licentious amusements and abandonment. Local people an' foreigners were attracted to di natural charm of di place an' businessman in di touris' industry began to develop di area. Di firs' hotel built was di Sundowner. Let us go 'ave a drink in di lounge or in di bar."

"The ambience is superb," he remarked, as he tasted the rum-cream that Pappy ordered.

"Oddah hotels sprang up," Pappy continued. "De Samara, de Mirage, Hedonism an' di Gran' Lido, I t'ink are di main ones. In days gone by, you could walk along di beaches an along Norman Manley Boulevard. Look what 'app'n'? You better watch you step when yuh walkin'! You could be trespassin' 'on private property, a big jump from di cockfightin' days!"

"Do they still do cockfighting here?" he asked.

"Dey probably do, but I can't swear," Pappy replied. "Do dey still do cockfightin' Raymon'?"

"I nevvah hear of any," Raymond replied.

"Some t'ings don't die easily. Dey jus' don't go away." Pappy murmured almost inaudibly.

"Well," said he, "it's no use mourning about it. Here we are. We may as well go back to the beach, till we are ready to eat. I may even go for a dip. How about you, Ray?"

"Sure," Raymond said, "I 'ave on mi bathsuit under mi pants."

"Well, I 'ave no bathsuit. Nevvah has use fo' one. An' I don't ink dey allow' you to bathe in you' birt'suit. I would 'ave to go to Hedonism," Pappy slyly remarked.

"At Hedonism yuh couldn' jus walk in an' go bathe naked. Yuh would 'ave to join one a dem nudis' club," Raymond explained.

"OK, let's go," Pappy said. "I hope dey don't charge fi di beachchair."

On their way, they were accosted by a man, just as they came from the lounge, who obviously knew Raymond. "Anyt'ing a bruk, tidday, Star?" he drawled.

"We not toleratin' touris' harassment!" Pappy snarled.

"Not today, Star," Raymond said. "Nutten naw gwaan right now!"

"Cool, Star! Cool!" the man said and loped away.

"I suppose dey will soon come to harrass us to rent a Dread or to buy crack," Pappy grumbled.

"Ray, do you know the bloke?" he asked.

"Yeah!" Raymond replied. "He is a rude bwoy from Town. Dey call him Spike. De police will soon pick him up. Dey know say him dey 'bout hustlin' an' a' hide same time from di Police, in Negril, but dey not lookin' fo' him. Robbery wit' aggravation. Di Police dem a gi him long rope fi ketch him."

While Pappy was lolling in a beachchair, and Raymond was cavorting with some girls in the water, he strolled along the beach. He saw Spike and went after him. "Spike, what are you selling?" he asked.

"Oh, jus' a lickle drap-pan an' a lickle peaka-pow an' t'ings," Spike replied. "I nuh innah nutten big, Boss. After nutten big nah gwaan!"

"What yuh think playing this week? You got a rake?" he asked.

"Oh, so you know 'bout it!" Spike pleasantly replied. "Dey playin' pregnant woman, number sixteen, dis week, Mi nuh know what TV gwine play. Ha mussi young gal or small car dem ha go play.'

"How do you know that?" he asked in pretended amazement.

"Well, I 'ave to tell dem somet'ing to make dem buy from me, accordin' to di runnin's dat I see goin' on an' di rake I get. Dey dependin' on me to tell dem somet'ing. Some can't t'ink fo' demselves an' dey buy what I say dem fi buy."

"So what happens when you tell them what to buy and they lose?"

"I 'ave to t'ink up somet'ing quick to tell dem," Spike replied grinning slyly.

"Should you see a mongoose running across the road would that be a rake? What would you tell your clients to buy?" he asked.

"Boss, yuh see a mongoose runnin' cross di road?" Spike asked excitedly.

"Yes, saw one." he said.

"Den nuh good rake dat, Boss? Yuh fi buy nine, twenty and twenty-nine, live or dead mongoose!" Spike explained. "Mongoose fi dead. Dead is nine an' mongoose is twenty-nine."

"But this mongoose wasn't dead," he bantered, "so why not buy mongoose only?"

"No, Boss! So long mongoose 'pon road, him either dead or gwine dead," Spike said.

He paid for nine, twenty and twenty nine, "If I win, how will I know where to collect my winnings?" he asked.

"Dat easy. Look out fo' a little card on dat light pole over dat side. Dere is always a person nearby fi tell which a dem numbers did win, an' where to collect you' winnin's from di banker."

He returned the pieces of drop-pan to Spike, "Keep these tickets," he said. 'If I win, collect my winnings for yourself. Keep the change as well. Who controls the business around here?"

"You ha' police?" Spike asked, trembling with suspicion and fear.

"No, I'm not," he denied. "I am just curious. Relax, Spike."

"Don't seh mi tell you! It come from Kingston," Spike explained. "Yuh know a man name Missa Chow? He is di big man! He is a mafia! He got a beach cottage wid high walls. Nobody can see what a gwaan in dere. Him got a boat name Sea Bird."

"Mafia! Sea Bird!" he exclaimed, and cursed himself for his spontaneous excitement. As he walked back towards Pappy still basking in the beachchair, he told himself that, for the present, he would not disclose this disconcerting bit of information about Chew and the *Sea Bird* until he was absolutely sure.

The journey back to Kingston was uneventful, except when Raymond and other motorists had to stop to allow a huge and leisurely Jamaica Red bull to cross the road at Middle Quarters. Pappy slept most of the way and Raymond remained silent.

Chapter 13

AN INTERLUDE-WEST KINGSTON ERUPTS

" *Wake up!* Wake up, Bat!" Pappy shouted in his ear
as he roughly shook him. "Hell a pop loose a Tivoli!
Di news deh 'pon tv. We miss some o' it already!"
With their eyes glued to the television, they listened:...*violence
which started a few weeks ago in West Kingston, has developed into serious proportions. Armed men from party strongholds in Rose Town, Tivoli Gardens and Denham Town are engaged in a fight with opposing groups from Hannah Town,
Whitfield Town and Rema. It was reported that the Rose Town
community was attacked Wednesday night and early Thursday
morning by heavily armed gunmen from Arnett Gardens and
Whitfield Town. By daybreak, the disruption switched to Rema
and Denham Town where gunfire was exchanged between the
security forces and gunmen for nearly half-hour.*

"I did hear gunfire," Pappy remarked, "but I thought it was
business as usual with gunmen ketchin' dem practice or celebratin'
a football win. I didn't t'ink it was anyt'ing serious."

"*Residents are advised to stay away from the area for their
own safety, until normality is restored,*" the television announcer

declared.

Pappy vehemently wagged a forefinger at the announcer. "If you did bet me that somet'ing like dis wouldn't happen, I woulda win!" he shouted. "I not leavin' my house until di war done! Cockroach no business in a fowl fight!"

"But it is not happenin' in Trench Town, Pappy," he teased. "Just now, you're not in the midst of it."

"Me sah?" Pappy exclaimed. "I goin' underneat' mi bed till di war over!"

"If I observed rightly," he bantered, "modern beds have no space underneath them to hide even a small child, much less a man of your stature."

"I am tellin' you dat from 1966," Pappy related, "in Western Kingston dere have been fightin' between di Police an' gunmen in West Kingston. Is time for it to stop now. I remember not so long ago when di Commissioner — I don't remember his name — wit' 120 policeman went to Tivoli an' gunmen shot at dem. Di gunmen put women an' children in front of dem to prevent di Police firin' back at dem. Dey say dat di gunmen escape' by a undergroun' tunnel. Until today, the Police can't find any tunnel. Many years ago, the whole o' Kingston lock' down when 120 policeman an' over 100 gunmen fought along Foreshow Road an' Denham Town for six days."

"Man! Incredible!" he exclaimed.

"Yeah!" Pappy continued. "It was worse dan Sam Sharpe riot an' Morant Bay Rebellion put together! Why Jamaicans like to fight so? Wait here come the midday news."

The security forces staging a raid in search of arms in the Tivoli Gardens area, were met with heavy gunfire this morning from men with sophisticated weaponry suspected to be AK-2's. At one stage, the security forces were pinned down under heavy fire. Since early this week, there has been unrest in the inner-city communities.

"I was hopin' di news would tell us what caused the flare-up. I suppose we will learn from the papers what cause' it. All I know is dat I not leavin' dis house! Is not my business! Why should I go out dere an' get shot? I am no hero!"

"I wish, Pappy," he replied, "that the situation was as simple as that, so we could sit back on our asses and relax, saying it is no business of ours. But it doesn't look good to me. When civilians violently confront the security forces, democracy is in danger, as you mentioned."

"It seems to me that the Prime Minister is about to read an Act of War," Pappy declared from the kitchen. "I better pack up an' go back wit' you to Mother Country. But I don't even have a passport an' I cant leave di house go look 'bout one. I 'ave to wait till t'ings cool down."

"And by that time," he teased, "you won't feel like leaving."

"You could be right," Pappy replied. "Did you look at the picture of dat brave woman with her newborn baby in her arms at KPH? She said that di war wasn't goin' to stop her from goin' home to the rest of her children who were waitin' for her to come home to look after dem."

"Is she brave or desperate?" he sardonically asked. "Necessity knows no law nor danger."

"Maybe both," Pappy sadly grumbled. "I hope dem stop dis bloody nonsense quick so dat people can go 'bout dem business in peace."

He spent the rest of the days of confinement watching television and playing two-man French domino with Pappy and trying not to listen to Pappy's incessant grumbling and repetitions. He had exhausted his supply of Matterhorns and two of his choice cheroots to the utter disgust of Pappy who abhorred smoking. There was no beer and Pappy refused to go on the Street nor would he permit him to go. "I hope di war soon done so dat we can get some fresh air," was perpetually chorused by a thoroughly disgruntled Pappy. "Dead people rottin' on street like dead dog! Jus' t'inkin' of it make mi skin crawl. An' we runnin' short o' John Crow!"

He phoned Chew on the third day in order to relieve himself of boredom and to avoid the griping of Pappy for a short while. "How are things with you in Allman Town, Man?" he greeted Chew.

"Allman Town is always calm and peaceful," Chew replied.

"People are going about their business, but they are staying clear of West Kingston. Everywhere has closed down in the West and I heard that several dead bodies are left rotting in the streets. How are you?"

Pappy has put us under siege, tight as a drum," he bantered. "We are running out of supplies. Can you send us some Red Stripe?"

"Ah! Ah!" laughed Chew. "When the strife is over. I do not relish being shot."

"What do you think is the cause of the trouble this time?" he asked.

"The cause is always the same. Defence of turf is everybody's guess," Chew lightly replied. "But it cannot be pinpointed to any-one particular cause. The Leader of the Opposition is claiming that this flare-up was politically orchestrated, while the Leader of the government feels that it is an act of criminality and therefore, against the State. I think that the crisis in West Kingston is more deep-rooted in poverty and neglect rather than politically driven, and it can he remedied by sustainable and consistent efforts on non-political groups working alongside the political representatives."

"What do you think about the Prime Minister empowering the army with Police-powers?" he asked.

"I hope it is temporary and that very soon there won't be any need. Such powers given to the army can lead to a Police State," Chew declared.

"Yeah, I agree," he replied. "There is always danger. The Prime Minister made a statement last night that there must be no part of Jamaica which is outside the control of the security forces."

"My Dear Friend," Chew replied, "the road to hell is paved with the best intentions. But the Prime Minister is right. He must see to the security of the nation as his supreme authority. I, however think that this scrap between the security forces and gunmen is be-ing blown out of proportion. Did you hear about that little fracas in Bradford?"

"Yeah," he replied.

"Nine hundred policemen were engaged in quieting the riot," Chew continued. "One hundred and twenty policemen and forty-three civilians were injured and thirty-six rioters were arrested, and it didn't even hit the headlines in the British papers much less the foreign press."

"Well our combative nature cannot be easily subdued. We are always finding a cause for fighting or we fight without a cause. I am wondering how gunmen in depressed areas procure such expensive weapons. There can be only one explanation. I suspect that there is an organization outside of Jamaica, probably drug-related, that is operating in the inner-city communities in pursuit of their own interests. The Police need to discover and seal off this source as quickly as possible."

"Alright," Chew abruptly replied. "You are saying a hell of a lot! I have to sign off. We will talk again."

Next morning, Pappy rushed out at the cry of the news-vendor and the thwack of the papers falling into his yard. "Look at dis, Bat! Massi mi master, war done!" he shouted excitedly as he re-entered the living room. "I hope dem don't start anymore! We need to forgive an' forget. A nation dat fail to forgive an' forget is boun' to perish!"

"Well," he sardonically murmured, "like in most wars, everybody lost and nobody won. When will we ever learn?"

Chapter 14

HARBOUR CRUISE. CHEW- "PIECE DE RESISTANCE"?

*P*appy was up early and as usual, perusing the newspaper, in front of the television. "Pappy, good morning," he greeted him. "I would think, having bleached your bones so hard yesterday, you would be busy repairing them in bed."

"If you find me in bed later dan six o'clock, call di doctor or di undertaker. Somet'ing gone wrong wit' me," Pappy replied.

"Did Raymond wake up?" he asked.

"Raymond?" Pappy coughed, snorted and chuckled. "Only a hurricane or a earthquake could wake him up at this time o' day! What's on your agenda, today?"

"I am thinking of just lazing around," he replied.

"Suits me," Pappy said. "I can use di car. You can 'ave breakfast when you're ready for it."

"You got up and prepared breakfast, since morning?" he asked, greatly surprised.

"It isn't much of a breakfast, just roast' breadfruit and some ackee an' codfish, wit' orange juice an' coffee."

"Sounds like a helluva breakfast to me," he remarked.

"Well," Pappy quipped, "Take it or leave it. You don't 'ave to eat it. Go to a restaurant."

He must have been dozing when Raymond left. Pappy returned about midday. "Dere is a madman standin' across di road," he said. "He has no clothes on."

"What is he doing?" he asked, peering through one of the windows that faced the street.

"Jus' standin' dere, lookin' at nuttin'," Pappy replied. "To lose your mind is to lose everyt'ing! Do you remember Mercedes?"

Mercedes was his cousin. "Yeah! We went to school together. She was very bright."

"She mad!" Pappy ruefully exclaimed.

"She was a bright girl. What happened?" he casually asked.

"It's a long story. Her husband was shot and killed one evening, ridin' his bicycle from work. She had two daughters, Joyce and Paula. Both were *Informal Commercial Importers* or higglers. Dem use' to sell escallion an' thyme an' such t'ings in Panama an' Curacao an bring back clothes an' shoes an' such t'ings to sell in Jamaica, makin' a good profit. It was good business until di bottom drop out. But Joyce got greedy. She get involve' in drugs an' died from poisonin'."

"How did it 'app'n?" he asked.

"She carry di drugs by swallowin' condoms packed wit' it. On her last trip, she found herself in the morgue, instead of on a plane. It was reported in di papers dat she had a cup of hot soup on her way to di airport, which caused a condom full of cocaine to burst in her stomach. At di 'ospital, dey found thirty condoms of cocaine in her stomach, not to mention some more in other parts of her body."

"Don't tell me!" he exclaimed.

"Oh, yeah! She found out too late dat hot soup an' coke don't mix!" Pappy said.

"A helluva menu that!" he exclaimed.

"But it didn't end dere fo' poor Mercedes," Pappy continued. "Her other daughter, Paula, was arrested for drugs. She is a nice girl an' she is my god-daughter. To bail her was di most I could do for her an' Mercedes, an' so I did."

"You seem to be makin' the bailing of offenders a vocation or a life' work," he remarked.

"Well, come to t'ink of it. Life is a one way road, isn't it? Dere is no turnin' back an' is no real satisfaction unless you relatin' to somebody, anybody for dat matter, in a kind an' useful way. An' don't do it because you hope to be rewarded in some place or di oddah called heaven. Jus' do it, because somebody need your help as much as you need anodder person's 'elp for yourself. We all need 'elp at some time or di oddah! Life is subtler dan a slick extortioner, a wily illusionist or a wanton whore! Life doesn't really love you, although you love life. Life will serve you for a short time — three score years an' ten dey say an' if you're lucky, maybe little more by reason of strengt'-if you're strong enough and if circumstances are in your favour to bend life to your will as you want it. But life will destroy you, as soon as life gets a chance to do so. Life is always devisin' or inventin' horrible ways to get rid of you, and dat t'ing call' life eventually succeeds. You can't win. But I am not afraid of life. Life excites me. I tell Raymond, every time I see him, not to be fooled by life, but de bwoy won't listen to me. I hope he will listen to you before you go back to Mother Country."

"You could make a good preacher, Pappy," he bantered. "You possess a convincingly pious mind. But on a serious note, what you just said is what I regard as the philosophical essence of life. I will speak to Raymond, I promise."

"Dat is how I see life," Pappy replied. "Not like your brother George. He wanted everyt'ing in life an' he wanted it fast. In di long run, see what 'appen to him? He lost everyt'ing! Paula was caught by Police wit' four oddah women an' charged wid obtainin' an' dealin' in cocaine. Accordin' to what Mercedes herself told me, Paula went to live wid a man without tellin' her anyt'ing. A friend of Paula gave Mercedes di address. When she went to the gate of an old house on Hanover Street, a man guardin' di gate, denied that anybody by de name of Paula Francis was livin' dere.

"Mercedes pushed past di man, shoutin' 'Paula weh you deh? Mi want mi daughter!' She felt a blow to her back, den di man who was at di gate, grab her an' t'row her out on di street. A man by the

name of Tony Brown came out on di sidewalk and threaten' her dat
if she ever return, he would kill her. Dat was di man Paula was livin'
wid!"

"Threatened to kill his mother-in-law, so to speak," he exclaimed,
"if she ever dare to visit her daughter! Rather shocking and unbelievable, ain'it?"

"Unbelievable as it may seem to you," Pappy sadly remarked, "
It did happen! Mercedes is a day-helper at one of those fabulous
houses in Cherry Gardens. She watch di decrepit house on Hanover
Street, at nights, wid' di hope of glimpsin' her daughter comin' out
o' Tony Brown's gate. Paula did not appear.

"One evenin' she saw Tony Brown standin' on di sidewalk, at
his gate. She held on to him an' shouted an scream' dat she wanted
see Paula. A small crowd gathered in a short time an' she shouted
dat if Paula did not come out to see her, she would go to the Police.
Tony Brown told the crowd dat Mercedes was a mad woman. He
incited dem to drive her from de street. Whores, pimps an' touts,
drugheads with sticks an' broken bricks, joined by scavenger dogs,
drove Mercedes up Hanover Street an' along East Queen Street till
a policeman turned dem back. The policeman listen' to her story
an' told her to report it at Central the followin' day. Poor Mercedes
could not afford to miss a day's work; she went to Central and
reported the matter. Late dat evenin', a beaten-up an' unconscious
Paula was dragged from a car an' t'rown at Mercedes' gate.
Mercedes was glad to get back her. She took Paula to the university hospital where she was detoxicated, but to no avail, for Paula
went back to Tony Brown in a couple of weeks. And then di Police
raided, as dey promised to do. Five half-nude women, includin'
Paula and a man was caught. Tony Brown either was not there that
night or he slipped away from di Police. To cut a long story short,
Paula was gunned down, like her father, on the street, the very day
I bailed her. Mercedes has since then join' di mad people on di
street."

"Well, it was very kind of you to bail her daughter. It's a pity
you went to so much trouble only to get her killed," he remarked.
"A brilliant idea came to me while you were gone. Do you remem-

ber that Chew promised us a sea cruise in the Harbour and along the southcoast. How about taking him up on it?"

"Me, sah?" shouted Pappy, "Water don't ketch me higher dan mi ankle when I go dere!"

"But you're not going into the water, Pappy? We are going into a boat. It is safer than church!" he protested.

"I know some church dat are less dangerous, an' I don't go to any o' dem, much less di sea!" Pappy grumbled. "Not over my dead body! You couldn't get me on a ship again, after I sail' on di S.S. lrpinia to Mother Country, an' you want me to risk my life in a little boat. Suppose a big shark decide to jump in di boat or bite out piece o' it? What goin' to appen' to all like me who can't swim? No, sah, leave me out of it!"

"We would be insulting Chew if we ignore his hospitable and friendly offer. Chew and I have been friends from childhood. If you turn down his offer, I couldn't look him in the face again. I don't think we will be welcome at his place again and you wouldn't have a second chance to outwit that tricky ice-dispenser."

"I'll be damned if I put my foot into a little boat!" Pappy swore. "An' dat is final!"

"OK, Pappy," he said. "I will go alone and leave you behind. I have never seen you as a coward."

"Me a coward? Take dat back an' shove it!" Pappy angrily shouted. "I am a cautious man, never been a coward in my life! Only a fool endanger himself when he don't 'ave to put himself in danger."

"I have never heard anyone say you're not a man to your word. You promised to consider Chew's invitation."

"Consider? Dat doesn't mean dat I accept. You takin' me for a fool?"

"No, a coward," he teased.

"No man ever call me a coward, yet!" Pappy furiously contended. "Since you come home, you 'ave been callin' me names. You call me a cynic, now you're callin' me a coward! What you plannin' to call me next?"

"I have not been calling you names, Pappy. I respect you too much to do that," he replied. "But if you don't go with me, I am going to think that you're a poor sport."

"I want no further argument with you on this matter. I simply not goin'!" Pappy said. "Item closed! New business!"

"OK! Item closed. I will call Chew and arrange for Sunday if it is convenient for him."

Chew was charmed and excited when he called. Chew said that he would be delighted to take them on the promised cruise on Sunday. He was also disappointed to hear that Pappy demurred. Pappy listened uninterestedly when he told him that Chew happily agreed to take him on the cruise on Sunday and that Chew was disappointed that Pappy was refusing to go. He took the car keys and told Pappy that he was going to the hotel to attend to his correspondence and other business. From the closet in his room, he took down his favourite hunting jacket. A present from a Russian agent, bought in St. Petersburg where he had worked on a diplomatic case, this jacket, blue, soft and silky, to the touch, was made from chamois leather from the Caucasus. It was heavily padded and had a large detachable fur collar so that it was cool in summer and warm in winter. He had fitted a spring-holster close to the left armpit in such a way that its bulge was not discernible on the outside.

He had practised more than a hundred times and regularly to unzip this jacket with his left or right hand and pull his gun with whichever hand, firing in a single fluid and deadly accurate movement, faster than the human eye, but had never had the opportunity to put his extraordinary skill to the test. He walked to the Datsun with the hunting jacket slung over his shoulder. When he parked the Datsun, he pulled on the jacket, went to the reception desk, asked if there was any correspondence or message and collected his room key. He upturned the divan bed, removed the Luger and shoved it into the spring holster inside his jacket. He gave the slight bulge a friendly pat, viewed himself in the mirror, and straightened the jacket. When he arrived at his grandfather's house, he re-hung the hunting jacket in the clothes closet.

Chew arrived punctually at ten o'clock. He had already donned his trunks under his slacks, and instead of a shirt, he had pulled on and zipped up his hunting jacket with Needham's Luger in it. He felt weak in his knees with surprise when Pappy rose from before the television. "Da's Chew blowin' outside, come, let's go!" Pappy said.

"You really coming, Pappy?" he asked in disbelief

"Well, I can't t'ink of anyt'ing to do today. So I say to myself, go drown yuhself!"

Chew admired his hunting jacket and when he explained that he bought it in Russia, Chew was impressed and expressed his desire to acquire one. He promised to inquire if they were available in the sportshops in London. Chew was a superb driver and within a short time they arrived at the cove in Hunt's Bay where the Sea Bird was berthed. He and Pappy were introduced to Buzzer who was captain and crew, all in one. Buzzer was a lean and slanky six-footer with a sly and unpleasant twist to his mouth. His eyes were mere slits in his Mongoloid face. His head seemed too heavy and he supported it by resting it on his collarbone. He acknowledged their presence with a mere grunt.

Pluto seemed to he a good sailor. He exuberantly leapt aboard with a short and deep "ruff-ruff!" Pappy refused to go aboard without a life jacket. Chew laughed, picked up an orange coloured jacket from the rail and assisted him into it, showing him how to pull the inflation ring, if an emergency should occur.

"You won't need this aboard the Sea Bird," Chew explained. "But if it makes you feel safer, the captain and the crew have no objections. You can have an inflatable raft as well. We can inflate it for you and tow you in it, if you prefer that to coming aboard. You can even swim in that life jacket from here to Cuba, sharks excepted, of course." Pappy eventually, without further persuasion and reassurances decided to clamber aboard the Sea Bird. Once aboard, he took off the hunting jacket and carefully folding it, put it in a secure place on the deck.

Buzzer skillfully guided the boat at low speed out of Hunt's Bay into the Harbour.

They were comfortably seated on the tiny deck.

"Here are some anti-seasick tablets," Chew said. "If you feel bad at any time, chew one and swallow it."

"Pappy may need it, but I am the proverbial old man of the sea, son of Neptune himself," he said. "You have a beautiful boat here, Chew."

"Thank you," Chew proudly replied. "So you know about boats!"

"I can handle one if I have to," he replied. "So, this is Kingston Harbour!"

"Yes," Chew replied, "But it is no longer the harbour I used to know. As you know, it is one of the few natural harbours of the world."

"Oh yeah?" he remarked, passing his eyes over the expansive horseshoe shape of the harbour, its deep blue waers and the purple heads of the distant mountain ranges.

"It is no longer the Harbour," Chew said sadly. "It is now a monstrous cesspool."

"What do you mean?" he asked.

"What I mean is that industrial, commercial and domestic waste is killing the Harbour," Chew shouted against the roar of the wind and the loud swish of water passing under the Sea Bird's keel. "At least thirty-six sewage plants empty untreated effluvia into the Harbour. About fifty percent of the sewage of Jamaica is dumped here. I am told that they dump over seven million gallons of untreated water per day. There is also industrial waste from several factories."

"I am not goin' to eat any more sea-fish!" Pappy swore. "An' of course, I don't swim. You jus' make sure I don't fall in dat water! As soon as I get back on dry land, no man nor woman will ever get me near di sea again!" Pappy's voice was vehemently high.

Chew pointed to the giant Causeway arching its back across Hunt's Bay to join Portmore, Edgewater, Independence City, Waterford and Bridgeport. "See that causeway?" Chew said. "It adds to the pollution."

"How does it do that?" he asked

"Well, it closes off Hunt's Bay from the sea and is causing massive silting which reduces the circulation of the water. The Mangrove swamps of Portmore were once the largest breeding ground for crabs."

He said that he did not know. Pappy said that he had heard something to that effect.

"Well," said Chew, "the crabs have died out. There is the Forum Hotel, what is left of it."

"That's an imposing building, but it appears to be abandoned," he said.

"That is an abominable waste!" Chew said sadly.

"All those lovely cottages gone to the dogs," Pappy said.

"Yes," said Chew, "there were dozens of them, some occupied by squatters, others their doors and windows, fixtures furniture stolen."

"Horrible waste!" Pappy shouted in disgust into the wind, and for his pains, got a mouthful of sea spray that choked him.

"I used to fish in Dawkin's Pond," Chew said. "But I don't go there anymore, for the canals spew filth from Braeton into it. The pollution is so great that shell-fish has disappeared."

"A critical situation," he commented.

"It is crucial!" Pappy emphasized, shouting above the whistle of the wind and coughing, once again.

Chew pointed to the other side of the Harbour as they drew away from Port Point.

"Over there is Port Royal," Chew said. "There are pipes spewing filth from Port Royal into the sea. You can see and smell it from here. I have seen it with my own eyes, septic pit cleaners drive their trucks down to the sea and run their hoses into the water. I no longer fish at Morgan's Cove because of the sight and smell of refuse floating in the water. At Gunboat Beach, according to the experts, six thousand tons of solid waste is washed up by the sea per year."

"I don't believe it!" Pappy exclaimed. "Six hundred tons, maybe, but not six thousand tons!"

"I wish it were six hundred tons!" Chew replied. "We would still be doing badly! Believe it or not, it is likely to be as much as six thousand tons. Better see for yourself."

"Do you t'ink dat we settin' di stage for a major epidemic?" Pappy asked.

"It is a threat not be ignored," Chew replied.

"Most people don't seem to be aware of what is happening near to them. They need to be environmentally conscious," he suggested.

"I agree," Chew replied, "Kingston is such a wonderful city. I am an environmentalist and the lack of official measures against air pollution in the city is really giving me the creeps."

"You're an environmentalist! You don't say!" Pappy exclaimed. "What dem do?"

"Yes, I am an environmentalist," Chew replied. "We advocate better care of our environment, proper disposal of waste and conservation of our natural resources such forests, rivers, sea and wildlife. I went to Palisadoes recently and despite the efforts of voluntary groups to keep the area clean of refuse and debris, what I saw appalled me. There was garbage everywhere. Old motorcars, rustin' car pails, construction waste, coconut husks, plastic bottles, other non-biodegradable stuff, you name it."

"I grieve over what is 'appenin'. It really hurts. Our people are slowly, but surely destroyin' demselves. We're self-destructin'!" Pappy mournfully remarked.

"All is not lost," Chew remarked. "Oh look! There are the Conference Centre and the Bank of Jamaica," Chew said. He ordered Buzzer to swing the bow of the Sea Bird around and to cut the engines, so that he could point out some landmarks to his guests. "There is the Norman Manley International Airport," Chew said, pointing towards the distant Palisadoes peninsula. "Did you know that a Concord once landed there? It created a lot of excitement throughout the Caribbean, at the time."

"Yeah, I recall," he replied, "It was in the London papers and on the BBC. It was the world's largest and fastest passenger plane."

'The radio stations, the Stock Exchange, the University that a talk show host says is an 'intellectual ghetto', the University of Technology, the House of Parliament, Kings House, Hope Gardens are all located in Kingston." Chew explained.

"It is a thriving city," said he, "and as I said before, a rather beautiful city too."

"Kingston is like a pretty woman with a bad leg ulcer which is not receivin' any drastic treatment to get well," Pappy said. "Look on what 'appenin' in Western Kingston?"

"Most cities have areas of depressed living on their fringes, Pappy. It seems to be a natural thing," he explained.

"That may be true," Pappy protested, "but I think dat in Kingston it is de worst!

"I wouldn't swear to that. You haven't been to Bangkok where six million people live in and around a single city, nor Calcutta with a population of four and a half million people, nor to Johannesburg, population approximately three million, nor Soweto with another three million, Nairobi with one and a quarter million people. I have been to these places and to a few overcrowded cities in other parts of the world. Kingston in and around is occupied by a little over half a million people. Not too bad at all, comparatively speaking."

Chew was greatly impressed. "It appears as if you have been everywhere, Bat!" he exclaimed.

"Yeah," he replied. "I have been to a couple of places, because of my job. Special assignment. I spent three months in Ankara working as a shop clerk in a Turkish bazaar while I spied on the proprietor's brother, to discover what he was doing with the large quantities of rifles and small arms he was obtaining from a gun factory in Argentina."

"Did you find out?" Chew asked.

"Yeah, I did. He was selling them to desert men at a huge profit. I spent another month in Ankara, this time as a eunuch in a rich Turk's harem while investigating what happened to a young English journalist alleged to have been abducted from a street of Istanbul by his servants."

"Did you find this journalist?" Chew asked.

"No, I found out nothing about her, but I learnt how to wrap and keep a turban in place around my head, as well as to bow and prostrate without tripping over my gown."

"Did you lose your balls?" Pappy coyly asked.

"No," he replied. "Why?"

"Dey cut out di balls of eunuchs," Pappy said.

"I was only disguised as a eunuch, Pappy, I wasn't a real one. An' nowadays, the eunuchs in modern harems are allowed to retain their balls, since they are not slaves."

"How about it Mr. Chew?" Pappy mischievously asked. "I learn dat priests have to be castrated to become celibate."

"That does not happen in the Church as far as I know, but with some orders of Buddhist priests." Chew explained. "Bat, you've been getting around, indeed!"

"Bats do fly around don't they? Cricket bats, vampire bats, rat bats and butterflies," Pappy remarked.

"He looks more like a panther to me," Chew said, laughing into the wind, as he ordered Buzzer to head out to sea. "Bat, are you a tiger or a panther?" Chew asked, looking intently at him.

"Maybe a cross between the two," he suggested.

"I still think dat Kingston is di wors' city." Pappy contended. We have too many gunmen."

"Gentlemen," Chew called out above a fresh gust of frolicsome wind that was fluttering about their faces and ears, "After such a long and enlightening talk, we ought to be hungry. How about lunch?"

"Yes," Pappy jovially shouted. "Let's have lunch before di sea-sickness start. I am so thirsty and hungry. I believe I will soon get it!"

Chew explained that hunger and thirst do not cause seasick-ness, it was caused by the motion of the boat. "So far, everybody seems to be doing well as far as seasickness is concerned. And of course, we have those anti-seasick tablets to chew on," Chew re-assured Pappy.

"Mr. Chew, I t'ink I prefer to chew some lunch dan to chew on pill," said Pappy who joined by the others, laughed at his own attempt at punning.

Chew climbed down into the tiny cabin and returned with a huge lunch hamper and an igloo. Pluto woke up and drew near with a "wuf-wuf!" erect ears and brisk wagging of bushy tail to get his share.

"Buzzer, you hungry?" Chew shouted

"Z i- zi - ye -ye

Yes! Buzzer answered

That was how Buzzer got his name, he surmised.

Chew handed a lunch box and a cold beer to him. "Pass these to Buzzer for me," he said. When he returned to the deck, Chew handed him another lunch box and a beer, as well.

"Pappy, Raymond and I were in Negril, yesterday," he said.

"Really It's a nice place," Chew remarked.

"Yeah, a very nice place," he said, in agreement. "My first visit."

"Did Raymond tell you that I have a villa there?" Chew asked.

"No, Ray did not," he replied.

"He probably forgot to mention it to you," Chew said. "It's occupied, all the time. Tourists."

"Do you know a Mr. Chow that has a beach cottage in Negril?" he queried of Chew.

"No," said Chew, "but I swear I have heard of him. Why do you ask?"

"He lives somewhere in Kingston and also owns a beach cottage in Negril. He also seems to be a big time gambler. We were told, that he operates peaka-pow and drop-pan in Kingston, as well as in Negril."

"Gambling is big business in this country," Chew remarked.

"Do you gamble, Fr. Chew?" he teased.

Chew smiled mysteriously. "I play a little peaka-pow and mahjong with friends for the fun of it. That shouldn't be called gambling."

"You're a man of the world, no longer a priest. I see nothing wrong wit' a sociable an' moderate bit of gamblin' among friends," Pappy declared.

"I was never a priest, Mr. Carter," Chew reminded, with a sad smile. "I gave up before taking the vows, because of circumstances with which you are familiar. I am rather a social animal than a man of the world."

"Oh, yeah! Pardon my error," Pappy apologized. But man of

di world an' social animal seems di same t'ing to me. I see no difference."

"Don't take Pappy too seriously, Chew," he intervened. "Pappy likes to gripe. Pappy and I are two-bit gamblers. We both hate to lose. Well, what's happening on the local scene?"

"We have practically all the works here, illegal sloth machine, lotto, horse-racing. It appears that drop-pan has been made legal. Surely, peaka-pow is next. We have been hinting at casino in a big way, to attract big-time tourists."

"Sooner or later, we are goin' to 'ave casino. No doubt about dat! We have to attract' tourists. We'ave di hotels an' drugs in place already. I even believe dat a little money-launderin' goin' on. Here come' Las Vegas Number Two, like how we 'ave Hedonism Number Two. Who is goin' to stop dem when di time comes?" Pappy grimly asserted.

"If they bring in casino gambling," Chew commented, "more tourists will come. More drugs and related crimes will come too. I doubt that we will be able to contain the many evils that accompany casino gambling. The times are like a flood, these days. It is taking us along with it. We cannot be left behind. There is very little we can do to slow down or turn around the times. We can't even make decisions about our own affairs in our own country, without some interference from outside."

"According to Bob Marley, we have to fight," Pappy announced.

"Call out the army," he shouted into the wind. An angry roar like great guns arose out of the sea and the deck of the Sea Bird was drenched with spray.

"Where are the generals?" he humorously shouted, and wind and salted spray filled his mouth and caused him to cough, like Pappy did.

"See dere now," Pappy in fright cried out, "di boat neatly went under di sea an' a shark could 'ave jump' into di boat! We better turn back an' land di boat!" He assisted Chew to reassure Pappy that they were safe.

When his grandfather regained his composure, he said to him, "Pappy, we have to float on the tide of human affairs."

"Oh, yeah," Pappy replied, throwing up his hands in a gesture of alarm, disgust and resignation. "What about me who don't know how to swim? Ah gwine drown!"

Sensing that Pappy was still upset, he felt sorry for him, and threw his powerful arms around the old man's shoulders. "Cheer up, Pappy," he said. "It isn't the end of the world. You and I may yet get a chance to turn it around. It's all in the game!"

"Or upside down!" Pappy humorously declared.

"Pappy, have another Heineken," Chew said.

"Big gamblin' now," argued Pappy, pausing to drink his beer, "I cannot see it as you two are seeing it. I see too many dangers in these get-rich quick-scams."

"Casino," I think will give this country a big lift," he suggested, eager to continue the discussion. "I have been to Las Vegas, Atlanta City, Aruba, Monte Carlo, Columbia, Curacao, The Bahamas, Dominican Republic, Atabasca and Acapulco-quite a few cities where casino is legal, and where tourism is flourishing and the economy is very strong. Casino is a multi-million industry employing thousands of people. Casino gambling would create jobs and decrease unemployment. It would increase foreign exchange and help to reduce the national debt. It would improve the standard of living for many, and attract foreign investors. The government ought to think on the great earnings and other advantages to be gained. It ought to see casino gambling as a means of battling with competitive marketing with other countries in tourism and other industries. I am in favour of it. There is a great price to pay, yes. But we pay for everything, don't we! Is there anything free?"

"Not even Salvation!" Pappy quipped. "You 'ave to pay di pipers an' you can't even call di tune! Dey play what dey feel like playin' an' expec' you to dance! I t'ink dat di government actin' correctly by lookin' at di proposals cautiously. I seh , 'No Casino'!"

"You can't have a greater evil than poverty. Poverty, not money, is the root of many evils," Chew declared. "We have to face reality and do whatever is expedient to alleviate the curse of poverty. Casino can help to overcome poverty."

"Sometimes de cure is worse dan de disease," Pappy grumbled. "Ever hear about de doctor who cure de disease by killin' de patient?

Chew was smiling blandly and listening attentively to Pappy, then he glanced at his Omega. "I hope that you have enjoyed this little ride in the Sea Bird, Pappy. I am sorry the time has run out so fast. We have to go now. I have an appointment."

"Thanks a lot Mr. Chew," Pappy replied. "I was about to move for de adjournment, but you took de wind out of my sail. This 'as been de most frigtenin' day of my life, but I 'ave enjoyed it. We better turn 'round de boat now and head fo' de shore, before de sea come an' wash us away. A storm might spring up!"

"Thanks a lot, Chew," he said. "I enjoyed the cruise immensely. The Sea Bird is a great boat and Buzzer handles her superbly."

"We must do it again," Chew graciously replied.

"Oh! Where is the bathroom?" he asked.

Chew pointed to the short ladder that led from the deck to the tiny cabin. Taking up his hunting jacket, he climbed down the ladder and entered the cabin. Fastening the door, he looked around for a place to hide the Luger. He had planned to drop it overboard unnoticed, but did not get the opportunity to do so. He found a narrow space between the cabin roof and a cupboard decorated with a red cross on the door. Satisfied that no one could discover it unless there was cause to remove the cupboard, he put on his jacket, removed the gun from the holster, wiped it with a rag and tucked it into the aperture. Zipping up his jacket he returned to the deck.

"You're dressed already!" Chew observed.

"It's getting a bit chilly," he replied.

After Chew bade them goodbye at their gate and drove off, Pappy said, "We have had a jolly good day."

"Yeah," he teased, "We didn't see a single hungry belly shark in the Harbour.

"Yeah!" Pappy jovially retorted, "Dey must have heard that I was comin' to visit today."

"Ah, ah!" he laughed. "Are you suggesting that you scared the poor little bastards? That wasn't my impression when a couple spoonfuls of spray came visiting on deck and nearly drowned us. Remember?"

"To tell you di trut', I saw my Maker, when di sea cover up di little boat we was in," Pappy unashamedly admitted. "It was dat time I thought di sharks was comin' for us!"

"I tell you what, Pappy, after that lunch we had aboard the Sea Bird, I am still feeling a bit peckish," he casually confessed.

"Me too," Pappy replied. "Never go to bed hungry, say I. It would be a national disgrace if a doctor performin' de autopsy should report dat you died in de night from starvation."

"But why would it be national disgrace?" he asked.

"It would be a sign dat the nation not takin' good care of its sick, lame, mad, old an' lazy citizens." Pappy replied, with a poker-face. "But di longer we stand here talkin', di hungrier we gettin'. Jamaican people believe dat you will get gas in you stomach, if you talk too much 'pon hungry belly. You will get colic, if you paint on empty stomach. Corn an' peas won't bear an' yam will grow hollow, if you plant dem on hungry belly. Don't take what ol' time people believe as joke!"

"Thanks for the advice," he replied.

"Well," said Pappy. "I believe dat a roas' breadfruit an' some ackee an' saltfish would do us well for supper."

"That sounds like supper for a king!" he exclaimed.

"Well, some paupers like me, who have to eat breadfruit an ackee for supper don't appreciate dat dey rich," Pappy jovially declared. "Dey must go to places like Sri Lanka, Bangladesh an' Afghanistan an' some places in Africa an' in Asia where di people eat locus' and cockroach."

"How about a dish of dog, cat or frog? In some countries these are considered delicacies," he remarked.

Pappy grimaced at the thought. "Don't spoil my appetite," he jovially shouted. "Man, four or six slices o' breadfruit an' ackee an' saltfish or Coconut Run-down wit' salt' mackerel floatin' in it, dere is nuttin' better dan dat!"

"The very thought of it makes my mouth water," he bantered.

"What?" Pappy exclaimed in mocked amazement. "Cats an'

dogs? Rats an' frogs! Not me!"

"Oh no, I mean roas' breadfruit for supper!" he replied.

"Ok, you go inside an' relax. I am goin' out a street to buy a big breadfruit an' some ackee. I 'ave fish in di fridge an' an open tin of chocolate."

The entire house, from rooms to hall, soon smelt of the breadfruit being roasted on the gas-stove, and of the saltflsh being boiled. He relaxed before the television, while Pappy was busy in the kitchen, but he wasn't paying attention to anything in particular.

Conversation over supper was brief and scrappy, since it seemed that both men were succumbing to the enervating and soporific effects of the cruise. "As soon as I finish eatin' an' wash di dishes an clean up di place, I goin' take a shower an' go to my bed," Pappy announced.

"This supper is joy unspeakable," he said.

"Thank you," Pappy replied. "Did you notice how Chew was uncomfortable when yuh ask' about Chow? What you t'ink cause' him to be upset?" asked Pappy. "Do you t'ink he knows somet'ing he doesn't want us to know?"

"Yeah, I noticed it myself or a number of things for that matter," he replied. "But you said that you cannot keep your eyes open, I suggest we discuss Chew tomorrow when we will have rested."

Deserted by Pappy, he sat before the television, mulling over the day's proceedings. It was an enjoyable day. The sea was calm, except for an occasional gust of wind that caused the boat to roll a bit. Pappy had gradually overcome his fears and the temperamental Pluto had sleepily kept to himself until lunch time. The discourse was animated, the beer was kept cool and the lunch of jerked chicken, plain rice and vegetables was superb. Everything was fine, except for a passing moment when he asked Chew if he knew Chow. Chew swiftly regained his suave and ingratiating stance of the rich and perfect host. He wondered about Chew's abrupt and urgent excuse for termination the cruise. It was clumsy, as well as suspect. But his mind was yielding no answers to the many questions he was asking himself. His speculations and lack of deductions were a counter-current taking a swimmer further and dangerously away from the shore. He concluded, with utter dissatisfaction, that since no light was coming out of the darkness to show him the way, he'd better follow Pappy's example, shower and go to bed.

"I am a sucker, Brother Burnel George Carter," he shouted above the hiss and vigorous splatter of the shower, "to get myself into a pickle with your messy affair. And Carter, I must tell you that you've left me in a mess I ought to pack up and hot-foot it for Mother Country, as Pappy would say. But once I pick up a trail, I can't leave off until I come to the end of it. It's a damnable offence of mine! You left no telephone number nor forwarding address. I know nothing about your business. I haven't a clue to go by. Just blew up yourself like that?

"You expect me to believe that, eh, Burnel George Carter? By George, I won't! For it ain't like you to do a stupid thing like blowing up yourself! You love life too much do a silly thing like that. You got to tell me something! Anything, that it wasn't like that! Ah, Man, you're all messed up! Where are your buses and cars? Your bank account? Your documents? You didn't have any? You giving me a runaround! Now you have me barking up the wrong tree, ol' fellah, when I begin to put my old schoolmate under the microscope. Throw a little light on the subject, Ol' Boy! Talk to me."

Emerging from the shower, his laughter was almost maniacal. "Ah me!" he said aloud. "Talking to the living is difficult enough, talking to the dead is indulging oneself *faute de mieux,* and an absolutely hopeless exercise. The dead never seem to want to communicate with the living. If Burnel George Carter was around, he would ask what kind of mumbo-jumbo was that - talking to the dead." But he shouted from behind the towel with which he was drying his face and head, "I could use any kind of mumbo-jumbo just now to prove that Chew is not involved."

The *piece de resistance!* The term flickered and flashed in his mind. Detectives are often trained to look at the obscure and remote for clues in their cases, and reconstruct the crime moving the pieces like pawns in a game of chess. Secret Service investigators are trained to do the opposite. Lord X, when briefing an agent for a special assignment impressed on that agent to look for what he called the *piece de resistance*. Lord X claims that the *piece de resistance* is as obvious as a sore thumb and smells just as bad. Lord X claims that the *piece de resistance* is always there begging to be noticed. It is ironic that the obvious can be so obvious that an agent could wander around it like a flea-ridden dog chasing its tail and missing it.

"Are you the obvious, Fr. Chew?" he mockingly asked, shrugging into an oriental robe of diamante blue, he had bought, with cap and slippers in Osaka where he was assigned to investigate an English professor's connection with the opium trade. His cover was blown, and he barely escaped, in time, a horrible death. "Fr. Chew, my hunch is telling me to keep an eye on you," he muttered. "You could be that sore thumb, the *piece de resistance,* too obvious to be missed. Are you the missing piece in this jigsaw puzzle, the joker in this poker game?"

"Piece de resistance!" were the last words that fell from his lips as he slipped into a deep sleep. It had been oscillating in his brain, while he lay awake, as if the words synchronized with the blips of the oscilloscopic second hand of his solar-electronic wristwatch.

Chapter 15

RAYMOND BITES THE DUST

*T*he multicolored neon lights of the Mangrove Club flashing intermittently from a thirty feet billboard could be seen for miles about the Portmore - Fort Henderson-Hellshire-Edgewater region. The night was pitch dark, so dark that the stars shone like bright pin-points from a barely discernible sky. The innumerable Portmore houses, the shop lights and street lights flickered and shimmered like yellow and white sequins on a black evening gown. "See di fu-fu-fu-fu-bu-bu-bu bwoy deh!" Buzzer hissed as he pointed out Raymond and Needham arriving at the club.

"Dem dey bwoy fi dead! So me say!" Scarface swore.

"No-no-no ki-ki-ki-kill dem. Bu-bu-bu-rrrruk dem rrrrrass," Buzzer ordered. Buzzer, Scarface and Bappis' had been watching and waiting in hiding for Raymond and Needham to show up at the club. When they arrived, Buzzer, after a great deal of angry hissing, managed to persuade his companions to wait a little longer.

Raymond swaggered inside the club and jacked himself up against one of the women who was sipping Ting at the bar. She was laughing and flirting with the guy on her left. Needham went to the lower end of the dancehall and unceremoniously dragged a young lady onto the floor contorting and grimacing to the music.

Raymond tapped the arm of the woman he had 'kotched' up against. "Hi, chile! You nuh long fi see me?" he greeted her. "What's cookin'?"

She continued flirting with the man on her left as if she hadn't heard. "Hey Vi," he tapped her arm more insistently, "Yuh nuh hear man ha' talk to yuh?"

"Cool!" she said to the man on her left. "Nutten naw gwaan Rayman," she replied to the man on her right. "Mi deh yah same way!"

Raymond pressed the small of his back more firmly into the edge of the counter and examined his Nike, shoved his hands deeper into the pocket of his jeans, while pretending to be viewing the small crowd in the hall. The glow of the psychedelic lights, the smell of perfumes, a pungent smell of ganja spliffs and the sweaty gyrating bodies swiftly began to soak into him with an erotic effect. "Vi, yuh nuh waan buy mi a beer?" he said.

"Mi nuh ha' no money, sah!" she replied. "Mi jus' did a tell Percy say t'ings thin! Nuh business no deh!"

"What you drinkin', Ray?" the man on her left asked.

"Heineken," Raymond replied.

The man ordered another Ting, a Red Stripe and a Heineken.

Buzzer said to Scarface, "Yu-yu-yu go-go-go hey-hey-heylp Pppppu-erchy gi-gi-gu-get dem out."

The young man who cleaned the club during the day and helped to wash dishes, glasses and pots and pans at night, crept up to Needham. "Missa Needham I want to talk to yuh, he shouted into Needham's ear. "It urgent!"

Needham followed the boy out of the crowd to the back end of the hall. "What is it?" he anxiously asked.

"Buzzer, deh bout!" the young man replied. "I see him was ha' talkin' to two men outside.

Needham looked around in alarm. Conscious of his gun hanging heavily in the waist of his pants, "Ha' weh him deh, Star?" he whispered to the youth, his eyes piercing and splitting the mass of light into small pieces.

"Mi nuh see him again," the young man answered, "but him deh 'bout!"

Needham wasn't feeling too good. He and Raymond had avoided Buzzer for two weeks, now. Buzzer was looking for them. He should have paid Buzzer his money.

That Buzzer did not make jokes passed through his mind. Needham felt for his gun and the hardness and closeness of it reassured him. "Make Buzzer go f—himself," he said to the young man who beat a hasty retreat. "After him nuh badder dan mi!" He could not, despite his bravado, control his guts knotting up with fear. He sidled over to where Raymond was socializing with Vi and Percy. "Man deh bout!" he said to Raymond. "We better ex' di spot! Leave eart'!"

"Vi, mi will see yuh. Ah right, Percy, see yuh anoddah time," Raymond said, fear and urgency creeping through his body.

"Alright, Raymond, will be seein' you soon!" Percy said in a friendly tone. Raymond and Needham had almost reached the door leading into the kitchen when Percy shoved a gun in Raymond's back. "Raise you' han' easy like," he growled. "Buzzer want see di two o' you." Needham also felt a gun jabbing viciously into the small of his back, and almost simultaneously, he was relieved of his gun. "Bwoy like unnu fi en' up in a handcart an' crocus bag," the man behind Needham growled, prodding him painfully with his weapon. "Move an' keep movin', Bwoy!"

Buzzer emerged out of the darkness, at the back of the kitchen. Raymond noticed that the customary bulge where Buzzer always carried his gun was missing, nor did he have a gun in his hand. His swift and stealthy mind began almost immediately to devise a ruse of escape, but his legs were trembling uncontrollably. He did not see the open-handed slap coming to him from Buzzer. It exploded against the side of his head and he fell to the ground. Percy savagely kicked him in his side and dragged him to his feet. "Di mo-mo-mo-ney! Ha' wu-wu-wu-weh it day?" Buzzer hissed.

"What yuh say?" Raymond squeaked.

"Buzzer seh where is di money you 'ave fi him?" Percy explained and doubled him over with a fist into his stomach. Raymond opened his mouth and spilled the beer Percy had bought him. He was too busily occupied to notice what was happening to Needham. Scarface's gun was ominously exploring Needham's nostril, under his jaw, behind his ear, below an eyeball, his chest, his crotch, as if searching for the most vulnerable spot in which to explode. "What mi fi do wit' him?" Scarface asked Buzzer.

"Fi-fi-finish wid d'-dis one firs'," Buzzer replied.

"Mi did gi-gi-gi' Needham di-di mo-mo-money fi gi' yuh, an' he l-l-lulos it." Raymond stammered and pleaded with Buzzer. He was desperately afraid with Percy's gun stroking one ear. The other was badly hurting where Buzzer had applied his open-handed blow, and he dared not lift his hand to scratch it.

"Give we a chance," Needham screamed as the muzzle of Scarface's gun jabbed violently at a most sensitive spot. "Mi will bring di money tomorrow!" Needham screamed. He could stand it no longer. He broke free. Bullets whizzed about him as he took his foot in his hand and ran into the darkness. He tried to skirt the Mangrove swamp to his left, but fell head first into the foul smelling water. Mangrove roots and branches octopus-like clutched at his arms and legs as he tried to emerge from the ooze and to force himself farther away from his assailants, among the slippery tangle of root, leaves and stem. Clutching a sea-fig trunk, he dragged himself wet from the mud.

Even before he had regained his breath, he felt his body all over for gunshot wounds. Feeling none, he shouted between gasps of air "Jah, mi nuh dead!"

"Damn!" he shouted when he discovered that he had lost a foot of his expensive Nike sneakers, while the other foot was filled with mud and water. He discarded the wet and mudded shoe, as well as his socks. All around was silence, except for the savage and strident music seeping from the club and the sounds of myriads of nocturnal insects in the swamp. And soon, too soon, the mosquitoes discovered him. Luckily for him, they did not attack those parts of his body that were muddy and wet. He began to jabber between chattering teeth when the chilliness of the night and of the water penetrated his skin and his crotch began to itch terribly.

"Jus' wait till I pick up mi oddah gun," he kept shouting as he slowly crawled through the mangrove towards the dry land. "I gwine shoot out dem blouse an' skirt! Dey will see who can lick shot!"

⚜

When he appeared for breakfast in the morning after the Sea Bird cruise, he noticed that Pappy was agitated. He wasn't reading the paper nor was he watching television.

"Morning Pappy," he greeted. "How are you, this morning?"

"Morning," Pappy grumbled. "Why you get up so late?"

"Hey," he lightly exclaimed. "You're having seasickness the day after the event, Pappy? That should have happened when you were merrily sailing, yesterday."

"If it was seasickness, I don't think I would be feelin' as bad as I do now," Pappy replied. "I just don't like the way t'ings are turnin'. It smells and I couldn't sleep last night."

"What is bothering you?" he anxiously asked.

"I t'ink you should leave dis matter alone an' go back to Mother Country. Mr. Chew wouldn't like us to know dat he is mix' up in dis. If Chew is mix' up in it what are we goin' to do? George dead already. Make him rest. Don't bother dig up him bones." Pappy advised.

"Listen Pappy, I can't close the investigation. It is too late now. If only to clear Chew of suspicion, we have to continue. George has not only been murdered, but he has also been robbed by person or persons not known to us. They have not only robbed and murdered him, but they have methodically set out to wipe his very memory from the face of the earth. Who hated him so badly? I need to find out. I may have to go to New York to unravel this whole thing. Only that I can't go until I find even one little positive thing to work on. I haven't found that yet. In fact, I believe that the key to unlock this case is here, but I am not going the right way to discover it. Let's forget Chew and begin to look somewhere else."

"Like where?" Pappy asked.

"That I dont know yet," he admitted. "But don't worry yourself unnecessarily. When we reach the bridge, we will figure out how to cross it. At present, we are going nowhere. The pieces don't seem to fit. People close to us seem to know things they don't care for us to know."

"Right," said Pappy. "I hope dat Chew isn't involved."

"So do I," he replied, "for Chew's sake. We have been friends from school days. However, let the shit hit the fan wherever it will."

"Ugh!" Pappy groaned in disgust. "Leave dat out of it. We talk enough filth yesterday. Let's not talk anymore today. I did not sleep last night an' now I'm havin' a headache."

He felt that he owed Pappy an obligation to get him out of the mood he was in. "I can cure that headache of yours, Pappy," he tried to cajole him.

Pappy looked warily at him. "Forget it," he warned.

"I wasn't thinking of painkillers," he explained. "I was thinking of taking you to breakfast and then how about a game of dominoes? A six-love or two ought to banish that low feeling of yours and here we are sitting down moping and doing nothing."

"Well, I had breakfast already and left some for you," Pappy replied. "I couldn't wait on your pleasure. But dominoes will be alright. Remind me to take di newspaper for dat ol' coot."

He parked the Datsun near to the light post on which the drop-pan card was stuck. He crossed the street, with Pappy in tow, towards the men under the guango tree. He noticed at once that the dice-players were not squatting in the dirt but had gathered around the young man with the radio-cassette player.

"How did he get bail? Pappy asked Ferdie.

"Mmmh! Mi hear say a don bail him, sah!" Ferdie replied disapprovingly.

"Who? A which don dat?" Pappy asked.

"I dont know a t'ing!" Ferdie asserted. "As how mi buy it, ha' so mi sell you! Nobody tells me anything, and I don't ask any question. This present day generation! They don't tell you anything, and they don't ask you anything either, till something happens to them. You bring the paper?"

"I said I wasn't bringin' anymore paper, you little runt," Pappy declared good humouredly.

"Anytime you feel not to bring the paper, don't put your foot down here!" Ferdie bantered.

"See yah!" Pappy snarled. "Is you own dis place? Since when you can tell anybody what to do from what not to do?"

The men around the radio-cassette player, paused from their listening to enjoy the rough and tumble exchange between Pappy and Ferdie.

"Look on dis runt, eh! Tellin' me not to come back down here!" Pappy playfully ranted. "What a feisty ol' man!" Pappy was addressing the tiny crowd which broke out into more uproarious laughter.

"Mi seh," Ferdie repeated. "If you don't bring di paper, don't put you' foot down here!" He appealed to the small group of laughing men, "All o' you, tell him not to come back down here, without the paper!"

"He mus' be t'ink dat I am any paper boy fi him!" Pappy shouted. "Hear sar! Yes sar! Dat is what you want? You want a servant-boy fi fetch an' carry fi you! Don't use me. You hear?"

Pappy drew the newspaper from beneath his shirt and threw it at Ferdie, "You waspy, eh?" he teased. "You're like one a dem ol' puppy dawg!"

"If you t'ink you bad," Ferdie warned, "Take you'self down here wit'out the paper!"

"Go away! Scram!" Pappy shouted to the delight of the group, waving his hands above his head.

After this bit of drama between Pappy and Ferdie had ended, the group returned to listen to the radio. "What is happenin'? No dice nor domino, today?" Pappy called.

No one answered.

"What's de score?" Pappy asked, joining the group which made some space for him.

"Jesas, him out!" shouted Bert, springing high into the air with his radio-cassette player on his shoulder.

"Who out?" Pappy loudly asked.

"Lara," Bert replied. "He make' t'ree 'undrid and seventy-five runs!"

They all listened intently to the commentator. He watched with amusement the men shouting, dancing and hugging one another.

"We teachin' Mother Country to play their own game," Pappy loudly commented.

"Him better Sober's score," Bert stated.

"Yes, man, him better dan Sobers," some of the group chimed.

"What unnu talkin' 'bout?" Pappy shouted. "In 1958, right here at Sabina Park, Sobers set a records of t'ree 'undred an' sixty-five runs not out against Pakistan. I don't remember di exac' date, but it was a Saturday, an' Sobers was only twenty-one years old. Di cricket mash up! The crowd was so worked up that they took to the field mashin' up di game wit' fifty-five minutes of play to go. What unnu young people know 'bout cricket?"

The group became very vociferous each and everyone giving his own account of the innings in animated language and gestures, as if he were actually there at the match. "Go away! Hush up you' mout'," Bert shouted at the group. "Any a yuh know 'bout cricket? Lara better dan Sobers!"

"No!" protested the tall thin man. "Di radio jus' say Sobers make t'ree undrid an' sixty run in one day. A which Lara can do dat?"

The smallest man in the group, anxious to pour oil on troubled waters, claimed, "Dem good fi true." He was greeted with, "A fool, yuh fool? How dem fi good? Dat cyaan happen in cricket!"

Eventually, the group became divided into two factions. One insisting that Lara was better than Sobers, the other the converse.

"Sobers is a Jamaican, him mus' better!" one group declared. This brought a howl of protest from the other group. They claimed that where you came from had nothing to do with the debate. The groups rejoined and turned to Pappy (he had been neutrally listening and watching all along) for an opinion, thus putting him on the spot.

"If one man make more runs than the other in one Tes' match, don't dat man better dan di oddah man?" the tall, thin man asked.

"I don't see it dat way," Pappy replied. "Sobers was the bes' in his time. Lara is di bes' in his time. You should not compare dem.

Dey can't be compared."

"Wisdom!" shouted the small man. "But as how t'ings ha' go now, I feel seh Lara better dan Sobers, still."

"Well," said Pappy. "Let everybody hold on to their opinion. Don't quarrel nor fight over it. It is only a game."

"True wo'd, Pappy," said the tall, thin man. "Irie, but we nah quarrel nor fight. Is talk we jus' ha' talk."

"Well, don't make you' talk sound like quarrel an' fight!" Pappy admonished and counselled.

"Lara good fi true," said Bert, shifting his radio-cassette player to his other shoulder, "Him better dan Sobers."

"You ever see Sobers bat yet?" the small man truculently asked him.

"You did see how Lara lick di ball off Curtis Lewis?" Bert retorted. "Which Sobers could a lick ball like dat?"

"Kiss mi granny! Where yuh stay an' see dem play? You cyaan see dem 'pon you radio?" asked the tall, thin man.

"Unnu start di quarrel again?" Pappy shouted.

"No, Pappy," Bert shouted in reply. "Is only a friendly talk we ha' talk!"

"Friendly talk!" Pappy grumbled. "Till blood get hot and angry words an' blows begin fly!"

"No, Pappy, we not like dat!" the men chorused. "We are decent people."

"Mi nah mash fly," said one of the dice-players. "But if anybody mash mi corn…" He flicked open his ratchet knife and his eyes rolled in their sockets.

"See mi Gad deh!"

Some of the group laughed.

"Put up yuh mastic, Star," Bert urged him. "Mind Babylon see you!"

You jus' say yuh decent," the small man reminded the diceplayer.

He looked calmly on, recalling what Pappy said, that these men didn't fight and quarrel among themselves. The group suddenly calmed down and returned to listen intently to a sports comment on the radio. *"You have just seen or heard how a great cricketer perform,"* the sports commentator said.

"Same t'ing mi say? Di commentator jus' say dat Lara greater dan Sobers," the tall, thin man said

"Quiet Man," the burly man ordered. "Make mi hear it fo' myself!"

"Lara displayed a magnificent performance today..."

"See deh now!" said the tall, thin man looking at the knife-wielder. "Ha' so man fi profarm mek dem say yuh great."

"Not everybody can perform like Lara or Sobers," Pappy counselled. "But you can do good whether by word, deed or by example, so dat people will always say good t'ings about you. In dat case, it not important who greater dan who."

"Wisdom! Irie!" the tall, thin man shouted

Pappy looked at his grandson who was standing aside, bemused by the scene that was being played out before him. "Since nobody in di mood to play domino, today we may as well go home," he said.

On the way home, he asked, "Do you know what I find most striking?"

"No, what is it?" Pappy replied.

"Those men! Why do they have to make so much effort to keep away from one another' throat?"

"Deep seated anger, hard life an' frustration, I guess," Pappy replied. "It is there wit' dem all di time. It doesn't take much provocation for dem to erupt."

"Which of the two is better, Pappy, Lara or Sobers?" he mischievously asked.

" I told you already," Pappy replied, smiling broadly. "We're not goin' to quarrel over it, are we?"

"No I should think not!" he replied.

"Well, Sobers has a very impressive Test Cricket record. Lara has just arrived. He has a long way to go to prove dat he is not jus' a flash in his pants," Pappy explained.

"Why didn't you tell them that?" he asked.

"An' make dem believe I takin' sides? No, sir! I avoid trouble!

Which o' dem do you t'ink is better?"

It was his turn to grin. "I think Lara is better because…"

"Hold your horses! I don't want to hear your reasons for believin'. You're entitled to your opinion, besides, I am hungry," Pappy stated.

They were enjoying a bucket of Kentucky Fried Chicken before the television when it was announced: *At about 11.30 p.m. last night, a man identified as Raymond Carter was found behind The Mangrove Club, Port Henderson, suffering from gunshot wounds. He was taken by the Portmore Police to the Kingston Public Hospital where he was admitted in a critical condition. The Police had not up to news time discovered a motive for the shooting. The police is seeking to contact one Joseph Needham who who may assist them in their investigation. Carter and Needham were seen arriving together earlier at the Mangrove Club. Anyone knowing the whereabouts Needham is asked to contact the Police .*

Pappy's chicken leg fell to the floor, as he listened to the news, and then he screamed, "Raymond!"

"Let's get to the hospital!" he grimly said. He backed out the Datsun onto the road. Pappy was so distraught that he had to send him back to lock the front doors.

"I hope dat Raymond not mix' up in anyt'ing," Pappy moaned.

"I hope not," he said.

At the hospital, their footsteps sounded heavy and hollow as they walked to the Male Casualty Ward. They had a long wait of several hours before they were allowed to visit Raymond's bedside. "He is serious isn't he?" he asked a nurse.

"He spent the night in intensive care," she replied. "He is stable now, but it was touch and go during and after the operation."

"What operation?" Pappy asked.

"The doctor took two shots out of his belly and two out of his chest. This patient is a superman!"

Raymond started to moan and toss weakly. The nurse looked at the dossier at the foot of the bed, went away and returned with a hypodermic needle on a tiny silver tray. "Excuse me, gentlemen, time is up," she said.

"Four shots! My mother! Dey meant to kill him! Poor boy!" Pappy uttered and groaned as they retraced their steps along the corridor.

As they entered the Datsun, he said, "I hope that he will be conscious tomorrow, hopefully, in order to tell us what happened. There is nothing we can do until he is able to talk to us."

"It's a police case," Pappy remarked. "But de Police is now so saturated and overburden' wit' unsolved murders an' robbery dat deh might treat it as jus' another case of shootin' an' robbery. Do you t'ink the shootin' of poor Raymond has anyt'ing to do wit' George?"

"I am not ruling out that possibility," he replied. "Though I don't seem to be getting my fingers on to anything that makes sense. There ought to be a lead somewhere. Everything seems as dense as a jungle."

"Well, let's 'ope he is able to talk to us, tomorrow," Pappy said, as they reached his house. "It has been a long day. Too much excitement for di likes of me. Dis is not good fo' my pressure. I goin' to bed!"

꧁꧂

The following morning, they went early to the hospital. There was an unusual number of policemen around and he felt an uncanny feeling of excitement. "I wonder what is going on now, Pappy," he murmured.

Two porters wheeled a body completely wrapped in a bloody white sheet past them as they walked the corridor.

"Das goodbye for dat one ain'it?" Pappy irreverently whispered.

"Don't say that Pappy," he gently admonished.

As they crossed the ward, they noticed that Raymond's bed was vacant. He felt Pappy's heart thumping violently, as he caught him just in time from falling.

"My Gawd! My Gawd, he is not here!" Pappy said with a groan.

"Take it easy, Pappy," he murmured. "They probably have taken him back to intensive care or to have his wounds dressed." But even as he said that he noticed an orderly vigorously cleaning the blood from the floor.

A doctor was swiftly summoned by the matron to see to Pappy who had passed out.

"It jus' 'appen' dis mornin'," an' almost hysterical nurse panted. "A man come in here and slash' di patient t'roat, den stick di knife in him chest. Not one time, but again an' again like him didn't mean to stop, right in front o' mi an' everybody. Den di man, di patient blood all over him, jus' walk out quiet like him nuh do nutten! Him didn't even take out di knife. Him leave it stickin' up in a di man!"

"What the man looked like?" Bateman eagerly asked.

"To tell you di trut' I can't describe him. He is a tall brown man, but him look like any other man who visit hospital. I see too much o' dem durin' di day fi pick out anyone special. Di Police been askin' de same question. Are you police?"

He said that he wasn't. He was just interested, because the dead man was a relative of his.

"Sorry," she said. "I hope the Police ketch him! Maybe the Police can tell you whatever you want to know."

Pappy surprisingly and despite his shock, regained some composure before the doctor arrived. "Is it really possible right here in de hospital?" a dazed Pappy repeatedly asked.

"Yes," said a very calm nurse who had come to Pappy's assistance. "Dis is not the first time that it has happened in dis hospital."

"It is a vicious act!" Pappy cried.

"Sar!" cried the excited nurse, rolling big eyes in a charmingly fat face and lifting them up to the ceiling, her mouth agape in wonderment and horror. "He didn't even pull out di knife. He left it stickin' in di patient' chest! Di brute! Di animal!"

"He seems to be very good with a knife," he calmly murmured.

A stupefied Pappy and his stoical grandson, walked from the ward and sat in the Datsun for a little while, he silently listening to his grandfather's expression of grief.

"What do we do now?" Pappy eventually asked.

"We have to find Needham fast, before the Police get to him," he said.

"Who is dis Needham?" Pappy asked.

"Raymond's friend. We heard on the news this morning that the Police is looking for him."

"Well, let's go, if we 'ave to find dis Needham. You know where he live?" Pappy urged.

"I haven't the least clue," he replied.

"Den how yuh gwine find him if yuh don't know where he live?" Pappy shouted in desperation.

"Take it easy, Pappy," he said. "We shall play it by ear. I know him. We shall visit a dancehall or a couple of dancehalls!"

"Me, sah? Never been to a dance in my whole life!" Pappy objected. "If we find him, what are you goin' to ask him?"

"Let's find him first," he replied.

"I knew somet'ing bad was goin' to happen to dat bwoy," Pappy mournfully murmured. "I should 'ave kept a firmer hold on him."

He, detecting chagrin and self-reproach in Pappy's voice, tried to reassure him. "Come on Pappy," he said. "Don't blame yourself. Raymond chose the road he wanted to take, so did George. He was no fool. He must have weighed the odds. He has not chosen the best of bedfellows."

"What do you mean? Dat your brother was a homo?" Pappy dryly asked.

"No, no, I don't mean that!" he replied. "It is a manner of speaking. I mean that he fell into bad company, probably drugs and all."

"Well, seh what you mean," Pappy grumbled ungraciously.

Pappy must have become a stoic overnight. He had retired to bed very glum the night after Raymond's death, which was not abnormal for a man who some hours earlier had received the shocking news of his grandson's violent and unexpected death in an hospital ward. He was intently watching the tele, the following morning, greatly composed as if it had not happened. His only surviving grandson had insisted on preparing breakfast, and was busy in the kitchen.

"Bat," Pappy called to him, "Di tele jus' report' dat another domino game was shot up las' night. The gunmen escaped in a white Toyota motor car, leavin' two of the players dead. A dead man was also found in a drum on Woodpecker Avenue. When will this killin' business stop? Why can't the murderers an' those who are prone to killing people-psychopaths dem-free themselves from what Bob Marley called *mental slavery?* Bob Marley stood up an' sang out for freedom and peace."

"There is an interesting article in the paper, this morning, Pappy," he said. "Did you read it?"

"Naw," Pappy replied. "I am in no mood to read this morning. I can't concentrate. Perhaps later."

"Well, listen to this," he said, emerging from the kitchen to pick up the paper and to select the particular section: *According to Police statistics, there were 964 murders in 2002 of which only forty-three percent was solved. Of this total number of killings twenty-seven percent was domestic; fifteen percent was gang related murders; Robbery twelve percent; Reprisals thirty-two percent; Drug related murders three percent; Political and tribal murders one percent, and undetermined murders seven percent."*

"What? Revenge killing is a whoppin' thirty-two percent?" Pappy exclaimed.

"Yes," he replied noncommittally. "Revenge tops the list!"

"We are in deep trouble!" Pappy said with a groan. "We are in great trouble! There are only two of us left. George and Raymond are gone. Dey are probably better off than us where they gone. You have neither chick nor child! Maybe jus' as well. For what a cruel world to bring children into?"

"Now, Pappy, don't be so morbid. I intend to give you a litter of grandchildren, the finest set of kids to be found any part of this world.

"A litter of pigs! I have to see dat first before I believe! I didn' know you was a hog," Pappy gibed, as he took the paper.

"Correction, Pappy, I didn't say pigs I said kids," he replied with pretended solemnity. "Will your Lordship have his breakfast now?"

After breakfast, Pappy buried himself into the newspaper, getting increasingly upset with some of what he was reading. "Why can't the media suppress bad news, and let us 'ave one happy day per week?" Pappy complained, moaning in disgust. "Deh jus' feed us, day after day, on sensation. What you 'ave to say about di matter, Bat? Don't you think di public should protest what dem getting as news an' lock down the media?"

He realized that Pappy was just being facetious to uplift his spirits. "Well the media is the mirror of the soul of the nation. The media couldn't be seen as responsible or even credible, if their journalists and newsmen report only good news. We also have to remember that a newspaper is a business in a competitive field. It has to present a saleable product that the public will care to buy. In fact, the media makes more profits reporting on war rather than peace. What news upsetting you now?"

"*Last night,*" Pappy returned to read the paper aloud, "*some men were having a game of dominoes at a home in Park Place, Maxfield Avenue. Two gunmen jumped from a white Toyota and shot them. Two died on the spot. The Police said that the motive was unknown. The people said that one of the dead men was the brother of a man who had given evidence against another who was found guilty of murdering the brother of the other man who was killed. The relatives of the dead men are now swearing revenge, for they were saying that they know who were the murderers.* No one is safe nowadays, not even when you playing dominoes. Domino is now a dangerous game!" Pappy cried ruefully.

"Dominoes has always been a dangerous game, Pappy, especially when you are bent on revenge," he teased, hoping to cheer up Pappy. "But if some people know who killed them, why don't they inform the Police?"

"Inform! You ought to know by now that that *'inform'* is a bad word! Reprisal holds everybody to ransom. It holds you. It holds me. It holds everybody! Think of the number of people killed this year, because some people value life to be of no consequence, and it use' to be *an eye for an eye* in earlier days," he cajoled, "and *a tooth for a tooth,* now if one so much as mash anybody's toe by accident or touch a hair 'pon dem head, they're demandin' the whole hog, and they not givin' you time to say. Pardon. I'm sorry! I know a time when man quarrel with man, an' they mad to kill each oddah, but de' only threaten each other. Nowadays, when a man threaten you, report it to the Police, then run weh or go 'ome go plan you' funeral! Revenge leads to retaliation, and retaliation leads to more acts of revenge. Why must people kill another? It makes no sense to me. It's sheer madness!"

"You will never know, Pappy," he whispered to himself. "You can never know!

"My heart bleed," Pappy sadly remarked, "when I look at all dis picture, in di paper, of a poor old lady standin' outside her burnt out shack, with her two piece o' belongings, an' her five grandchildren. She told di cameraman dat gunmen kill di children's parents an' den return an' burn her 'ouse. Hear what she said to the newsman, *"Mi ha'fi leave now, doah mi no ha'no way fi go. Mi hear say dem diddah come fi bu'n mi 'ouse, but mi nuh did believe anybaddy could a cruel so fi leave mi an' di poor dead lef' granpickney dem out a door!"*

"Cruel, indeed, but no matter 'ow heartless dey may be, dey should still have respect for poor old people an' children," Pappy concluded.

"Women, children and the aged suffer most in a war," he concluded sardonically. "Men can only die once."

Chapter 16

TWO MORE BITE THE DUST

*I*t was dark outside, except for a solitary street light. They had no desire to dine, but to sit before the television, repeatedly discussing the tragic end of Raymond and reviewing their strategy to find Needham. "It will be like lookin' for a needle in a haystack, as dem seh in Mother Country," Pappy grumbled.

"If we only knew the joints where he and Raymond used to frequent, I believe finding him would be easy," he stated. "As it is, time is against us. The Police might get to him before us. Then they might arrest or detain him, thus making it almost impossible to talk with him. Time is running out."

They did not have to go looking for Needham. There was a faint and hurried rap on the door. "Missa Bat! Missa Bat," someone was softly calling.

"Who is it?" Pappy sharply asked.

"Is me Needham, Raymond' friend, sah! Is Missa Bat dere?"

"What do you want wit' Missa Bat?" Pappy asked.

"I want to talk to Missa Bat, bad, bad!" Needham replied. "Opin di door, please, sah!"

"That's him," he calmly declared. "I recognize his voice. He sounds scared and desperate." He went to the window, cautiously drew the curtain aside and verified by the street lamp that it was indeed Needham. "Let him in, Pappy."

Needham slipped past Pappy and stumbled into the room. "Dey lookin' for I to kill I," he cried in terror.

"Who lookin' for you?" he asked.

"Syndicate," Needham whimpered.

"Syndicate!" Pappy shouted. "Who is Syndicate?"

"Why is Syndicate looking for you?" he asked, without waiting for answers to the first question.

Needham slumped into a chair, and was trembling like a leaf. "Dey kill Ray," he replied. "Ray seh he don't want to work for Syndicate anymore. Somebody go an' tell Missa Chow."

"Missa Chow? Do you mean Chew?" he asked.

"Yeah, mos' people call him Missa Chow," Needham said.

"Why dey want to kill you?" Pappy asked.

"Because I an' Ray was bredrin an' I know who kill him," Needham replied.

"Who killed him?" Pappy asked.

"Buzzer!" Needham screamed hysterically. "Buzzer is a murdarah!"

"Ah, now I see!" he murmured. "I begin to understand! What sort of work were you and Raymond doing for Mr. Chew?"

"I don't work for Missa Chow. Ray work fi him." Needham answered.

"What sort of work?" he asked.

"Fishin'," Needham replied.

"Fishin' for drugs!" Pappy suggested.

"Yeah," said Needham. "Buzzer and Raymond, de go in di Sea Bird an' pick up di drugs from out di sea."

"From out di sea!" Pappy exclaimed. "Mi mother!"

"Dat ought to be easy," he replied. "Parachutes!"

"Dese drugs people stop at nutten," Pappy, grumbled. "Deh pack it all in mules, sausage an' Easter bun."

"Who are the people in Syndicate?" he asked.

"Missa Vinton, Missa Chow, a man dey call Diamond Toot, an' a woman in Miami, dey call Kersene Ile. Missa Vinton, he is the chief one. Me use' to work on Missa Vinton' bus as di 'ducta. When Babylon took Missa Vinton an' carry him go jail, Diamond Toot' t'ief everyt'ing Missa Vinton 'ave."

"I see!" he exclaimed. He looked at Pappy as if to say, I am thinking, I now know why George had to be killed. The *piece de resistance,* the sore thumb, at last!

"Tell us more," Pappy urged Needham.

"Missa Chow control' business in town. Diamond Toot an' Kersene Ile control business in Miami."

"What is Diamond Toot's real name?" he asked.

"I don't know," Needham replied.

"Do you know the real name of the woman you call Kersene Ile?"

Needham said that he didn't know her name either. He surmised that Needham, Raymond and Buzzer were minions, pawns in the game.

"You said that Buzzer killed Raymond. Why didn't you go to the Police?" he asked.

Needham was on the verge of hysteria again. "Babylon?" he screamed. "No, Boss!" he pleaded. "If I inform on dem, dey same one will call I infomer an' lock up I. Den ask I man to tell dem more, an' when I man cyaan tell dem anymore, dey beat I wit' a bag o' wet sand and shock I wit' electric wire to tell dem more."

"If dat is true, da's police brutality!" Pappy grumbled.

"Some Babylon don't like informahs, Boss," Needham explained. "Dey tell gunman dem a who inform on dem an' de gunman dem sen' dem bredrin go waste dem.'"

"Waste them?" he asked. "What do you mean?"

"He means," Pappy coldly explained, "to kill you. Dat is what waste you mean."

"Babylon wicked, Boss!" Needham exclaimed.

"Pappy, could that be true?" he asked.

"It's a popular belief dat di Police cannot be trusted with confidential information, I don't t'ink dere is any foundation for it. It was probably started by criminal elements to discredit the Police and make people afraid to give the Police information. I t'ink it is part of strategy of killin' or threatenin' to kill witnesses who could help the Police? Di police do 'ave provisions for secrecy of information and for the protection of witnesses. I doubt, as I said before, dat dere is any foundation for di belief dat di Police leak information to criminals, though in the best of families dere are black sheep. Dere are bad policemen and dere are good policemen. If dere is any truth in di allegation, I am sure the Commissioner an' di superior officers would not countenance it."

"I not tellin' Babylon nutten," Needham insisted. "I prefah dead firs'!"

"Alright, we won't go to the Police, " he promised, "so long you don't try to hide anything from us. As I understand from what you said, Syndicate is the name of a posse, isn't it? How are Chew and Diamond Toot' connected? Which of them is the don?"

"No, Boss, Dere is no posse. Some yout' try a t'ing, but Missa Chow tol' dem not to use dah name, Syndicate, for him usin' it already."

"Tell me about Diamond Toot'," he ordered.

"Diamond Toot' don't live here. He live in Miami. He go an' come. He an' Missa Vinton own' di Mangrove Club. When Missa Vinton go a prison, Diamond Toot' sol' di club to Missa Chow. Ray was di manager of di club. I 'ave a sister workin' in di club. She name Lucilda. She is a go-go dancer workin' dere. She can tell you 'bout Diamond Toot'. She was his queen."

"I see!" he exclaimed. "Pappy, it seems to me that the pieces of the jigsaw puzzle are falling into place."

"I t'ink I see di picture," Pappy replied, sarcastically. "Your brother, Burnel George Carter, under di false name of Vinton Case owned a club in partnership with a man called Diamond Toot'. I am sure dat is not his real name. I also t'ink dat Needham has not told us everyt'ing. I don't want to say dat he is lying, just yet, but he is hidin' some t'ings he don't want us to know. How about dat, eh, Needham? Tell us everyt'ing."

"Yeah," Needham replied. "Diamond Toot' seh dat Missa Vinton seh him fi sell di car an' di bus and di club an' close down everyt'ing."

"So Diamond Toot' cleaned out Mr. Vinton's office and his apartment before the Police arrived. Is that so?" he asked

Needham laughed wildly. "I don't know how Diamond Toot' get de apartment from de Police, but he cleaned it out long ago. Diamond Toot tol' Raymond dat Missa Vinton put him in charge of everyt'ing."

Pappy was furious. "You mean to tell me dat Raymond know all about what was goin' on, an' he said not'ing to us? He kept it to himself. Dat boy nuh easy!"

"We have to find that Diamond Toot'," he savagely growled. "He owes us an explanation."

"He is a hard man to find," Needham croaked. "Sometime him here. Sometime im in aneddah place. Him go an' come. I man don't see him since Missa Vinton blow up."

"Maybe he know' how George blow up!" Pappy shouted.

"Hold your horses, Pappy," he said. "Good God," he said to Needham, and his voice was hard and sharp, "Why have you come here to tell me this, now that Raymond is dead? Don't you think it is too late? What do you want me to do about it? Raymond is dead. You will be next!"

Needham did not answer. He was dumb with fear. He was frequently wetting his dry lips with his tongue, and his body shook as if he had ague.

He did not press Needham for an answer

"Raymond seh if anyt'ing happen to him to come to you," Needham blubbered.

He did not believe that Raymond said any such thing to Needham. He had a good guess why Needham had come. Needham was desperately seeking a place to hide.

Needham needed protection. Needham was a hunted rat. Needham was hoping that he would save him.

"Needham, can you stay with your sister, the go-go dancer for a few days?" he almost gently asked.

Needham nodded. His lips were too dry and his fear too great for him to answer.

"OK," he said. "Go to your sister and lie low, until I decide what to do. I hope to work out something for you."

He told himself that he had to do something quickly. He had to devise some means of protecting Needham. He recognized the importance of Needham as a link towards closing the gap in his investigation at which he had been working without much headway for almost a month. There were still pieces of the jigsaw puzzle that did not seem to fit. Probably he should grill Needham before sending him away, but he decided to delay the grilling till they met again. When Needham was driven by more fear or vice-versa, he would be impelled to tell what he knew and not what he chose to tell. He sensed that Needham was withholding information, probably holding an Ace close to his chest waiting for an opportunity to play it to his profit. Needham was evasive, over-cautious and rapacious. He felt that Needham distrusted him. "I think that we can let him go now, Pappy," he said. "I think that he has told us enough to work on."

"Yeah, more dan enough!" Pappy said sorrowfully.

"Needham, give me your sister's address and telephone number," he ordered. "On no account must you attempt to contact us. We will keep in touch with you, Understand?"

He made a mental note of the address. Needham did not remember his sister's phone number.

"OK, be on your way," he ordered.

Pappy rose to let Needham out. He paused for a moment with Needham at the door. "Be careful now. Remember to lay low," Pappy was briefing Needham. Then two shots rang out. "Lord have mercy," Pappy cried out as he was slammed back into the living room.

He instinctively threw himself to the floor on all fours. He crawled towards the light switch and plunged the room into darkness. It took a moment to pull his Beretta from its secret compartment, but a warning flashed in his brain not to use it unless it was absolutely necessary. Trained to focus his eyes and pierce the darkness like a cat, he was a more than stealthy and dangerous match for any assailant in the dark. He crawled to the door, but swiftly drew back into the darkness of the room because of the light of the street lamp. There were three or four shots fired further down the street. He wanted to slip outside, but he could not get beyond the street light illuminating the front doors. Not hearing any unusual sound that may indicate the still presence of the intruder, he pushed the doors shut, then re-switched on the light and crawled towards his grandfather.

Pappy winced and clenched his teeth. He stared at his grandson as if he were not seeing him. "Look like de end of de road. Get a priest. Pray for me," he murmured from bloodied lips, before slipping into unconsciousness.

He pulled back Pappy's shirt and shuddered at the damage to his chest. "Goodbye, Pappy," he said almost unemotionally. "This is only the beginning of the road, if we believe what the preachers say."

He replaced the Beretta in the secret compartment of his valise and went to the phone to call the Police. But while he dialled, a police car with wailing siren drew up at Pappy's gate. Several others followed filling the once very peaceful street with their strident and melancholic wails.

A police officer listened to his story, while a group of policemen were keeping back a crowd from mobbing the house. He did not mention Needham. The officer jotted notes in a black book that looked too small for his huge fist. Another policeman was drawing chalk lines around the body.

"He is dead. Cold stone dead!" remarked the policeman who was drawing Pappy's profile on the floor."

"Your name and address, sir?" the officer asked.

He gave the officer his address and asked his name. He liked the officer at sight. The officer looked efficient and there was a freshness and exuberance about him as if he was new to the job and liking it.

"I am Detective Sergeant Richardson," the officer proudly informed him. "Your address?"

He gave a British address that, as far as he knew, didn't exist, but was entered in his false passport.

"So you is a visitah!" the officer said. "Do you know di victim?"

"He is my grandfather," he replied.

"How long did, you know him?" the officer asked.

"Practically all my life," he replied, slightly amused.

"Sorry!" said Sergeant Richardson. "What did you say is di victim's name?"

He was amused by this line of questioning, since he used it at times. He knew the technique as oblique questioning wherein a similar question was repeated off-hand and the two answers compared for verification or to discover discrepancies in a statement or evidence. Lawyers regularly resort to it in cross-questioning a witness.

"How was he killed?" Detective Sergeant Richardson asked his ball point pen poised above a page in his little black book.

"He was shot! By whom, and why, I do not know," he answered.

Detective Sergeant Richardson murmured. "Shot an' killed about midnight!" and wrote the words in his book. "Although he is dead," he explained "we have to carry him to de hospital for a doctor to pronounce him dead. According to law, he is suffering from gunshot wounds and he is not dead until doctor seh so."

He said that he understood that, and the officer went to the telephone. At that point, a policeman came in to report to the officer that another body had been found atop a zinc fence a few blocks down the street. "Hell pop loose!" the officer exclaimed. The Detective Sergeant stared at him. "Do you know who shot your grandfather an' why?" he stolidly asked, once again.

"I am a visitor, home on vacation as I told you before," he answered. "How could I know that? I know nothing about my grandfather's business."

"It is possible you could know the motive," Detective Sergeant Richardson retorted. "I don't take nutten for granted. Is it attempted robbery? This happens at times to foreigners comin' home to visit their relatives and to enjoy a vacation at home. It is also happenin' to returnin' residents. Thieves tend to target them. Was it attempted robbery? What do you t'ink?"

"I don't think so," he replied, "since I saw no one. No one attempted to enter. My grandfather is not a visitor. He has lived in this house for the greater part of his life. He heard strange sounds outside, he opened the door to investigate and he was shot."

"Always a wrong thing to do! I tell people everyday what to do when they hear strange sounds outside their homes at night, yet they do the wrong thing every time," the officer said. "Whenever you hear strange sounds outside your house, at night, don't turn on your inside lights. Never open your door. Never stand before a window tryin' to see what is going on outside. Make a whole lot o' noise. But people won't listen an' learn until they get shot. An' then, if you learn the hard way by getting shot, it is too late to correct the mistake for you're dead!"

"I am posting a policeman to guard this house," Richardson said. "Come to Denham Town Police Station tomorrow morning and give a full statement."

He did not sleep that night, not with the body of Pappy lying on the cold tiles and covered with a white sheet, the babel of voices on the street in front of the house, and the policeman smoking, incessantly clearing his throat and irreverently walking in and out of the house.

At early dawn, two men in a hearse, came for Pappy's body. Two burly detectives, a photographer and a finger-print expert came the same time. He was relieved that the expert did not ask him for a print and the photographer complied with his request not to take a photograph of him, but he had to answer the questions put by the detectives all over again. An hour or so after, he refused to give an interview to a batch of eager news reporters.

He was under the impression that morning had taken a long time to come and was marching away just as slowly. Except for a large and dank patch of blood on the floor of the living room, and the single policeman lolling about and a group of curious spectators and mourners loitering on the street in front of the house, there was little evidence of the hubbub of the night. He was shocked at the sight of his haggard face in the mirror. He didn't feel hungry, but he was getting exhausted and nasty. He shuffled out of his clothes and fully turned on the shower. The coldness of the water was like good medicine and he subconsciously shed the weight and the pain of sorrow and bitterness from his shoulders. He told himself, while he was shaving that he should not blame himself for his grandfather's untimely and violent death, though he must admit that he had inadvertently and indirectly subscribed to it, and that he could not leave the island without avenging his murder. He actually exulted in the vibration of the electric razor against his skin and the aroma of Brut shaving cream and lotion which he applied generously to his face. Satisfied with the improvement of what he saw in the mirror, he pulled on a pair of dark pants, Cashmere fawn coloured turtle neck jersey and sockless, gray patent leather loafers. He told the policeman that he was going to Denham Town Police Station, locked the house and leaping into the Datsun, literally bulldozed his way through a battery of newsmen and onlookers.

He considered himself lucky to meet Detective Sergeant Richardson just as the officer was about to go off duty. The officer was very obliging and detailed a policeman to take his statement. He informed the officer that he was moving to his hotel.

"Wherever you are, keep in touch with the Denham Town Police," Detective Sergeant Richardson advised. "We may need your assistance. We might even detain yuh as a suspect."

"Thank you, Sergeant," he replied. "You can call me Bat if you like. All my friends do. I ask you to assist me with the autopsies for my grandfather and my brother. Can I come to discuss it with you tomorrow?"

"Come in the afternoon anytime. Your grandfather's body is at Madden's."

"My brother's body is also there," he said.

"Sorry!" said the officer noncommittally. "You mean that fellow who got his throat cut at KPH?"

"Yes," he replied. "That is the one."

"And now your grandfather got shot?" asked the officer. "Are you sure, you fellows not in drugs or something?"

"Pappy was a respectable gentleman in his community," he asserted. "The people on the street and his neighbours will swear to that. It is obvious that Raymond was involved. But what he was involved in, I do not know. It is for the Police to find out. I am visiting from England. This has been my only visit in many, many years."

"We shall surely find out," Detective Sergeant Richardson pleasantly said. "I must be going. I hope to see you tomorrow."

He woke in his hotel room just in time to listen to the afternoon's newscast.

❧

The body of a man about twenty-eight years old, identified as Bernard Needham a.k.a. Joseph Needham alias Rambo, of no fixed address, was found atop a zinc fence in Trench Town. It is suspected that he was the victim of a gang reprisal. Apparently, he had failed in his bid to scale the fence in order to escape his pursuer(s). Needham was a member of the disbanded Syndicate posse. According to police report residents of Fourth Street said that at about 10.30 p.m. last night, they heard gunshots. Needham's body was discovered half an hour later on top of a zinc fence he had failed to scale. Needham was wanted by the Police for robbery with aggravation, shooting with intent and wounding Ernel Ascott of Hannah Town and Roland Vickers of Trench Town. A gentleman of Trench Town, was held up and shot to death at his home at about 10.15 p.m. last night. He was identified as...

"This is a country of melodrama," he murmured. "If that rascal had not been killed, I could have been arrested for aiding and abetting a wanted man." He switched off the television. After all, he was there when Pappy was killed. He didn't want to hear a hashed-over version of what happened. He phoned *Room Service*. "I will have black coffee and toast, please, as well as the newspapers and a cold Red Stripe, he ordered. While having his frugal breakfast, he scanned the papers for news of Pappy and Needham's death. "Nothing yet," he murmured, "the newsmen haven't been able to put their scripts together in time for the newsrooms."

After breakfasting, he pulled the Datsun from the parking lot and drove to Portmore. He sensed a morbid stillness about the place. He felt for a cigarette and lit it, though normally he would not have done so when on the hunt. He crept from the Datsun and seeking cover behind a beached boat, watched the Sea Bird sleepily and gently tugging at its moorings. "Nothing going on there," he said. "Buzzer is probably asleep after a busy night."

He put out the cigarette and pocketed the stub. The deadly quietness sharpened his senses, as he swung himself aboard the Sea Bird. "Buzzer," he called softly. There was no response. "Hey Buzzer, you haven't got home yet from your little foray, last night?" He slipped the Beretta from his waist and screwed on the silencer. Having swept the upper parts of the boat with keen eyes, ears and nostrils, he picked up the smell of fresh blood above the rawness of the sea. Then he noticed the traces of blood, as if a body had been dragged from the little deck towards the cabin. "Hey what happened here?" he exclaimed. He pulled on a pair of gloves and tried the door of the cabin. It was locked, but it didn't take a minute for him to pick the simple lock, and he stopped short at what he saw. The floor of the tiny cabin was covered with gore. He bent forward and touched the lifeless and sprawled form of Buzzer. "Someone got here before me," he said. "The amateurs have messed you up. I would have done a neater job with a single shot. They are coming back, I suppose, to take you on your final trip across the Harbour. Sorry, I can't wait around much longer to see them, but I don't think you will be coming back."

He looked around the cabin from where he stood, then gazed at Buzzer's body again. "Who did this to you, Pal?" he murmured. "Whoever did it, had it in for you bad, bad, bad!" He calmly shut the cabin door, unscrewed the silencer, slipped the gun back into his waistband and climbed over the side of the Sea Bird. He told himself as he returned to the Datsun that his work was cut out for him and to keep ahead of the Police he had to work fast, very fast. He drove along the Port Henderson road, admiring the sea from the road on the edge of the cliff, past the Lazaretto and beyond Fort Clarence and easily found The Mangrove Club overlooking the infamous Green Bay. He parked under a coconut tree that had on no coconuts and absorbed the view. The haunting strains of Eric

Donaldson's Festival winning song, "Sweet, sweet Jamaica", passed through his mind and he was tempted to add "Jamaica, no problem?" to it, but he was reluctant to live such a lie so late in the day. He drew a breath of raw, salty sea air into his lungs, instead.

The shutters of the club were down, though its thirty feet high neon sign was still flashing faintly. He found a door open and walked in. He was greeted with the foul smell of stale sweat, stale sex, stale beer and stale dust and dirt. An old woman was sweeping, while a big boy was piling chairs on the tables. On the countertop, a young man was softly snoring, with the back of his head resting on his arms.

"What you want, Man?" the woman cackled. "Don't yuh see dat di club close?"

"I am looking for Lucilda," he replied.

"Lucilda? No Lucilda work 'ere," she said.

"Is Dallie him want," the boy explained.

"Oh, you mean Dallie!" the old woman cackled. "She gawn home lang time an' di man she gawn wit' nuh want see yuh neither. Him 'ave gun!"

The boy stopped stacking the chairs and grinned knowledgeably at what the old woman was saying.

"Oh, I understand," he replied. "Seems everybody has a gun these days!"

"Yes," agreed the old lady. "Everybody killin' everybody. Soon dere won't be anybody lef' fi kill. God soon come!"

He laughed mischievously, "I agree with you, Ma'am. There won't be anybody left to kill anybody."

"Come back tonight an you will see Dallie," she advised.

"About ten or so," she grumbled. "No 'oman suppose fi gwaan so! She nuh see she soon done!"

"What do you mean?" he inquired.

"Me nuh business," she cackled. "Me deh yah fi drink milk nuh fi count cow! But she gwine go to hell! Come see fi yusself."

"That's a good idea," he said. "I will come see for myself Goodbye."

"Den you naw give me somt'ing?" she asked, stretching a

wrinkled and dirty palm towards him.

He took a Jamaican hundred dollar bill from his wallet. The boy was eagerly staring at him. He gave him a fifty, as well. The old lady said thanks. The boy said nothing.

He drove back to the hotel, refitted the silencer to the Beretta and tucked it under a pillow. Then he secured the door and threw himself on the bed. He wasn't taking any chances.

He woke at about 8.00 a.m. He called Room Service and ordered fried eggs and bacon, bread, fruit, coffee and the newspapers. He lit his last cigarette and recollected that he had not removed the stub he had in his pocket. While having breakfast he worked at his plan. He had to fit all that was to be done, the joint-funeral of Pappy and Raymond as well as other matters, within a time-frame that must culminate with the exact date and time of his departure from the island.

He planned to see Detective Sergeant Richardson that afternoon. He hoped that the officer would have some news for him regarding the autopsies in order for him to set the date for the funerals. He intended to visit Chew. He did not want Chew to be suspicious. He was working out the correct moment to confront Chew with the murder of George, Pappy, Raymond and Needham, as well. He planned to confront him shortly after the funeral. He had arrived at a deduction that Chew was responsible for these murders directly or indirectly and he was going to give this theory his best shot. If it worked out, he would go after Diamond Toot', as quickly as possible.

He glanced at his watch and was surprised that it was already three o'clock. He got into the Datsun and drove to Denham Town to see Detective Sergeant Richardson.

"I thought you had run weh," the officer bantered. "I am supposed to seize your documents, until we are satisfied that you did not kill your uncle."

He was relieved that the officer was kidding. "Am I a suspect?" he lightly asked.

"Everybody is suspect until proven otherwise," the officer replied. "I don't take anyt'ing for granted. That's why I am a detective sergeant and not an ordinary policeman. At what hotel are you staying?"

"I told you already," he replied.

"Eh? My memory must be gettin' bad!" the officer remarked. He took out his little black book and scribbled in it.

He silently credited the officer with a good and shrewd memory. His psyche which became occasionally active was sending a warning signal to his brain to tread cautiously with this clever detective. He could not afford to disclose his undercover, for instance, as there would be too many questions. On the other hand, Detective Sergeant Richardson was unaware of serving as a very useful ally.

"The autopsies will be held at ten o clock tomorrow morning at Madden's. You're presumably the nearest of kin. Be sure to be there to identify the bodies," said the officer consulting his black notebook.

"I am very grateful to you," he said. "Thanks!"

"NO big t'ing!" the officer replied. "It is my duty to get post mortems done, everday, except Saturday and Sunday."

The following day, he attended the autopsies and discussed the funeral arrangements with the undertakers. Pappy was going to be lucky. He would get his last request, since Fr. Wildish agreed to commit his body as well as Raymond's. He called Chew and expressed his desire to see him that very afternoon.

Chew greeted him warmly and conducted him to the lounge. Pluto flopped his tail two or three times on the carpet as a gesture of greeting. He was conscious of, and secretly impressed by the knowledge that the now friendly Pluto could in the next moment become a formidable attacker unleashing over forty kilograms of savagery at the bidding of his master.

"I was thinking that you would have gotten in touch with me before," Chew said as they settled at the psychedelic bar. "Ice! Ice! Ice!" the ice-dispenser squeaked.

"Could you shut up that thing?" he asked. "It is stirring up unpleasant memories."

"Yes, of course! I am sorry about Pappy and I miss Raymond dearly," Chew said, as he pressed a button on the dispenser and brought it to a standstill.

He listened patiently as Chew spun a ream of encomiums and tribute to Pappy's throwing in a few for Raymond. "Good boy, Raymond," Chew said.

He was sick with aversion and anger at Chew's hypocrisy and felt like strangling him then and there. But of course, he would have Pluto to contend with.

"I hope that the Police pick up the killers soon," Chew continued.

"I hope that they will, before I leave," he replied.

"When do you plan to leave?"

"I intend to leave on Sunday, shortly after the funeral."

"So early?" Chew asked.

"Yeah," he replied. "I had not planned to overstay my vacation. I have to get back to work." He was satisfied that Chew was completely at ease, and he was hoping that nothing untoward would disrupt his plans in the three days he had to execute it. "The autopsies were done this morning. I have made arrangements with the undertakers for the funeral to be held at Dovecot, 2.00 p.m. on Saturday. There is nothing to hold me here after that. I came to tell you."

"I will be there at the funeral," Chew said.

"Well, thanks for the beer. I must be going," he said.

"Come anytime," Chew invited, stretching out both hands to clasp his. "Bat, I am sorry your vacation is spoilt. And apparently you haven't discovered any foul play in George's death."

"Yeah," he lied "Apparently! I am going back to England to lick my wounds. I hope to return next year."

"What will happen to Pappy's house and his affairs?" Chew asked.

"Thank you for reminding me," he replied. "That was the main thing I came to discuss with you. I am asking you to take care of the house. Rent it out or something. I don't think that Pappy had any money in the bank to talk about, and as far as I know, he owed no one."

"Is there a will?" Chew asked.

He laughed. "I haven't gone through his effects and papers. But it is hardly likely that there is. Pappy used to say that what he possessed was not worth the ink, paper or effort to write it down."

"A will is important," Chew said, "Even if you have nothing of much consequence to bequeath, you should write a will."

"I agree," he replied. "I must be going."

"I will take care of the house for you," Chew promised. "See you at the funeral."

"Thanks for the support," he said. "Be seeing you." As he went towards the Datsun, he told himself that if Chew had any fears about his knowing too much about him he had cleverly succeeded in defusing that fear. He drove to the news offices and arranged the funeral announcements. He stopped by the guango tree on his way back to the hotel. The tall, thin man was the first to greet him.

"Mi sorry seh Pappy dead. Mi ha' go buy 'dead' dis week. Pappy is a good man. Him wi mek I win!" the tall, thin man said. "Pappy is a good man!"

He was slightly amused by the incongruous tribute of the tall thin man (it did not occur to him to ask his name) but he was relieved that he did not ask for money to buy the rake. "May you win," he said.

"Did you bring the paper?" Ferdie mournfully asked.

He was not surprised at the impropriety of the request. He placed his hand on the old man's shoulder. "Pappy cannot bring you the paper any more. He is dead!" he said

"I didn't mean that," the old man explained. "I just want to see for myself in the paper that Pappy, my old friend, is dead. I weep till my eyes dry. I 'ave no tears left."

The old man was trembling like a leaf and his tears were flowing freely. Bert, his grandson, put down his radio-cassette player, wrapped the old man in his arms and led him away.

"Yeah," he said to Bert. "Take good care of him. You're lucky. You have some one to care about. I have no one left."

Everybody by the guango tree wanted to hear about the funeral arrangements. He had to repeat them again and again. They all wanted to go. He took some money from his wallet and gave it to the tall, thin man. "Buy everybody a drink," he instructed. "Buy Ferdie a news-paper and if there is any money left, buy 'dead'."

"Thank you! Thank you, Missa Bat!" the dice players and the little man shouted. The big, burly man was too sad to say anything. He held down his head and kept picking up the dominoes allowing the pieces to fall slowly, one by one, from his apparently nerveless fingers.

"Sorry, I can't stay any longer. Fellows," he shouted. "I have a number of things to do."

"Irie!" mournfully said the big, burly man. "See you at di funeral!"

On his way back to the hotel, he retooled his memory on a number of details he must attend to. "I must call to confirm my flight."

He also told himself that he had to go to Hertz to settle his account with them and to arrange for their car to be picked up at the hotel on Saturday at 6:00 p.m. after the funeral. He would use taxis from thereon.

Chapter 17

IF YOU LOVE ME HONEY, YOU CAN HAVE ME WITHOUT A DIME

*H*e dressed at 8.00 p.m. He slipped on his safari jacket, but decided to leave the Beretta. Unarmed and with-out a conventional weapon, he had saved himself at least one occasion in Accra where he was investigating an African dealer in precious stones. He had to use his bare hands and he carried a garotte since. He wore a heavy gold chain around his neck, but it wasn't gold. It was tough steel. It had a platinum edge that by a flick of wrist could become a garotte to slice through a man's neck. The heavy St. Christopher's Cross dangling from it was a lethal weapon, when the chain was wrapped around his fist to form a knuckle-duster or swung like a ball and chain.

The Mangrove Club was over-conspicuous under the dark, starry sky by its tall multicoloured neon sign that flashed, 'Mangrove Club Welcome', once every minute. The music was abysmally loud and the hall was steaming with sweat, cigarette smoke and the pungent smell of marijuana. He walked over to an unoccupied table and sat facing the stage. His watch was showing ten. The performance on stage had apparently just begun. He pulled a cigarette from a new packet and with his eyes glued to the stage, began to make his contribution to the smokiness and smells. Nobody could accuse him of being indifferent to the torrid performance that was taking place on stage. "If that voluptuous, gyrating woman is Lucilda," he murmured, "she is a beautiful piece. What in heavens name mek Caribbean woman so beautiful and desirable? The sea? Or mixed breeds?"

Lucilda sang in a throaty sort of contralto. Her smile was electric, her laughter infectious and intoxicating. Her costume was intended to reveal rather than to conceal. She had a detached quirk of pushing her pelvis forward, arching her back and sweeping back her long hair with long, purple painted nails as if to say, "Ah will kill you wid it". She was singing, "If you have the money. I have got the time, Honey. But if you love me, Honey, you can have me without a dime." He was sure that he had heard that song before. Was it in London or on Broadway? He couldn't recall.

"Luz, yuh firin' awright!" one of the men shouted above the whistling and 'meows'. Some men called out, "Do di bicycle!" The tiny band changed to a hectic beat and she worked the number. She was everybody's darling. The howls and yells were deafening as she pulled off her sequined rag of a skirt and threw it at one of the men who deftly caught it. The howls and yells became louder as she worked at her G-string. Some men were shouting, "Di Bottle Ride! Give us di Bottle Ride!"

He had no idea what they were shouting about. A waiter came up just as the lights were dimmed, and he ordered Rum Crème. From the sudden hush and the harsh breathing of the men, he suspected that something out of the ordinary was about to be performed. He glued his eyes to the stage while he enjoyed his iced Rum Crème. Two sinuous girls joined Lucilda on stage. Their breasts were nude and nubile. The rest of their bodies was barely covered with tassels and sequines, G-strings, loads of costume jewellery and shiny black high-top boots. Their dancing with Lucilda was accentuated by a single spotlight that played on to the stage. Then the light was further dimmed. A red light flooded the stage and supplanted the spotlight. A waiter appeared with three bottles of

Red Stripe beer on a tray. Each of the women took a bottle and entered into a rather erotic act, juggling with the bottles and sucking at them from time to time. There was a sudden pause in the music and then a clarion call which he recognized as the opening bars of Beethoven's Fifth Symphony. This gave way to a torrid reggae beat during which Lucilda, with a twist of her hand, tore away her G-string and threw it among the men. Some of the men went into a tackle in quest of this prize. The girls on stage were dancing closely together, then they convulsively separated, as the lights changed from green to blue.

"Go deh, Dallie!" the men shouted. The waiter returned and took away two of the bottles on his tray for all to see. One of the girls danced before Lucilda holding her bottle aloft at first, then slowly and convulsively bending forward and pointing the mouth of the bottle towards Lucilda's abdomen. The two women danced approaching each other closer and the men egged them on, with coarse jokes, whistling and clapping. They danced closer until the hall was plunged into darkness. When the lights came back, and the dancers separated, there was no sign of the bottle.

"Good God," he swore. "The old lady was right!"

And the men, having been raised to orgiastic levels, some of them, yelled, cheered or applauded like infernal demons, and shouted lewd jokes at the dancing girls, at the end of the Bottle Ride. Each man had probably entered a dreamy or imaginary passage in which he was vicariously wishing that he was working in place of the bottle that had disappeared.

He placed a five-hundred dollar on the table and beckoned to a waiter. "Bring me another Rum Crème and tell that young lady who swallowed the bottle that I want to see her."

She came to the table five minutes or so later. "Sit down, Dollie," he invited her. He handed the five-hundred dollar note to her. "You deserve more than that for your act."

"I suppose you want to see how I do it?" she coyly asked. "Yuh want to see close for you'self where the bottle went?"

"I guess so," he replied. He liked her laughter, hoarse and melancholy like the sound of turtle doves.

"I rather like your voice," he remarked, "and I love the way you toss your hair from your eyes as you danced."

"Like this?" she asked, casting back her hair with long purple painted nails.

"Yeah," he replied. "Just like that!"

"It's no big thing," she said. "It's just a big, long wig. My real hair is short and I wear false nails. Do you like them?" She held them up for him to inspect them.

"Yeah, I like them," he replied. "Have you heard about your brother?"

"Yes," she calmly replied, "they killed him."

"Who killed him?" he asked.

"Buzzer," she replied. "I been tellin' him over an' over that he would come to a bad end. He wouldn't listen to me."

He could not see whether she was crying or not, but he noted a break in her voice. "See there now, is the same t'ing I tell him! Him 'ave nobody to blame. He wouldn't listen to nobody!" she said.

"Your brother told me about Diamond Toot'. He said that you and he were lovers. I want to know more about him and anything you may know about Syndicate."

"Are you a police?" she asked.

"No, I am not. I was Raymond's brother," he told her.

"You t'inkin' of takin' over from them?" she asked.

"I haven't decided what to do. I am trying to learn all I can first," he replied. "I don't want to talk to you here. Can we go to your place?"

She hesitated, then nodded her agreement. "When the show over," she said. "Where is you car?"

"My car is a blue Datsun. I parked near to the coconut tree. I will wait for you in the car," he told her. He watched as she wove her way back to the stage, adroitly avoiding the hands of the male patrons, and stopping to acknowledge the platitudes and compliments of a few.

"Some piece of woman that!" he complimented.

Lucilda instructed him as he drove to Independence City. "Where I live is easy to find to those who want to find me," she remarked.

He took her remark to mean that she sold sex. Probably that was the more lucrative side of her vocation.

"Here is Passage Fort," she said. "Turn left. This is Florida Drive. Continue drivin' until you come to Middlesex Avenue. Da's all. Now drive slow an' look for a Monkey an' a Rooster on top of the gatepost."

"Ah, here we are!" she said. "The Rooster is you. The Monkey is me. You can't miss it nex' time."

He laughed softly at her humour. Then she started to sing, "If you got the money. I have got the time."

"Suppose I haven't a dime?" he teased.

"Then you wastin' your time, Mister!" she retorted. She leaned heavily against him as they went to her door. By the time he got the door open, she was piling all over him. "What you want to know about Diamond Toot' can stay till later," she whispered into his ear.

"Condoms! Have you condoms?" he asked. Something was about to explode inside him. He had not had a woman for over a month. She released him and took a box of "Hot Delights" from a drawer.

"How did you know my brand?" he teased.

"All the big man dem ask for it," she lied, nibbling away his body into little bits.

She was like a thoroughbred horse. She didn't seem to be able to run out of steam. "You say you're a monkey?" he complimented her. "You're more like a run-away train."

"You're not too bad a locomotive either," she retorted.

He admired her intelligence and humour. "You're pretty smart!" he remarked.

"In my game, you have to be smart to survive," she gravely replied. "Don' you like smart girls?"

"Yeah," he replied. "Some women are terribly dull."

She laughed dryly. "I 'ave met some pretty dull men too," she remarked.

"Yeah, I guess so," he replied.

She started to play with the chain around his neck, trying to weave it into the hair on his chest.

"Lay off!" he ordered. "This chain is not a plaything. It is a weapon."

"I don't believe that," she said.

"See for yourself," he said and sitting up, he tugged at the St. Christopher's Cross and flicked the chain in a single fluid motion. He placed her finger gently along the platinum edge. "Careful now," he growled. "See this cross? Feel the weight of it. You can crack a man's skull with it, or cut through his neck like a razor, if you know how to use it."

"You are a dangerous man!" she whispered.

"Yeah, you can call me that," he growled.

She released her breath with a tiny scream. "My Gawd. You not goin' to kill me?"

"No," he said, caressing her all over again. "Tell me about Diamond Toot', Chew and Syndicate. Is Diamond Toot' a dangerous man?"

"I love dangerous men," she murmured, drawing a tentative forefinger down his stomach.

"Come off it, Dollie," he growled. Tell me about him."

"Me 'fraid!" she whimpered. "He will kill me, if I talk."

"Do you want your brother's murderer to go free? Is that what you want? Probably you prefer to tell your story to the Police. You're in the business with them, aren't you? If we don't do something about him, he will kill you, anyhow, because you know too much. Where did that bottle go by the way? Show me how you did it."

"Dey don't seem to notice that I wear flesh coloured leotards under my G-string," she began to explain.

"You lie!" he merrily exclaimed. "You can't wear anything under a G-string!"

She rose, went to her dresser and returned with a tiny balloon which she inflated. He was surprised to notice the replica of what looked like a Red Stripe bottle, label and all.

"My partner hold the bottle so and squeeze out the air, then she knead the bottle between her palms so, as we dance close. The bottle soon become like chewing gum and she roll it into a little ball and stick it inside her leg."

He laughed some more. "A simple illusionist act!" he exclaimed.

"What you say?" she asked. "Is a bad word dat?"

"No," he explained to her. "It is a word we use to describe the tricks of the magician. You know who is a magician ain't it? People enjoy being tricked by an illusionist who fools them into believing that his tricks are supernatural."

"It's true that people like to be fooled," she agreed. "They like tricks to be played on them. When I tell men how my little bottle trick is done, they don't want to believe. And those who believe like to tell their friends that's not how I do it. They have their own nasty version."

"Do you know Mr. Chew?" he asked.

"Yes, I know him. When Mr. Vinton built the club, he use' to visit often. Then when Mr. Vinton was arrested, Diamond Toot' told me dat Mr. Vinton seh he was to sell the club to Mr. Chew."

"I see!" he exclaimed. "What did he do with the money?"

"I don't know," she replied. "He never told me."

"Did he mention that Mr. Vinton told him to sell out his buses and his cars and to clean out his office and his house and probably his bank account, as well?"

"No," she answered. "He never mention' it."

"Your brother said that Diamond Toot' stole everything my brother had and then blew him up."

She was horrified. "Needham never told me anything," she cried. "I did not know what was happenin'."

"Needham said that Syndicate set out to kill him and Raymond. Why would Chew want to do that? Or was it Chew?" he asked.

"That is not exactly true," she explained. "Buzzer gave Raymond a gun to sell to a man from England. Needham spend half of the money and Raymond spend the other half. Buzzer and his friends came to the club and shot up Raymond. Needham escape' by jumpin' an' hidin' in di swamp. Then Buzzer send one of his friend' to kill Raymond in the hospital. I told Needham that Buzzer would catch him one day."

"How do you know all of this?" he asked.

"Needham tol' me when he came to borrow money from me to pay Buzzer. I didn't lend him, cause he never pay me back whenever he borrow' from me."

"Tell me about a girl by the name of Paula. I understand that she was a friend of yours," he said.

"Paula? How do you know about she?" Lucilda asked.

"If you know what you're looking for, it is easy to find where to look," he remarked. "Tell me about her."

"Gawd!" she whispered and closed her eyes.

"Tell me about her!" he growled. "Who spiked her drink that night? Who raped her?"

"I don't know about it!" she denied.

"Go ahead. Tell me," he gently urged her, his voice losing its steel to become calm, reassuring and persuasive. "Your brother drugged her in a bottle of Pepsi wasn't it? A man by the name of Tony Brown ordered Needham to drug her!"

"I don't know," she repeated in a distressed voice. "I work in the bar when I am not dancing. I wasn't at the bar that night. I took Paula to the club. Tony Brown promised her a job. I don't know what happen' to her."

"You couldn't know what was happening because you were high yourself, weren't you?" he mildly accused her. "You took your friend to the club and threw her to the wolves. You knew what was going to happen to her, didn't you? You had the same experience, didn't you? Tony Brown drugged and raped you, and then you lived with him, because you had to survive on drugs, he gave you. Are you still on drugs?"

She started to sob. He couldn't decide whether to be sorry for her or not.

"She was going on bad," Lucilda cried. "Dey took her upstairs to sleep it off. I know not'ing more till mornin' when I see her. 'Paula what 'appen to yuh?' I ask' her. She look sleepy an' foolish and she said, 'Mi nuh know. Nutt'n nuh 'appen to mi. Yuh see anyt'ing 'appen to mi?'"

"Poor kid!" he murmured. He patted her arm gently. "It is

alright! I have nothing against you. I just wanted to know."

"What are you going to do?" she ceased her sobbing to ask.

"I don't know. Maybe nothing. Rest it!" he replied.

"I am afraid they will kill you," she cried.

He laughed at her sardonically. "Don't worry, Darling. Small-timers and vermin do not find me an easy man to kill," he boasted.

"Tony Brown' real name is Damascus Brown!" she suddenly announced.

"Good God!" he shouted. The information hit him like a bomb. He was dumbstruck. He quickly recovered and asked her. "How do you know that?"

"I have two children for Diamond Toot', a boy and a girl. He said that he want' the boy to have his father's real name, Damascus Brown."

"Now I see!" he exclaimed. 'The Road to Damascus' reverberated in his head. Pappy, he remembered, once made an allegorical reference to the Damascus Road, but for the life of him, he could not recall in what context Pappy had used it. "I have been blind," he said aloud. "If I had only seen what I am seeing now, I could have saved myself and others a lot of pain! Where are the children?"

Lucilda burst into tears. "Diamond Toot' stole them," she cried

"What do you mean? Where has he taken them?" he inquired.

"He told me that he gave them to a woman by the name of Kersene Ile in Miami, as he want' a future for them. I want Junior and Jodie, back." She wept and could not be consoled.

As tough as he was, love for women and children was his weak spot, his Achilles' heel! "OK," he said, "I will try to get Junior and Jodie back. I promise. They are illegally in the United States. It ought to be easy to get them out."

"How are goin' to find dem? America is a big place!"

He mischievously grinned at her. "If you see chickens, Mother Hen is always near. If you see Mother Hen, chickens are not too far away, and sometimes Father Cock. I will find them. Have you photographs of Father Damascus and Damascus Junior and little Jodie?"

She took a small snap folder from the dresser and handed it to him. Diamond Toot' looked like any ordinary and harmless, doting father.

"Mmmm!" he cleared his throat. "Beautiful children! Bald-headed Mr. Damascus Brown a.k.a. Tony Brown a.k.a. Diamond Toot' is a handsome fellow. He used to treat you well?"

"Yes," she replied. "He is a very nice and kind man."

"Kind!" he loudly exclaimed. "Kind to some and very cruel and unkind to others. It is all in the game! Never mind! I will get you back your children."

"What is your name, Lover Boy?" she asked.

"Call me Bat," he replied.

"That is not your name," she pouted. "What is you real name?"

"That's good enough for now," he replied. "The less you know about me, the better off you will be. Give me your phone number. I will keep in touch with you."

He swiftly dressed, took out his wallet and gave her another five hundred. She pressed the two five hundred dollar notes into his hand. "Bat, you are very nice. You make me want to live. I cannot take your money." She held on to him, kissed him and seductively sang, "If you love me, Honey, you can have me without a dime."

Chapter 18

RETRIBUTION

*T*he funeral of Pappy and Raymond, accompanied by a marching band of Trench Town and by uniformed groups (he was learning that Pappy was a patron of civic and social organizations in the community of Trench Town) was a gala affair of which Pappy would have disapproved, if it were possible for him to have anything to say about it. A good number of mourners from Trench Town (many of whom did not know that Pappy existed until he died) Ferdie and the Guango Tree Posse of Dice-gamblers and Domino-players (the tall, thin man named them for the occasion) as well as friends of Raymond, turned up. They filled the Dovecot chapel until there was no standing room, the rest of them spilling on to the pathway and among the multicoloured bougainvilleas.

There was a wake on the eve of the funeral, at the guango tree. The mountains of bread, fried chicken and gallons of mannish water, and white rum – Heineken and Red Stripe beer turned out to be more expensive than he had estimated. There was singing chatter, laughter and domino playing (Pappy would have loved that) chaired by the burly man, that lasted until morning light. To top it all, Ferdie had chartered a bus to convey the Guango Tree Posse to Dovecot, without consulting him, and then asked him to pay the bill.

Fr. Wildish caught the flu. He had telephoned Bat that he couldn't even rise from his bed. When Ferdie heard, he was overjoyed, and declared that Fr. Wildish's failure to put away Pappy for good was an "*act of God*". Ferdie had disapproved of Fr. Wildish from the start. Ferdie claimed that none below the rank of a bishop could appropriately send Pappy on his final journey. Ferdie was, there-fore, happy for the opportunity of hiring his own brother-in-law, Bishop Bray, minister of the Born Again New Testament Church. Bishop Bray, a Pentecostal minister-and he did bray-was a burly, amiable and handsome six-footer who looked like an Afro-Ameri-can quarter back with an aura of affluence about him. He had a voice that was loud and raspy, and an infectious and rather healthy laughter.

Bishop Bray danced and pranced behind the caskets of Pappy and his grandson Raymond, bellowing in his gravelly tone his ser-mon which was interspersed with an occasional whoop of triumph and alleluias. "Give thanks an' praises, Brothers. Give thanks and praises, Sisters fo' God is good!" he shouted, pointing a forefinger of reprimand at the congregation of friends and mourners. There was no known relative present except Bat. "Cephas Carter an' his grandson Raymond Carter, are now with the Lord!" Bishop Bray assured the congregation. "Fi yuh time will soon come! All of you, one by one, two by two! God will receive you in his kingdom!"

Despite the solemnity of the tragic occasion, and of the chords of sorrow that were plucking on his heart strings and of the opening hymn, *Now the labourer's task is o'er /Now the battle day has past* ... he was amused at the antics of Bishop Bray who jigged and pranced and ran a gamut of accents alternately from Jamaican pa-tois to English, and a southern American twang. Although Bishop Bray was briefed on the circumstances of the deaths, he on the contrary, insisted that they were acts of revenge. "*Vengeance is mine, saith the Lord. And I will recompense!*" was the text of his sermon, yet he quoted half-dozen or more of other irrelevant texts on other issues. As if he was paid for saying so, Bray asserted that Pappy and Raymond had gone to heaven. "Gord has lock' them up in his strongbox — you know, strongbox in a bank — and not even the devil can broke the strongbox of Gord! The devil, Brothers and Sisters cannot broke that bank! Therefore, don't think about these people in the casket. "They safe! But you think you safe? Think about yourself, about your own soul, and I don't mean you' shoes' sole-ah! You must be born again-ah! Born-ah of the spirit-ah! Of the water-ah and of the blood-ah!"

Throughout the service, he ruefully wondered, Raymond for sure, but what had Pappy done to deserve this? He had tried to accede to Pappy's request to get him a priest. He looked at Pappy's casket, and sadly murmured, "It isn't my fault, Pappy. I tried to get you a priest, but we were down on our luck! Your friend, Ferdie, has the last laugh, after all!"

"The labourer's task is o'er!" Bishop Bray shouted. "It's over! Over! They are now in heaven!" Bishop Bray set out to describe heaven, as if he had been there and was just returning to earth. "There is no pain nor sorrow up deh! No labour in heaven! No night up deh!" he shouted, pausing to mop his profusely sweating face, and to let loose one of his infectious chuckles or laughs or whoops.

He wondered how Pappy would adjust to life in heaven. No pain nor sorrow, he could understand, but no labour? Pappy would soon be bored to death! As for no night, he could not visualize Raymond existing without a night club and nocturnal activities. He would soon desire to return to earth. The problem is how would they escape from *Gord's strongbox?* He privately scoffed at the novelty and absurdity of Bishop Bray's claims until he suddenly pulled up to ensure himself that in respect for his dead grandfather and for his dead brother, he shouldn't be indulging skeptical views at that particular occasion.

Bishop Bray kept hammering away at the *wicked hearts of men.* "The wickedness of the times is the sign of His comin'!" he pranced, shouted and sweated. "The comin' is near-ah. The end-ah is near-ah!" Bray shouted until he was hoarse. "Vengeance-ah is mine-ah! Will someone say Halleluj-ah? I want to tell-ah all you' people-ah to get right wit' Gord-ah! Get it right-ah wit' Gord-ah! And do it now-ah! Will someone shout 'alleluja? Shout HALLE-

LUJAH!" A thin and bony old woman wearing a red white and black turban with two pencils and a pair of scissors stuck in it, and a bunch of wilted flowers held aloft in her right hand, jumped from her seat and started to shout, "Alliluyah!" This triggered off the pent-up emotions in the chapel like adding a match to a gasoline drenched woodpile. A murmur of amens rippled throughout the congregation, then exploded into a torrent of alleluias like the rat-tat-tat of an antiquated submachine gun.

"Pandemonium now," Bat muttered to himself and retreated outside for a breath of fresh air. He was uncomfortable with the excessive exuberant exultation, though he knew that uninhibited vocal expression was characteristic of Jamaicans. When Bishop Bray felt that it had gone on long enough, like Christ in the story of the tempest, he called an abrupt halt. "Peace! Be still!" he shouted, and Bat returned to his seat. While he was outside, he whimsically told himself that he hoped that Pappy would forgive him for letting him down. Pappy was probably there in the chapel, probably hovering over his body along with Raymond and George, and enjoying (or frowning) at the melodrama that was being performed before his casket.

"You are blind," Bishop Bray continued. "Blind-ah! You're blind like Paul on the road to Damascus!"

Bat sat up at the mention of Damascus and listened intently, thereafter, to Bishop Bray's preaching.

"Seek salvation, but you must firs' drop the scales from your eyes! All those who have scales on their eyes, put up your right hand and say amen." A sprinkling, mostly women, threw up their hands and shouted amen. "You ha' fi enter salvation with your eyes open, Brothers and Sisters," Bishop Bray screamed, jumped about, laughed and whooped.

"You ha' fi wise like a serpent an' harmless as a dove, fi mek Satan no t'ief salvation from yuh! Unnu hear what mi say? A blind man can't enter salvation unless the scales fall from his eyes. Do I hear anybody say Halliluyah amen?"

"The goodly bishop has a good thing going," Bat mused.

At the graveside, they sang, *We shall meet on that beautiful*

shore, and he tried to visualize, with a flash of humour, Pappy re-
monstrating that he wouldn't step in any water deep enough to cover
his ankles. After Bishop Bray had pronounced the commendation
which concluded the interment of Cephas and Raymond Carter, he
gave the Bishop an envelope with his pay for which the Bishop,
mopping his face, profusely thanked him. "How do you like the
funeral, Mr. Price?" Bishop Bray asked.

"Pardon?" he replied, then suddenly recovered himself that Price
was his assumed name. "Oh, you did a mighty job! Thank you."

After everyone had left, he lingered by the graveside. "Pappy,"
he murmured, "Farewell, old fighter! I hope, next time, when we
meet, you will say that you had forgiven me. Tell St. Peter to go
easy with George and Ray. Ask George how could a bright and
intelligent man mess up his life and cause the rest of us such grief? I
wish you better luck with Raymond, this time around. I hope that
you manage to get him to speak English. Tell him I say he is to keep
away from bad company. Should you run into Fr. Chew, tell him,
Sorry, no hard feelings, but a man has to do what a man needs to
do, and also tell him that I hope Pluto is now a gentle angel dog!"

Chew was there in a black tuxedo, black felt hat and a black
tightly rolled umbrella to match. After the funeral, he asked Chew if
he could drop in on him to discuss a few details regarding Pappy's
affairs. "Would seven o'clock be convenient?"

"Yes," said Chew. "Seven o'clock will be fine."

Back at the hotel, he changed into dark pants, black jersey,
black sneakers, making sure to tuck a pair of black skin-fit gloves
into a pocket. He cleaned the Berretta, checked the magazine and
screwed on the silencer. He fondly handled the gun, knowing that
he was about to part with it, then he shoved it into the back of his
pants, the silencer resting uncomfortably cold and heavy against his
buttocks. Very rarely did he carry a gun in this position, preferring
a shoulder holster.

He called a taxi and arrived at Chew's supermarket at eight
o'clock. He had alighted from the taxi at a gate three or four houses
down the street and deliberately walked to the side-door with the
electronic eye. He was perfectly calm and at ease as the little panel

near to the bell switch blinked, ENTER. Chew opened the door and let him in, smiling suavely

"You're late," Chew said.

"Sorry about that," he apologized. "Had to do some last moment shopping for a gift for my fiancée, and some last minute packing. I hate packing."

"Most men do," Chew replied. "Come along."

He walked towards Chew's psychedelic lounge, with Chew before him and Pluto leading the way. He felt very bad inside with the unwelcomed thought of what he had planned for the dog. He stepped to the right of Chew. There was a dull pop! Pluto, without a single yelp, tumbled over, feet beating the air, his huge head and tail spasmodically flopping on the carpet.

Chew jumped forward and spun around as if he was the one who had been shot. "Easy now!" he snarled, savagely poking the mouth of the silencer into the small of Chew's back. "Keep your hands up, walk slowly and sit in your chair."

"You shot my dog!" Chew wailed.

"Sit down, Chew," he growled, gesturing with the gun at the chair. "I am not playing games." He stepped past the dead dog and pulling up a leg of Chew's pants removed an ugly Mauser 9mm pistol from a leg holster. "You have always been a poor liar, Fr. Chew," he said. "You told me that you do not carry a firearm. You can tell from a man's eyes, if you have been trained to that sort of thing, that he has a weapon concealed on his person and that he intends to use it, if and when he gets a chance."

"You killed my dog," Chew whimpered. "Why you had to kill him?"

"Sorry about Pluto," he sarcastically apologized. "But at times three is a crowd. You wouldn't want Pluto, to listen to what we are about to discuss, would you? He probably wouldn't like the rough stuff that might occur."

"What do you want?" Chew croaked. "Money? Are you a gangster like your brother, George?"

"What?" he exclaimed. "The pot cursing the kettle? We shouldn't say bad things about the character of the dead, should we? I don't seek blood money, in fact, my job is to seek out and bring dealers in blood money to justice."

Chew shook and trembled in his chair as if he was having ague.

"Chew, I am going to tell you a story," he said. "Listen carefully. You may fill in details if you wish or correct me wherever I go wrong. You know, as a fact, or you guessed that Diamond Toot' a.k.a. Tony Brown a.k.a. Damascus Brown, your friend, murdered George, to please a woman in Miami, the ex-wife of George, known in Jamaica as Kersene Ile and in Harlem as The Horse, just a little bit of reprisal killing, and also because he had plundered everything that George possessed, while posing as his friend and confidante. You did not tell me that you are the top-man in Syndicate. You tried to convince me that George accidentally blew up himself in the process of making a bomb. Give a dog a bad name and hang him, sort of. You were getting hot and uncomfortable with my nosing around and you sent you hit-man, Mr. Buzzer, to stop me, in order to cover your tail!

"Buzzer killed your right hand man in the drug trade, my brother, Raymond. Probably you knew about it. Probably you did not. It is for you to say. Buzzer killed Raymond because he gave him a gun to sell to me, and Raymond and his friend, Needham, failed to hand over the money. Needham was on the run, because he knew that Buzzer and his friends were searching for him. Needham told me a lot. By the way, Needham told a lie on you that you sent Buzzer to kill Raymond and himself."

Chew stiffened in his chair and fixed his gaze on the dead Pluto. He paused for Chew to speak, but Chew remained silent.

"Good!" he sardonically remarked. "Now that we seem to understand each other. I will continue the story. You sent Buzzer to kill me at Pappy's house. While he was waiting for an opportunity, the door opened and there was Pappy and Needham standing in the light! Needham whom Buzzer wanted so badly! The sudden and unexpected appearance of Needham so excited, confused and unnerved Buzzer that he fired at Needham and missed, but hit Pappy. Then he chased Needham, caught up with him and shot him.

"You became annoyed with Buzzer when you knew that he had

bungled your job. You went to the Sea Bird and killed Buzzer in cold blood."

He drew a bead with the Berretta, the ominous silencer pointing at a spot where the apex of Chew's nose joined his brow. "I am going to kill you, Chew," he snarled.

"Mother of God, pray for us!" Chew screamed. "Don't play God, Bat! Call the Police! I will confess!"

"What were you playing when you sent Buzzer to get me?" he shouted. "What do you call the cold-blooded murder of Buzzer? Did you give him a chance to confess?"

Chew was biting his lower lip so hard that his blood ran down his chin.

"You might have saved Pappy's life and the others as well, if you had confessed from the start what was going on. We don't need a jury to pronounce you guilty as charged, Fr. Chew," he sardonically growled. "You're guilty!"

Pop! Chew bolted upright and fell back, as if a mighty hand had lifted him and a mighty fist had smashed him in the face.

He pulled on his gloves and took up the remote gadget where it had fallen on the carpet. He fiddled with the keys and the bar stools sprang out from the floor, the ice-dispenser began to run the length of the counter, forward and backward, squeaking, "Ice! Ice! Ice!" He suspected that there was a secret compartment in the panelling of the walls. He continued manipulating the keys until a panel slid back to expose a small metal chest. He decided to ignore the chest as he had no time to devote to discovering the combination. He took up one of the packets piled on a shelf, punched a hole into it with a forefinger and tasted his finger tip. "Ugh!" he exclaimed. "The real stuff! Millions of dollars worth!"

He got out his handkerchief, wiped the Berretta and the Mauser and placed them on the shelf then slid back the panel and put the gadget in his pocket. He walked around the lounge carefully searching for electronic cameras and sound recorders. Satisfied that there was none, he stood over Chew's body, then stooped and crossed Chew's hands on his lifeless breast. "Sorry ol' Fellah!" he reverently murmured. "You would have become a terrific priest!"

He stepped out and used the remote gadget to pull the doors of Chew's lounge together, listening to them lock in their channels with a sharp click. "Good!" he said aloud. "It will take some time and trouble to force these doors open without this remote controller."

As if in afterthought, he tore out the wires of the electronic eye that led to closed-circuit monitors. He stepped out of the side-door and pulled it shut with the gadget which he then slipped into his pocket. He stripped off his gloves, tucked them into his pocket, and crossed several streets in a north-easterly direction, before hailing a taxi and mingling with the night crowd. He walked down the Street towards his hotel. He looked at his watch, as he stepped into the foyer of the hotel. "Mission accomplished in a little over two hours!" he murmured.

He stayed in bed all day. He had gone earlier to the desk to check out. He neither ate nor drank, but smoked one of his cigars. He had already packed and he kept the television on, particularly for the news. He was relieved that up to his departure from the hotel there was no news of Buzzer nor of Chew. "I must remember to send Detective Sergeant Richardson a gold cufflinks and tie-pin set and a 'Thank-you note,'" he said to himself as he left the hotel, in a JUTA limousine.

When the BA jet was in flight, he began to unwind. Depressurizing himself of tension was not a pleasant experience. He ordered a dry martini and yet shook and trembled, as his irresistible reflections were recalling sad impressions of the irrecoverable price he had just paid. "Too great a price!" he murmured. He had lost his beloved grandfather, Pappy, and his brothers, George and Raymond. He had killed his childhood friend, Fr. Chew. He felt sick and he hurried down the aisle to the lavatory. He wanted to smoke, but a warning signal kept flashing "No Smoking." He reflected while sitting on the cramped lavatory seat, on his road to Damascus. He was tired. He was tired of intrigue. He was tired of the man-hunt. He was tired of diplomatic hypocrisy. He was tired of the dehumanizing effect to himself of killing. "I must be getting old!" "But I must see this thing through to the end, before I hang up my gloves! I promised a mother to get her back her children. I have to keep my promise! I shall avoid killing their father when I find him, although he deserves to die. After all, I am not God, as Fr. Chew reminded me. I shall hand him and Kersene Ile over to the DEA. They will find enough stuff on them to pin and nail them for the rest of their lives. They will be having enough leisure to reflect and repent."

He flushed the toilet and returned to his seat. He ordered a double martini and, when the stewardess announced supper, he was already relaxed. He ordered steak and was told that because of the mad-cow disease, beef was not served. He, therefore, ordered fish, and rice and peas with vegetables. He asked for earphones to enjoy the movies. He picked up a back number of the *London Tabloid* and read a brief account tucked into the third page of the paper — barely noticeable — and entitled, *Jamaican Prime Minister Heterosexual.* Pappy had mischievously requested him to investigate and inform him what the word, chi-chi-man meant. Now that he learnt from the tabloid what it meant, there was no Pappy to tell it to. "Jamaica? No problem!" he gloomily muttered. "Most Jamaicans are a resilient, kind and happy people. There is hardly any other country with so many holidays and festivals or with a richer culture. The sun shineth. The land is green, but there are many hardships to be overcome. The senseless killings must come to an end or the darkness will not go away. Jamaicans deserve better than what is prevailing in the country." He was enthused with the popular slogan, *Lift up Jamaica.* "Jamaicans, wherever they may be, should strive to lift up the little island in the sun."

He decided then and there that he would try to do his part in a grand uplift from whatever small corner he might find himself. Feeling better with his new commitment, he picked up a colourful holiday brochure from the compartment before him and softly exclaimed, "Ah, Cannes! That's the place for a holiday! I have never been there! I think I will take Sonja there and cool out for a couple of days."

He set aside the brochure when the meal trolley arrived. After he had eaten, he began to think of his next venture. "After that holiday in France," he said softly to himself, "I shall pay Mr. Diamond Toot' and Madam Kersene Ile a visit."

When he reached his flat, he phoned Sonja. "I am back, Sonja," he called.

"Why didn't you call to say when you are coming back?" Sonja complained. "I can't cook a steak because of the mad-cow disease nor lamb chops because of the foot and mouth disease. I haven't seen any mad-cow meat anywhere and I detest sheep. They are stupid and smelly."

Sonja always sounded petulant, but he enjoyed her grilled steak. "You have enough time to cook fish, Darling," he jovially replied. "I shall arrive in forty minutes."

"Make it an hour and forty minutes," she said. "I am still in a state of undress, and you did not tell me that you were coming. I hope you have not been playing any of your funny tricks, taking off without telling me where you were going. If and when we get married, there will be no more of those hanky-panky games!"

"I did tell you that I was going to Jamaica, Darling," he replied.

"Bat, listen to me! You must have been dreaming that you told me," she cried. "You told me nothing! Promise me that there will he no more of these Secret Service games," she demanded. "I detest them worse than sheep!"

"Sonja," he gravely said, "while I was aboard the plane, on my way home, I was thinking the same thing that there will be no more assignments after this. I am going to Miami on my very last mission. I call that mission ROAD TO DAMASCUS. When I have accomplished what I set out to do, I shall return to tell you a long story."

"I adore stories," she said, "but I don't like lies. I detest lies. Promise me you won't tell me any lies."

He crossed his fingers, "I promise," he continued, "Thaw the fish! I will be with you in forty minutes. I will cook it!" he said.

Printed in the United States
33351LVS00003B/61-489